LEAGUE OF LOVE
Volume One

Caitlin's Hero

Mandy's He-Man

DONNA GALLAGHER

League of Love Volume One
ISBN # 978-1-78184-571-4
©Copyright Donna Gallagher 2013
Cover Art by Posh Gosh ©Copyright 2013
Interior text design by Claire Siemaszkiewicz
Total-E-Bound Publishing

.

CAITLIN'S HERO

Dedication

To my editor, Amy. The universe was smiling on me the day my manuscript landed on your desk. Thank you for believing in my voice. Your encouragement, support and frequent *hugs* have made my dream become a reality.

Chapter One

Caitlin normally swam laps at the same time as Riley had his squad training. If she had to be up early to drive him to the pool, she figured she might as well do something productive with her time instead of sitting around waiting. Caitlin never put on weight. She knew she was lucky in that regard, because some girls were always trying one new fad diet after another, but she did like to feel fit and healthy. Caitlin had a hearty appetite and was almost embarrassed by the amount of food she needed to keep her body fuelled.

She was neither short nor tall and her long legs, average hips and small waist were all in proportion. The problem with swimming—although she loved being in the water—was that wearing a swimsuit made it easier for people to notice her D-cup breasts.

Firm and round, they appeared to stick out rudely and she thought they looked out of place on her body. Caitlin and her breasts had not got along since puberty, when they'd seemed to grow to an enormous size almost overnight. Her enjoyment of participating in sports had taken a beating at the cruel taunts from other teens. At one point, Caitlin had actually considered breast reduction surgery.

That, of course, would not be possible — at least for the foreseeable future. Not after all that had happened recently.

Caitlin fingered the bracelet on her wrist lovingly, and pushed those sad memories from her mind. She always revelled in the solitude of swimming laps once she got started. It calmed her to listen to herself breathe in and out while her arms and legs sliced through the water, stroke after stroke. Just being around water soothed Caitlin.

The other bonus of early morning swimming was that there was no need to worry about the harsh Australian sun burning her very pale skin. Giving herself one last pep talk about the water being warm once she got wet, she headed out to the swim deck, trying, as usual, to push her mop of hair under her pink swimming cap.

As Caitlin did some stretches in preparation, she noticed the players from the local rugby league team on the other side of the fifty-metre pool. Most of the players were walking up and back in a lane, laughing and pushing each other in mock fights. All except for *him*.

Caitlin had observed the giant of a man before. In fact, on many occasions she had actually sought him out with her eyes. *Why wouldn't you?* she thought to herself. He was gorgeous — such a perfect specimen. Caitlin had watched him stretching his large body, which rippled with the mass of well-defined muscle that made up his impressive physique. Caitlin had also watched him standing, sitting, walking, running and swimming, all in such a skimpy pair of swimmers that not much was left to the imagination, and Caitlin had found she had a good imagination when it came to *him*.

On more than one occasion she had dreamt of him, waking to find her body sweaty, the ache in her core unbearable and moisture coating her panties. Caitlin had begun touching herself to try to ease that unfamiliar longing—quietly, discreetly, her strokes reluctant at first. The thought of masturbation had been disturbing, somehow wrong.

But not wrong enough to stop. On those occasions, she would inch her fingers towards that throbbing, hot place. She'd slide her hand down the front of her panties, past the layers of curls that covered her folds.

It was always the same. She'd visualise his broad shoulders and washboard abs and her breath would start to come in little puffs and pants, her nipples pulling tight. Caitlin always felt them forming hard button shapes even before she'd let her free hand touch them. She would touch and rub her sensitive nipples as she imagined his face—that sexy, yet sombre-looking face.

There was something about him that drove her to this point. Nothing and no-one else had ever caused Caitlin to caress her own body in such a way. This uncontrollable need was new, coinciding with her awareness of his existence. She'd slip her finger in between her folds. They were always slick and warm, and she'd begin to move that finger in a circular motion. Tiny sparks of something indescribable would start to form beneath her finger, her body striving towards some place, some ending to fulfil her ache. As she focused on the memory of his deep voice, which she had overheard when he'd spoken to his teammates, she'd imagine him talking to her, touching her. She'd pretend it was his fingers plucking at her nipples and his hand creating so much havoc within her body.

Finally, knowing she was nearing that peak that caused her so much bliss, Caitlin would find her clitoris, the place that held the release of that pleasure spike, and she'd rub furiously at it. Push and circle, hard and fast, assaulting her own body until finally the gratification came, a wave of pleasure and relief washing over her slick, wet body, leaving her breathless, boneless, sated.

Caitlin both loved and hated to remember those times she lost control. She'd heard that masturbation was a normal human need, but it didn't make her feel any less uncomfortable with her own actions.

Seeing him in such a state of near nakedness didn't help. Shaking off her silly, girly fantasies, her stomach fluttering in response to her wilful thoughts, Caitlin stepped onto the block and did a graceful racing dive into the water. For the first few laps she tried to find her rhythm, reprimanding herself for her body's response to the man by chanting a mantra over and over in her head. "I don't have time for men, I don't have time for dating, I don't have time for men, I don't have time for dating..."

Previous forays into the dating scene hadn't filled her with much confidence. These so-called dates were nothing but a bunch of octopus-limbed disappointments who seemed to think buying her a drink, or dinner, gave them the right to grope her at will. Just the thought had Caitlin angrily pounding her arms into the water.

* * * *

Brodie James was tired. Not sleepy, but that bone-deep, weary kind of tiredness that made you feel as if you were dragging yourself through life. He was feeling all of his thirty years at the early morning recovery session.

Yesterday's game had been a hard-fought grind, ending disappointingly in a loss for Brodie's Sydney Jets. Brodie's battle-fatigued body reminded him painfully of every tackle and knock it had taken. It wasn't just the game, though. Brodie could not pinpoint what it was that was making him feel so old and jaded. He was living the dream. This was the life he had worked so hard for. He was playing rugby league at the top level.

Brodie had lived and breathed rugby league from the time he could hold a footy. He was good — some even said the best. Brodie didn't go much for that sort of talk, though. He was successful, sure. His thirteen years at the top level were testimony enough. He had captained his club, state and country, and earned a good living doing what he loved. What more could he want?

Maybe that was exactly the issue. What more did he, Broderick Patrick James, want from life?

Just thinking about it gave Brodie chills, and that wasn't because he was waist deep in a swimming pool. These recovery sessions were just a part of the routine that was Brodie's life. He had to contend not only with his aching muscles, but with the antics of his younger teammates as well. Full of the exuberance of youth, these pups were good at riding him about his age. They respected him, though, despite their good-humoured cheek, and they were keen to learn all they could from him.

As his teammates laughed and horsed around, Brodie's attention was drawn elsewhere. She was here again. Brodie had seen her swimming laps at the pool many times. Something about the way she walked, or stood, or swam caught his attention. Maybe it was how her elegant arms seemed to effortlessly slice through the water.

He had watched, fascinated by the way that, no matter how hard she tried, she never completely managed to corral that red mass of curls under her swim cap. There were tendrils always haphazardly poking out. He wanted to tuck them away for her just so he could feel their texture. He wondered what her hair would feel like up against his chest—a bad move on his part. His body had an immediate reaction to the sexy thought, forming an ill-timed lump in the front of his tiny swimming briefs.

Brodie was shocked at this physical response. He had been with his fair share of women. Not lately, though. Lately he just hadn't really bothered. He could never tell, these days, if the many offers were made due to his high profile.

That thought reminded him of the big mistake—his now failed marriage. At first, Lila had seemed to be every man's dream. She'd said all the right things about wanting a family and the normal trimmings. It wasn't long, though, before Brodie had realised that what Lila said and what she actually meant were two entirely different things. Lila had wanted everything she could get. The memory of her was enough to remove that tight feeling in his trunks.

Sighing, Brodie took one last look in the direction of his redhead's swimming form as her arm lifted and curled back towards the water's surface. A glimpse of shiny metal caught his eye as it flew from her wrist to plop right into the water next to her. It looked to Brodie like a gold bracelet. She went on swimming, unaware of what had just happened. Without another thought, he ducked under the lane rope and swam towards the spot, diving to the depths of the pool in search of the lost piece of jewellery.

Chapter Two

I'm not getting into a rhythm today.

Caitlin scowled to herself. Her mind just wouldn't stop. She didn't know how to slow down the relentless wave of disaster that seemed to have swallowed her life since the tragic loss of her mother and stepfather in a car accident twelve months ago. Life had taken an abrupt change of direction that day, as the welfare of her ten-year-old half-brother was thrust into her care.

The memory was still so clear in her mind. She had rushed home after university to sit with Riley, so her parents could go out and celebrate their tenth wedding anniversary. The police crash investigation had concluded that her stepfather's car had been speeding when he had lost control, crashing into a telegraph pole and killing them both instantly. The end result had been that she and Riley were alone.

The next few months had been full of problems and tough decisions. With no life insurance and not much in the way of savings to help them, Caitlin and Riley had been forced to sell their family home. After paying out all legal and funeral costs, there was enough money left over for them to buy a small, one-bedroom flat in an old, majestic house in Ashfield, an inner western suburb of Sydney. The once opulent home had been converted into four apartments—two ground-floor garden flats and two upstairs flats, complete with French doors leading onto their own verandas.

Caitlin and Riley had settled into their new home as best they could. Riley slept in the bedroom, sharing closet space with his sister. Caitlin slept on a foldout sofa bed in the living room, which she made up every night and packed away again in the morning. The kitchen was large, with space for a small dining table and four chairs. The bathroom housed a beautiful clawfoot bath, pedestal sink and toilet, and there had been plenty of room to add a washing machine and dryer as well. The best feature of the new home was the large windows. Starting from nearly the ceiling line, they fell to a few feet from the floor. They were finished with deep stone ledges, perfect for sitting on to read, or just to gaze out onto the gardens.

Caitlin had shelved plans to finish her Bachelor of Music Performance since she'd had to find a way to support her diminished family. She was lucky to have befriended June, the pensioner living in the other ground-floor apartment. The old woman, also alone, had filled the role of adopted granny in Riley's life. June was happy to spend time with Riley when Caitlin was working and, in return, Caitlin drove June to the shops and to appointments. Caitlin was thankful she had been able to purchase her compact green Daihatsu to run everyone around.

Finally coming to the realisation that she wasn't enjoying her swim, Caitlin abruptly stopped mid-lap.

Thinking maybe a hot shower and cup of tea would work better this morning, she started to climb the rungs of the ladder to exit the pool. As she reached up to grab the handrail, she noticed her bare wrist with horror.

Her heart stopped. The bracelet that had once belonged to her mother — given to her by Caitlin's biological father, a man Caitlin had never met — was missing.

"What else can go wrong in my life?" she whimpered to herself. "I've lost my mum and now my bracelet."

Brodie found the bracelet on the first dive. It sparkled up from the bottom of the pool as if waiting for him. Grabbing the little gold links in his hand, he pushed back up to the surface. He made his way to the side and, in one smooth movement, lifted himself from the water and sat on the pool's edge, where he watched the bracelet's owner continue swimming, unaware of her loss.

Some of his teammates had stopped to watch Brodie. JT shouted out to him, a question he didn't quite catch. Brodie just waved at them in such a way to suggest that all was okay as he waited for his chance to return the bracelet to its beautiful owner. Brodie watched as the girl abruptly stopped swimming and headed over to the ladder, as if she was about to exit the pool. He jumped up and started towards her.

As she climbed the rungs of the ladder he saw her hesitate and look at her arm. Brodie could tell she was becoming agitated. Her eyes took on a wild look and her face, already a beautiful, pale, porcelain skintone, appeared to go even paler. Not liking to see her in such distress, Brodie almost ran the remaining distance between them. When he finally reached her, she had turned her back to him—ready to dive in, he guessed, to begin a search. Brodie reached out and placed his hand on her shoulder to stop her.

"Excuse me, miss. I believe you lost this while you were swimming."

Brodie held up the bracelet in his free hand at about her eye level. As if in slow motion, she turned towards him. She looked at his hand as he offered up the gold trophy, then her eyes met his. Brodie felt as though he had been hit in the chest with an impact harder than any rugby league opponent had ever delivered. His breath was knocked from his lungs as he gazed into the biggest, deepest emerald-green eyes he had ever seen. It was as if they burned deep into his soul.

It was then that the most unexpected thing happened. As Brodie stood, mesmerised, she actually leapt onto him, throwing those elegant arms around his neck, encircling his large frame with her long legs, all the while raining small kisses down his jaw. Hell, his cock sprang to life immediately as she pressed her impressive breasts, with pebbly nipples, into his bare chest. Over her head, in the distance, he could see JT and the rest of the team stare, open-mouthed.

She spoke—she was almost sobbing. "Thank you! Oh, thank you. You are my hero. You don't know how much this means to me!" She emitted little breaths that teased his skin.

Brodie, not wanting her to stop, didn't move. He wanted to embrace her so badly. The heat from her skin was electrifying and he felt so alive, as if every nerve had reawakened. He felt brand new.

Just as he had made that incredible discovery, the woman wrapped around him went stiff. She gasped and disengaged from him. He felt the loss immediately, as if someone had flicked a switch and taken away his soul. He just stood there like a big, stupid statue.

Her face had gone a beetroot red. Snatching the trinket from his hand, she hugged her arms around her body as if to hide it from view. But as he dragged his eyes from her wet-dream-inducing figure to her face, he could still see the look of desire in her eyes. She took off like a jackrabbit, running away in the direction of the ladies' locker room.

Brodie just stood there, trying to breathe again, as he watched her cute little behind move away from him, her long legs eating up the ground quickly. Brodie thought she looked nearly as good from this angle. Those round globes of her sexy backside made his hands itch with longing. He could almost imagine the soft skin against his palms.

He wasn't sure how long he stood there, but eventually felt a towel being shoved in his face. Brodie heard the sound of a familiar chuckle, and his mate Jon Thomson—JT—spoke.

"Hey, Cap, I think you had better wrap this around you, or jump back in that cold water before you get arrested for indecent exposure."

With that, his mate actually pushed him, towel and all, into the water. Brodie felt the chill from the pool on his throbbing erection as he hit the surface hard.

* * * *

Caitlin was shaking as she leaned against the shower stall wall and went back over what had just happened. What on earth had possessed her to jump all over him? One minute she'd been full of despair and gloom over the loss of her beloved bracelet, the next, she was in the arms of none other than *him*. She had actually thrown herself at the man and latched on.

Her arms and legs were still tingling from the touch of his skin. As she had wrapped her limbs around him, she'd noted how masculine his body was. It had invoked a feeling so foreign to her, she'd felt as if her body were some sort of chocolate that had just melted on him. It had felt so good and natural, as if that was what she had been waiting for.

Sexually, she had certainly responded. Her nipples were still so hard they were almost too painful to touch. She was wet and throbbing between her thighs, so hot and bothered, but most of all, embarrassed. Maybe the strain of the last year had been too much for her and she was actually in the throes of a nervous breakdown. She sighed to herself.

My goodness. What must he have thought of her as her traitorous nipples poked him in the chest and she all but molested him poolside? She groaned at the thought. Someone as gorgeous as him could have his pick of women, and had probably been embarrassed by her outrageous behaviour. He would surely think of her as just some silly girl. The man had not moved a muscle—not one. Maybe he was used to women literally throwing themselves at him. Suddenly it occurred to her that Riley and his friends might have seen her acting so disgracefully, and she felt sick with worry.

That realisation forced her to think rationally again. Caitlin focused on quickly drying and dressing. She was running late and Riley would be waiting for her. As she looked down at herself, now dressed in her favourite chocolate-brown tracksuit, her uncontrollable mind recalled the melted chocolate image and began to head off down that path again.

She roughly dragged the brush through her hair in the hope that maybe pain would curtail her errant thoughts.

"Stop it!" she said aloud, directing the firm voice at her reflection in the mirror. As she headed towards the door, a little, panicky thought entered her mind. There was the possibility *he* might still be out there.

Taking a deep breath, she put her head down and crept outside.

Riley was waiting impatiently for her as he kicked at the brick wall with the toes of his new runners.

"C'mon, sis, I don't wanna be late for school again, and I need something to eat," her young brother grumbled at her.

Caitlin's response was out of her mouth before she could stop herself. "Stop that, Riley. You'll wear out your new shoes and you know we can't afford another pair just yet."

Caitlin could have kicked herself with those shoes. It wasn't his fault he was growing so fast. She was becoming a huge grouch, always nagging at him. He was such a good brother, never causing any real trouble. She would have to think before she spoke or acted.

Riley just bent down and picked up his bag, shoulders slumped, as he headed towards the exit.

Riley Walters was a tall boy for his eleven years. He had red hair and green eyes, the same as his half-sister. They were brother and sister—it didn't matter that Cate's dad hadn't been his dad. Riley had always known his father had loved her just as much as he'd loved Riley.

Riley felt bad for Cate. She had given up so much to look after him because of that accident. He tried not to think about it. He knew it was hard for her, too. Harder, even. He wished he could stop being stupid and upsetting her.

He loved swimming and squad training, but he always felt guilty at the extra strain it caused. It wasn't just the money, but the early morning starts as well. When he was older he'd be able to get himself to training so Cate could sleep in. It was especially hard for her if he had a swimming carnival or trial early on Saturday mornings, because she finished her singing gig so late on Friday nights. Still, Riley knew that his sister would be up and cheering him on every single time. It made him so proud when he could win and repay her faith in him.

Riley tried hard at school too, hoping that one day he could get a good job so his sister could go back to university and be young again.

As they left the pool, Riley thought about telling her how he'd seen his favourite footy team here again. He had watched the game on TV last night and was upset his mighty Jets had lost. He reckoned the ref had been unfair and had penalised them too much.

"What's the point? Like she'd care, anyway— grumpy and nagging at me today, and it's not like she'd even recognise a Jet if he was standing in front of her," Riley grumbled under his breath.

Little did Riley realise how correct those words were as he looked up to see his sister standing, unbelievably, directly in front of one of his all-time favourite players.

Maybe I'm magic and my thoughts are coming to life. He chuckled as he watched his sister and Brodie together. He shook his head, mouth gaping open.

Caitlin had been looking at the back of her brother's drooping head. She knew he tried so hard to be good. Life had dealt him a rough hand already, but she had no doubt that Riley would overcome these hurdles. She was going to encourage him to set his goals high, then help him achieve them. It was the least she could do in memory of her mother and stepfather's love for the little boy. She still remembered the joyous look in their eyes as they'd introduced her to the green-eyed bundle wrapped in blue, and the way they'd made her promise to love him as much as they loved her. She fiddled with her bracelet as the memory of her mother's face came to mind, but the bracelet unexpectedly triggered a new image. It was the face of a huge man with big, brown eyes and a tasty, square jaw.

"Oh, my," she said. "I really need to stop doing that."

As the last word fell from her lips, she realised that the brown eyes and square jaw were, in fact, in front of her, and the lips in between seemed to be moving. Oh, Lord, he was talking to her and she had no idea what he was saying. Dressed in a black tracksuit and runners with a towel draped over his impossibly broad shoulders, he lounged against the wall with his arms folded casually over his chest and his long legs crossed at the ankles. He appeared to be waiting for her.

Caitlin stopped in her tracks. Riley also stopped and stood with his mouth open, staring at her. What was going on? She looked away from Riley and back to the figure against the wall. Riley elbowed her hard in the ribs. *Ouch,* she thought, or maybe she'd even said it out loud, since Riley nudged her again, more gently.

"Hey, Cate, aren't you going to answer Mr James? You're always telling me it's rude to ignore grown-ups if they ask you a question."

Brodie was a little taken aback by the 'grown-up' comment from the kid. He wasn't sure if the boy was making reference to Brodie's age or not. Even the 'Mr James' remark was a kicker. The kid obviously knew who he was. Maybe she did as well.

Compared to the kid, he was old, he supposed. In fact, as Brodie took a clearer look at the girl, he realised he was a fair bit older than her too. If he was lucky, she was maybe twenty, which — although legal — would still be ten years his junior. He grimaced. He could see the headlines now.

Australian team captain in teen sex scandal. Caught with enormous hard-on at local pool.

The papers never let truth get in the way of a good story, had a habit of twisting the facts to sell a few more editions. Rugby league had been taking a battering in the press lately, with scandal after scandal. Some of the bad press was due to stupid, irresponsible dirtbags who didn't deserve to play footy, but most of the stories were beat-ups used to boost ratings and inflate newspaper sales. He resented the way they seemed to want to turn the public against the game he loved.

Brodie had just wanted to see her again. *Just once,* he'd lied to himself. He could still feel the tingling sensation of her lips on his jaw, where she had pressed those sweet little kisses. His cock twitched at the thought. He had even considered asking her to meet him for a drink or something. Nothing serious, of course, but he'd thought maybe some more time exploring her fine body might be just what the doctor ordered. Seeing her now, standing there looking all innocent and timid, those emerald eyes so smoking hot that they were melting him, made him want things that he shouldn't. Her under him, those green eyes full of passion and need as he slammed his cock into her pussy. Would she be timid in his bed? Could he make her scream his name as he bought her to orgasm? But something inside Brodie, some fearful premonition, told him that having her would be too dangerous. 'Not good for his career' was what he deluded himself into thinking, while a voice in his head also warned him that maybe once he had her, he might not want to let go. He decided it was not going to happen. Ever.

So why, then, did he not just walk away?

Needing to move before he became a puddle on the floor, Brodie pushed himself from the wall. He closed the distance between them with one big stride, then stopped in front of her and held out his hand.

"Hi, I'm Brodie James. I didn't catch your name earlier."

Chapter Three

Caitlin gazed at the outstretched hand, then reached for it as if caught in some sort of magnetic field. His name was Brodie, he had said. He wanted to know her name, and she couldn't speak. Brodie was looking at her, his smile lighting up his face and making the world seem dim around him. She stood there just staring up at him, holding his hand, the heat building up her arm and making a quick path throughout the rest of her body, down to her toes. She was sure they had curled. She blinked once, twice. He was still there, with an amused but sexy look in his eyes. Had it been hours, minutes, or just a few seconds? She had no idea. Her world had stopped.

Hearing Riley's familiar voice saying her name, she dragged her hand from Brodie's. Reality instantly returned to her and she felt colder at the loss of his touch. She finally managed to find her voice.

"Caitlin. My name is Caitlin Walters."

Riley was actually jumping up and down on the spot. She had no idea why. Focusing her attention back towards Brodie James, Caitlin wondered if she should apologise for her earlier behaviour, or thank him again for returning her bracelet. She began to explain that the bracelet was her mother's and she had been terrified at its apparent loss.

As she took a breath and opened her mouth to continue, Brodie pressed his finger lightly over her lips. Caitlin slid her tongue out of her mouth at the sizzling touch. Wanting to explore him, and momentarily forgetting about Riley and what he might think, she brushed her tongue against the digit. Hearing Brodie groan, then growl sent Caitlin into a spin. Had she done something wrong? And if so, why did Brodie's response send her emotions haywire? There was only one thing she could do — run.

Caitlin grabbed Riley by the hand and dragged him as she fled. She could hear the shock — or was it horror? — in Brodie's voice as he called after her.

Even with Riley complaining next to her, Caitlin didn't stop running until she reached her little green car. Finally breathing again, she grabbed the keys from her bag, unlocked the doors and threw herself inside.

She sat gripping the steering wheel with both hands, trying to prevent her heart from jumping out of her chest. Caitlin knew it wasn't just the dash to her car that had her in such a state. The day had only just begun, and she was an emotional and physical wreck. She turned to Riley to see him staring at her, fury all over his young face.

"What was that all about, Caitlin Walters?" he almost shouted. "I had the chance to meet the Australian Test captain, the Jets' — *my team's* — captain. One of my favourite players, and what do you do?" he snapped. "Run away. Nice move, sis."

His face showed signs of concern for her. The boy was obviously too young to notice, or to understand, the slightly terrifying sexual attraction she had felt for his hero.

All she could manage in response to his outburst was a shake of her head and a soft reply. "I don't know, Riles. I just don't know."

Her brother turned from her and looked out of the window, muttering to himself. It sounded to Caitlin something like, "The guys will never believe it anyway." She wasn't sure what he meant by that. Was it that the guys would not believe she'd fled, or just that the captain of the Jets had been at the pool? Caitlin's head was spinning and rational thought was lost on her for the moment.

But Caitlin knew that no matter how much her emotions had her in a tailspin, the day was still ticking by and she had responsibilities to attend to — the first sitting, sulking and hungry, next to her. It was time to get moving.

* * * *

After a quick breakfast, Caitlin had dropped a still grumpy Riley at school. When she returned home to prepare for work and tidy their modest home, she busied herself packing away her bed, returning it to its usual day position as a sofa. After throwing a load of wet towels and swimming gear into the washer, she changed into her black and whites. Caitlin had been very fortunate to find employment as a waitress at a friendly, local Italian restaurant, conveniently located a short drive or comfortable walk from home. Caitlin did the lunch shift from Monday through to Friday. To her delight, the owner of Mia's Restaurant, Angelo

Donetto, also employed her as a singer on Friday and Saturday evenings. Caitlin loved singing above all else. Music had been her life before the accident. To get paid to do what she loved seemed almost immoral.

The other half of her duo was a portly Italian man named Roberto. Roberto could play anything on the piano—you only had to hum the tune a few times and he could play it. They performed myriad genres. From country to pop, or rock to swing, if a customer wanted it, they could usually deliver. For that reason, the pair had developed quite a following of regulars who returned week after week to savour the taste of good, homemade Italian food while enjoying the entertainment.

Singing was the one time Caitlin felt truly confident and in control. It was as if an alter ego took over when she held a microphone to her lips, and she was finally comfortable in her own skin. She lost herself in a dreamlike state whenever she performed. What was more, the generous tips she made from those nights went a long way towards helping to pay the price of Riley's swimming squad fees. The situation was a good fit—something she loved was paying for something *he* loved.

As she left to walk the short distance to work, Caitlin noticed another moving van was blocking her car. It wasn't the first time she had been inconvenienced this way. There were always tenants moving their belongings in and out of the rented apartment upstairs. "Just as well. I wanted to walk," she muttered as she waved to her elderly neighbour, June, who was out in their shared garden. Caitlin went to speak to the woman, remembering that she still needed to confirm June's ability to sit with Riley this Wednesday night, as well as her two usual nights.

June was usually found pottering around the little garden, pruning, planting and encouraging the most beautiful range of colours to appear.

"Good morning, June, the garden's looking lovely. You really have the touch." Caitlin saw the look of pride in the old woman's eyes at her compliment. "Just beautiful. It really cheers me up seeing all that colour, just like listening to a good piece of music. Which reminds me—are you still good with looking after Riley on Wednesday night?"

June broke into a huge smile. Caitlin noticed a light twinkle shining in the older woman's eyes as she repeated her favourite mantra.

"I'm always glad for the company, dear. Happy to have someone to watch my programmes with, and our Riley is such a good boy. We like the same shows. It's no bother at all."

June was such a gift. Caitlin knew that any programmes watched on those nights were Riley's choice and that June just pretended to enjoy them— especially on Friday nights, when football was shown on free-to-air TV. She doubted the old woman enjoyed that sort of entertainment at all.

As usual, June gave Caitlin a lecture about all work and no play, trying to encourage her to have a life of her own, a chance to find someone to 'fill her heart's desires', or some such romantic notion. Usually, Caitlin just laughed off these conversations, but today her imagination took hold and as she headed off to begin her work day, she daydreamed about her hunky hero and the way he had felt beneath her body all the way to the restaurant. It made her step a little lighter than usual.

Chapter Four

"I can't believe it—you of all people, Brodes."

"What? 'Me of all people' *what*, JT? That smirk on your face is really starting to piss me off. What can't you believe?" Brodie asked.

"Ice-cold Brodie James, leader of all men, getting a woody at the public pool over some little redhead piece of tail. *That* is what I can't believe, Cap. What were you thinking? Can you image the press getting a photo of that particular sideshow? Brrr... I shudder to think," the enormous, dark-haired man said, theatrically shivering in response to his words.

Thinking about the fiasco at the pool again, Brodie still couldn't believe she had run from him. She'd actually taken off like a scared rabbit. JT and the boys had been in hysterics. The memory of JT folded over holding his stomach, laughing at his expense, made Brodie curse under his breath.

They had ribbed him at every opportunity throughout the day's second training session. He had managed to silence a few of the young upstarts by dropping them hard on their behinds during tackle practice, he thought smugly as he sat in the sheds, undoing the laces of his sponsored boots and trying to not let JT's comments get under his skin. But it was true, and he knew it. He had imagined the very same thing as JT at the time, right down to the headlines in the paper. The fact remained that he had lost his cool, lost his head, so to speak. Because of her.

Every time he shut his eyes, images of those beautiful eyes and that face flashed into his mind. The memory of those cute bowed lips and her tongue poking out between them made him sigh with the loss he now felt. Made his cock awaken in interest.

Get it together. Now is definitely not a good time to be sporting a hard-on, not with this group of hyenas ready to rip me to pieces, he reminded himself of the young players surrounding him in the noisy dressing room. But how he wished he could have kissed those lips and explored every inch of that mouth. *Such a waste.*

It was then that Brodie heard a conversation that made his blood boil. Rage consumed him as he registered the voice of one of the young bloods of the Jets. It sounded like the new halfback, Mitchell Harris, nicknamed Rookie.

"Well, it's not like you could blame him. The girl was a hard-on on legs—did ya see the size of her rack?"

Brodie could not believe his ears as another male voice chimed in.

"Keep it down, Rookie, if the Cap hears ya he'll blow a gasket. But I think you're right. I'm a legs man, myself, and did you see the way she wrapped hers around Cap? Just thinkin' about them wrapped around me, all long and shapely…"

He had heard enough. It was the derogatory comment about the size of her breasts that got him, and before he could stop himself he went into a thunderous rage, berating all in earshot about their stupidity at speaking so uncouthly.

"What is wrong with you people? For God's sake, Rookie, can't you and the boys keep your minds out of the gutter for a minute? Haven't any of you learnt anything from the speeches and workshops the league hierarchy have sat us all through? What if someone was talking about your mother like that, Rookie? Hey, she's an attractive woman — perhaps I should have a shot at her? How would that sit with you? Well, Rookie? Answer me," Brodie roared at the suddenly sullen younger player.

The Australian Rugby League had devoted time and resources to trying to create a better image of football and footballers' behaviour, especially with regards to their treatment of women, and Brodie now invoked those lessons angrily.

"I'm sorry, Cap, we were just foolin' around," the other stunned youngster said bravely.

"Settle down, Brodie." JT now stood between Brodie and their other teammates. "The whole team's been watching you, Brodes — watching you watching her — for weeks now. There's even been a sweep, placing bets on when you'll work up enough courage to go and pick her up. Hey, no one guessed she'd end up doing it for you."

JT chuckled, obviously trying to lighten the mood and calm him down. He wasn't too keen on the idea that he had been the centre of this sort of attention.

"The young blokes were starting to think that there was something really wrong with you and that maybe you'd gone off chicks," JT added, grinning. "But I told 'em you were just on a go-slow, concentrating on protecting their backsides and trying to win us a few games." JT winked before moving away, returning to the job of stowing his gear into his sports bag.

Brodie, seeing the looks on the men's faces, finally realised that he had been well and truly set up. He'd fallen for the prank hook, line and sinker. The boys had been winding him up, teasing him. And they had busted him and his weakness for one Caitlin Walters.

* * * *

Brodie had a busy day ahead of him. He had a meeting with a local restaurant owner to go over the arrangements for using his venue for a fundraising night. The menu and entertainment was all to be taken care of by the owner of Mia's Restaurant, Angelo Donetto. The hundred-and-fifty-dollar-a-seat dinner was nearly sold out, and all money raised at the event was to be used to purchase specialised sporting wheelchairs, after the costs were taken out.

There were various types of titanium chairs designed specifically to cater to the needs of different sports. Most of these chairs were priced over the three-thousand-dollar mark, which made them difficult for the young, physically disabled athletes and their families to afford. Sport had been such an important factor throughout Brodie's life that he could not bear the thought of financial problems forcing a child to give up their chosen sport, at any level.

Brodie had met an inspirational young man who competed in marathons, and had been made aware of the boy's huge potential. Despite not having had the opportunity to make use of a top-of-the-line wheelchair for his last event, the boy had still managed to finish in quite a competitive time. Brodie hoped that with the state-of-the-art equipment he was about to receive from this fundraising, the boy would be able to compete at the same level as others, and maybe even enter the next Paralympics.

Many footballers worked hard away from the footy field, television and newspaper cameras—doing varied charity or volunteer work, meeting with sick kids at the children's hospital, or holding special training camps for young people. Unfortunately, most of this work was never put under the spotlight. It was always the worst actions that drew the most publicity.

After crunching the numbers, Brodie anticipated that even after costs, with all fifteen tables of ten sold and plenty of donated auction items up for grabs, he would clear well over sixteen thousand dollars. That should be enough to purchase at least five chairs— maybe a couple of chairs specially designed for track, a couple for court, basketball and tennis, and the marathon chair, of course. With that thought bringing Brodie a sense of great accomplishment, he decided to head on home. Being able to give help where it was needed was one of the by-products of his high-profile career that he actually enjoyed.

It had been an eventful day, Brodie reflected, as he parked his black Range Rover Vogue in its usual spot in the garage of the waterfront apartment block he owned. After grabbing the sports bag that held the training gear he'd used earlier that day from the boot of his car, Brodie headed up the private stairway. The spiral staircase led to the balcony and back entrance of his personal apartment. He stopped for a few moments to admire the view of the busy Parramatta River and to watch a passing RiverCat—a public transport catamaran used to ferry passengers to and from the city. It really was a great view, and one he hadn't stopped to admire for a while.

He remembered when he had first moved out of the lavish Hunter's Hill home he had occupied with Lila, how much he had enjoyed sitting back and watching the many boats that used this waterway go by. Since it was a popular thoroughfare that led to the spectacular Sydney Harbour, the river view was always changing. Boats puttering to and from the harbour foreshores, heading up to the many sites worth a visit—the 'Coathanger' bridge spanning the distance between the central business district and North Sydney, the Opera House, the waterfront Taronga Zoo or the Botanical Gardens, to name a few. Sydney Harbour was one of the most famous harbours in the world. Brodie loved his home by the water. The picturesque view was a relaxing diversion and a welcome change from the tumultuous life he'd endured while married.

No way did he want to dwell on the past and ruin his memories of today. Lila had a way of doing that to him. He couldn't help but wonder if Caitlin would treat him better. A ridiculous thought altogether, considering how little, if anything, he knew about the emerald-eyed beauty. Was that a good thing or not? He was still considering this question as he slid open the glass door leading to his home.

Chapter Five

Caitlin had not been inside the swimming complex at Leichhardt since her meltdown on Monday, preferring to do a drop-and-run from the safety of her car. She certainly had not looked for Brodie. Well, that was what she kept telling herself. The disappointment she felt at seeing Riley's smiling face coming towards the car on both days was hard to explain.

It was Wednesday, and Caitlin had a lot of errands to run. Along with her usual lunch shift and singing at the private function in the evening, she had also promised to do a quick shopping run with June. Caitlin enjoyed the little shopping trips, which usually included sharing coffee, doughnuts and a side order of conversation with her neighbour.

June was also quite handy with a sewing machine, and had been making a new stage dress for Caitlin with diamantes and sequins hand sewn throughout the black fabric. Caitlin had been so excited at the last dress fitting—she was looking forward to finally getting to wear the costume at tonight's event. The dress was incredible. *Even on me,* she had thought the last time she'd tried it on.

She had admired her image in the mirror—the neckline was just low enough to show the tops of her breasts, but not enough to make her feel self-conscious. The material seemed to hug her body gently, stopping just above the knee, the sparkling extras twinkling when she moved. Caitlin thought the new outfit would be a good addition to her stage wardrobe, but would never have dreamed of wearing the dress on any other occasion. Unless she was on stage singing, Caitlin preferred to blend into the background.

After settling June and Riley in front of the television with instructions for serving the lasagne she had made earlier, Caitlin went to dress. She wore her best black bra and matching panties under her new dress, and a pair of black stilettos to finish off the outfit. As the stage lights were bright and unforgiving, Caitlin usually wore makeup to perform—a layer of foundation, a quick brush of powder and rouge, finishing off with eye shadow and a touch of mascara to highlight her eyes, combined with a nice, bright lipstick. She wore her hair loose around her shoulders and gave it a quick fluff in front of the mirror, quite pleased with the results.

Grabbing her coat and keys, she went to the lounge to say she was leaving. It was a shock to see the look of surprise in Riley's eyes when he saw her outfit.

"Caitlin Walters, what are you wearing?" he choked out. "You look so different—I mean, in a good way. So grown up!" He giggled.

June playfully slapped at him to shush and winked at Caitlin, smiling as she added her thoughts. "You look beautiful, Caitlin. Go sing your heart out. Maybe someone will be there to catch it tonight, my girl."

* * * *

Caitlin arrived at Mia's a little early but wanted to have a quick meeting with Roberto about the final playlist and what was expected from them for tonight. Angelo had told her the night was a fundraising event. The tickets cost one hundred and fifty dollars each, and all seats had been pre-sold. Caitlin was amazed that so many people would pay so much for a dinner at Mia's that would normally cost a quarter of the price. It was a good feeling to know people out there cared enough to help others in need. She'd have loved to donate her share of tonight's wages, but then she wouldn't have enough for Riley's swimming fees. However, she decided she'd donate any tips she might make.

As Roberto started tinkling at the piano keys, Caitlin knew it was time to make her way onstage. Angelo had created a small alcove perfect for a performance area. The stage floor was raised up a couple of feet above the main room's floor level and further enhanced by a brick archway that also gave the performers a private spot, out of the public eye. The archway created a divide between the main floor and raised platform. As Caitlin stuck the playlist on the brick wall, out of eyeshot of the main room, she noticed some of the guests arriving.

The spotlights were still off, so Caitlin had a good view of the room. She could see Angelo nervously buzzing around. He was still waiting for the organiser to arrive and had hoped to introduce them, so Caitlin could receive any last-minute directions needed for the night to run smoothly. From her spot peeking out from behind the archway, she oohed and ahhed at some of the outfits the obviously well-to-do guests were wearing—designer handbags and expensive jewellery were plentiful in the room tonight. It wasn't the usual clientele of Mia's Italian Restaurant, and she worried that she might not be up to the task of entertaining such a group.

Reminding herself that the people were not really here to be entertained by her and Roberto, but to raise funds to buy wheelchairs for children, Caitlin motioned to Roberto that she was ready to begin. They had decided to start the night off with a few slower songs—background music while the guests enjoyed their meals, not even bothering to turn on the stage lighting because the night was not about them. Caitlin heard the familiar introduction to one of her favourite songs, the theme from the latest *Titanic* movie. It wasn't to everyone's taste because of its original singer, but it was still one she enjoyed performing. As she lost herself in the music, all nerves and apprehension she'd previously felt disappeared. She felt so at home on the stage.

* * * *

Brodie was late.

He hated not being punctual, but he had taken too long in the shower. He had been haunted by the memory of Caitlin Walters many times over the last few days and every time he thought of her, his cock stood at attention. It was becoming a problem, and he had taken to relieving himself just so he could function like a normal human being, without the ache of his constantly swollen cock distracting him.

As he had stood under the spray with his eyes closed, soaking up the warmth of the water on his still muscle-fatigued body, he had thought of her. The feel of her legs wrapped around him, her pebbled nipples pushing against him... And he had let his imagination take over.

Brodie had picked up the soap, made a thick lather in his hands and grabbed his cock, which was stiff as a post. He had begun to roughly stroke up and down as his imagination took off.

He could almost taste her nipples as he drew them into his hungry mouth, the fullness of her breasts pressed hard into his face as he drew those nipples further behind his lips and teeth, nipping gently at them, suckling and lapping first at one breast, then the other. He could imagine the little gasps and groans that would come from her as he lavished attention on her beautiful body...

All the while he'd stroked his length up and down in a ruthless rhythm, feeling the tightness in his balls as his ejaculation had neared.

She took hold of him, put her soft, silky fingers around his cock, the feeling of her hand on him incredibly making him harder. She pumped her fingers up and down, before exploring the circumference of his swollen head, playfully delivering a few faint taps, before returning to pump and stroke the whole length again. She tentatively touched his balls, and he sighed at the intense pleasure as she rolled them gently in her hand...

Brodie had felt the release as it travelled up his shaft and exploded from the end of his cock. He gave another few good, long pulls as the spurts of his cum mixed with the running shower water and washed away. He'd closed his eyes and leaned his head on the shower wall as his body had recovered, as the sensations and his imaginings disappeared along with his watery essence.

"Shit, I really need to get laid," Brodie had groaned. "I'm back in my teenage years, wanking every bloody shower again. It's disgusting."

Then, to compound the problem and add to his agitation, just as he was about to leave, Lila had rung. She had ranted at him hysterically, something about the water heater system at the house being broken, preventing her from getting ready for his fundraiser.

Brodie didn't know what angered him more, the fact she had bothered him at all about *her* house — as if it was his problem and he should fix it — or that she was coming tonight. He had sold the tickets himself, and she certainly would not have got one from him, so where, then, had she got it? Someone he knew had obviously given her a ticket, or was bringing her. *Great news*. When was she going to stop embarrassing him, sleeping with every Tom, Dick and Harry? *Apparently never, or at least not tonight*. He loudly slammed the door of his car. The aggravation from Lila never stopped.

Brodie found a car spot at the rear of the restaurant, in what appeared to be a private car park, probably used for staff. There was room for many cars, yet only two spots were occupied. Brodie hoped the owner wouldn't mind him parking there as well. He really needed to get inside and greet everyone, so he hurried around to the front entrance. As he pushed the door open, he was immediately struck by two questioning thoughts. Where was everyone? The place was so quiet. And who did that hauntingly beautiful singing voice belong to?

When Brodie's eyes had adjusted to the lights in the restaurant, he was relieved to see his first question was unfounded. The place was filled with people sitting quietly, listening to the voice apparently coming from the dark stage area he now spotted at the back of the room.

Brodie's attention was immediately taken up by Angelo, the restaurant's owner, who was checking to see if it was okay to start serving. He explained he had been waiting on Brodie's arrival. Letting the man know that this was acceptable, Brodie also explained tonight's schedule again to the nervous owner. He'd wait till between the entrée and the main course to make his welcome address, and between the main and the dessert he would auction off the various donations and memorabilia pieces he had gathered.

Brodie never quite made it all the way to his table, just left of the stage—he was stopped by nearly every guest. A handshake here, a kiss there… It was quite the job, being the host. It actually got to the point that he thought his welcome speech would be redundant. Was there anyone left in the room he hadn't personally welcomed? Still, as empty plates were being whisked away by efficient wait staff, Brodie made his way to the stage, stepping onto it from the front. The music had stopped, clueing him in that he was up.

As the stage light blinked on, Brodie noticed an older, plump man sitting at the piano. Maybe the voice had been a recording, he mused as he took the microphone from its stand. It was already on and ready for him to begin his spiel.

He delivered the usual welcome, thanking everyone for their generosity, and gave an explanation as to what was being auctioned, why and for whom. This brought rounds of applause from the dinner crowd. Brodie was comfortable with public speaking—since he was the captain, it was usually up to him to do interviews or make comments after a game. One of the hardest things to do was to talk to a reporter seconds after the final siren sounded, especially after a loss. He had done his fair share of this sort of function before, so speaking to this crowd of familiar faces was no problem. Soon he was ready to finally take his seat, but before he could, the door to the restaurant burst open. With the lights shining in his face Brodie couldn't quite see who the late arrivals were, but he knew, just by the commotion, that Lila had arrived.

* * * *

Caitlin had forgotten to grab a glass of water before starting her first set — she left Roberto to finish a piano solo and slipped out to the kitchen. As she took a swallow of water, she heard the male voice welcoming everyone to the night. Caitlin got a fluttery feeling. Did she know that voice? Was it the same sexy voice from Monday? Shaking her head, she tried to clear her mind.

"Honestly, I'm really losing it," she whispered. "What on earth would Brodie James be doing here at Mia's, using my microphone?" She laughed at what she dismissed as her own silly imagination. Clutching the glass of water, she headed back to the main room, careful not to get in the way of the busy staff heading out to serve steaming hot plates of home-made pasta.

Angelo was standing in front of the side entrance to the stage, smiling broadly.

"*Perfecto!*" her boss said, his Italian accent strong as he pinched his fingers together and touched his lips, making a kissing sound. "You sing like an angel, *bella*, as always." Caitlin could not help the warmth that stole over her cheeks from Angelo's compliment.

He was waiting to introduce her to the organiser of the event, the man on stage, Angelo explained, and as Caitlin looked around him to get a better view of who her boss was talking about, her heart skipped a beat. She blinked, looked again. She could not believe it. Brodie James was on her stage. It was all Caitlin could do not to drop the water she was holding. She clenched the glass tighter.

How on earth was she going to sing again, knowing he was watching her? She started to feel all hot. Perspiration beads dotted her forehead.

Who am I kidding? He probably won't even remember me anyway. Still, it wouldn't hurt to freshen up a little. Caitlin excused herself from Angelo quickly, mumbling about visiting the ladies' room, having drunk too much water. She held out the glass for him to take from her still-shaking hand, noticed the look of concern on his face, but couldn't stay and explain to Angelo why she was acting so erratically. Then she turned and fled once again, away from this man who caused her body and mind to react in such unfamiliar ways.

She couldn't stay hidden in the ladies' all night, though. As Caitlin started heading back to the stage, she watched Brodie step off it. He was just a couple of feet away from her. He hurried towards the front door. Looking in that direction, she understood why. In the doorway stood the most attractive, sexy, tall blonde woman Caitlin had ever seen. She appeared as if she had stepped straight from a catwalk or centrefold. Her clothes seemed almost explicit because of how little flesh they actually covered.

Reality cut deep into Caitlin's heart. This was the sort of woman that men like Brodie were attracted to, not skittish young girls who made fools of themselves.

It was okay—it had been a nice fantasy while it lasted, and the bonus was she still had her mother's bracelet after all, thanks to him.

After nodding to Roberto, Caitlin started singing the next song listed, a newer release from a young country singer branching off into pop. It was ironic considering the situation, that there would be no Romeo for her Juliet. Not tonight, and not in this crowd of people. She was not in their class at all. Trying to ignore her hero in the crowd, she focused on the very large, intimidating man at the table to her right. He looked a little familiar, as did a few other young men who seemed to be grinning up at her. She turned slightly away and tried to return to the almost dreamlike state she could achieve while singing, not wanting to ever think about any good-looking men again.

Chapter Six

Brodie stepped from the front of the stage, plastered a fake smile across his face and headed for the door to 'welcome' the late arrivals. As he walked closer to the noisy, attention-seeking woman—as he'd suspected, it was Lila—he finally realised who was accompanying her. It was none other than Jack Edwards, the scandal king, a reporter whose name was attached to nearly every article that had attacked Brodie's beloved sport over the past few years. He was furious. What the hell was his ex-wife doing here at his function with Edwards?

Talk about nightmare scenarios. The way his ex was dressed was enough to fill the papers with scandal fodder for days. As usual, Lila wore an outfit that didn't cover much at all. He'd never understood her taste in such revealing clothing. It embarrassed more than impressed him. It was the only area where Lila believed less was better.

The whole place seemed to stand still. Everyone's attention flicked from Lila to Brodie, as if they were watching a game of tennis. Just as he reached this most unwelcome pair of guests, he heard the music and the gifted singer resume. With the music distracting him momentarily, he almost didn't see that Lila was closing in. He was sure she was intent on placing a kiss on him.

No way! He quickly took a step away from her scantily clad body, placing a hand up to separate them. He grabbed the tickets from Edwards' outstretched hand.

Brodie double-checked the tickets and found them to be genuine. He'd known they would be. He requested bleakly that Lila and Edwards follow him. As Brodie turned and headed towards the only table with empty seats—his table—he now understood the reason the two seats had remained empty as the dinner began. He guessed he could stop worrying about who had not shown up. What was the world doing to him? He felt a little paranoid about the position he now found himself in. A whole night of having to be sociable with Lila and Edwards was ahead of him. He could only find one upside to this, and that was seeing JT's reaction.

As Brodie reached his seat he diplomatically, yet somewhat grudgingly, assisted Lila to get comfortable. *Maybe with a fork sticking out of her behind.* He finally had the chance to sit down and enjoy the beautiful music, but as he started to sit, his attention drifted towards the stage. The spotlight had been left on and now he could see that there was a singer, and the voice had not been a recording. His gaze locked on to a pair of huge, emerald-green eyes looking back down at him. He couldn't believe it was possible. His Caitlin was the owner of that beautiful voice he had been listening to all along.

There she was, standing not more than a few feet away from him. His heart raced, stopped, raced again, and he realised he was caught suspended somewhere between sitting and standing, staring at the most gorgeous woman he had ever seen. She was no girl. He had been wrong. Caitlin was all woman.

Her luscious red hair was spiralling down past her shoulders, which were encased by the sexiest black dress. Showing just enough cleavage and just enough leg, she glittered, as if covered in a thousand twinkling stars. An angel for him, sent from heaven and with such a sweet voice! He just wanted to take her in his arms and hold her. He imagined peeling that clingy dress slowly from her body and kissing her, from those creamy-coloured rounded swells that appeared at the top of her dress—his mind instantly transported back to his shower and erotic imaginings—all the way to her toes, lingering in many spots in between.

Brodie had to get a grip. *Either sit or stand*, he told himself forcibly. So he slumped into his chair, his engorged cock pushing painfully against the zipper of his pants. He squirmed, trying to ease the pressure, mesmerised by her voice, her body. Caitlin. He had to have her. But he couldn't use her that way. It wasn't his style, and since he had made the decision not to form any long-term relationships—not after the last one had ended so disastrously—Brodie now faced one hell of a fucking dilemma. As that thought pushed its way into his captivated and equally confused mind, he felt the hairs rise on the nape of his neck.

Lila looked at him, then back at Caitlin. She knew him. A frown lined her Botoxed face before it was quickly replaced with a sinister smirk. Lila was going to cause trouble.

"Finally joined the dots then, Cap," said a familiar, gruff voice.

It was coming from JT, his best mate, who had been sitting at the table with a few of the other Jets players and their better halves, probably making bets on how long it would take for him to recognise her.

"Took you long enough, buddy."

Caitlin had to continue singing, though she wasn't even sure how the words kept coming from her mouth. She was looking right at him when he noticed her. As his chocolate-brown eyes locked on to hers, they seemed to grow as big as dinner plates. He didn't sit or stand, but just seemed to be frozen somewhere in between. Caitlin wasn't sure if he was angry with her or not. She was confused by his reaction, thinking it was probably due to the beauty queen sitting next to him, whose long, blonde hair was so straight and shiny. Brodie was probably worried that Caitlin would embarrass him again. Who could blame him, after the way she had flung herself at him? He didn't need to worry, though. She knew her place.

As she dragged her gaze away from his handsome face, she noticed that his girlfriend had a frown on hers. But immediately she thought she must have misread the woman's expression. What on earth could the beautiful blonde possibly have to frown about when she was sitting next to Brodie James?

Three more songs. Caitlin could make it. Then she could take a break from his unrelenting gaze. She would duck outside, cool off and get a breath of fresh air. The temperature inside the room had skyrocketed. Caitlin knew Angelo would be frantic over the obvious problem with the air conditioning. She felt as if she was melting. Heat rolled over her in waves, from the soles of her feet through to the top of her head. It was almost torture, a feeling Caitlin had never experienced on stage before. She normally felt so comfortable and relaxed.

Chapter Seven

Brodie had not even noticed the untouched plate of food in front of him until JT punched him playfully on the arm.

"If you're not going to eat that, send it up this way. It's too good to waste."

Brodie saw the amused expression on his friend's face as the big man leaned towards him and spoke quietly, so as to not be overheard.

"That's the one from the pool, isn't it, mate? Careful. Looks like you've got it bad, and the way you're undressing her with your eyes..." He winked. "I'm worried you're about to drool, mate. Cruella over there is lapping it up, and by the way, what the hell is *she* doing here? Watch your back, mate. I think you've got trouble ahead."

Brodie turned his attention from JT to Lila, or Cruella, as JT insisted on calling her these days, and realised his teammate was probably right on the money.

JT had been with Brodie through every step of the messy marriage and subsequent divorce. Brodie liked the fact that JT was one of the few things that Lila hadn't got, and it wasn't through Lila's lack of trying, either. Lila had made it her personal mission to try and entice as many of Brodie's mates or footy opponents into her bed as possible, before and after the divorce.

JT had a radar for trouble, and Brodie wished he had listened to his friend's concerns before the wedding. Brodie had thought he'd been in love back then. Lila had played the role of devoted girlfriend, then fiancée perfectly — or at least, she had when Brodie was around.

Brodie had been like a plucky rooster, strutting about town with glamour on his arm and feeling the envy of every man in the trendy nightclubs they'd frequented. It hadn't been long into their marriage that the glamour had stopped hiding Lila's petty, vindictive and greedy streak.

League players' lives were actually lonely ones. They were away from home and family regularly. Frequently travelling long distances to games in places like North Queensland, Brisbane, New Zealand and Melbourne was standard. Brodie had also spent many weeks at a time abroad as he played for his country, then captained the national team against Great Britain and France. Not that Brodie was complaining — he loved playing and had done well out of the game, as had JT.

A few good contracts, sponsorship deals and endorsements, with the money wisely invested, had set Brodie up for life. He had purchased property for a song when the market was down and turned a profit. He just had a knack for making money. The income and fame was what had attracted Lila. She had certainly enjoyed his money, but she sure as hell wasn't getting her claws on any more. Brodie often lamented the overgenerous settlement he had made in order to get a quiet divorce. Now, as he pushed his plate towards his friend, he noticed the genuine look of concern on JT's face.

"I'm okay, mate," Brodie said with a grin. "Good to know you've still got my back."

"Always, Brodes, and you know it. It's a bit of a viper pit in here tonight. Bad organisation on your behalf," he said jokingly. "Certainly wasn't expecting that lowlife at our table." JT nodded towards Jack Edwards, then continued to shovel food into his mouth. After a few forkfuls he stopped eating and added, "It's almost enough to put a man off his food. What's going on there?"

Brodie just shook his head. "Trouble. What else? Maybe I should have paid a little more attention to the last-minute changes Angelo made to my seating plan," he answered. "I've got to start the auction. Keep those big paws down, JT. You don't need any of this stuff, and in fact, half of it was yours, anyway." Brodie laughed as he got up from the table.

Jon Thomson loved a good cause. He was a sucker for one. And he loved a win and would go to any lengths to get one — legally, of course. His mindset was a dangerous and expensive combination at a charity auction. As a result, he had a garage full of items he had no real use for. It was a bit of a standing joke around town that JT was invited to nearly every event going. Not that anyone else but Brodie would give him a hard time about it to his face. JT stood at a hundred and ninety-eight centimetres — or six foot five — and was a hundred and twenty kilograms of pure muscle. Jon Thomson was fierce on and off the field, never taking a backward step and loyal to the end.

Brodie remembered the first day the two had met. Both big men had eyed each other up and down, stalking like tigers waiting to pounce, each feeling out his opponent for any weakness. They had trained side by side that day, pushing each other to the limit. Neither man had wanted to be the one to break first. After weights, push-ups, pull-ups, tackle bags and finally running, each had almost fallen, exhausted, to the ground. It had taken the coach explaining that he needed two props on the field to end their pointless competition. He'd asked them to try not to kill each other, as he had a whole game plan centred around them and didn't have time to make another. Having been given a lifeline to end the feud without showing weakness, both men had headed towards the sheds.

They had hardly made it back, swaying and close to collapse, but a mutual respect had been established, laying a foundation for them to be mates for life. Ten years later, Brodie and JT, still leading the Jets, had won their fair share of games and battles. They'd had some lean times too. But one thing had never changed — they had always had each other's backs.

Brodie didn't think he'd ever be able to take the field in opposition to this man. Luckily, the Sydney Jets had managed to retain both players, and hopefully that situation would never change until they both retired. The alternative was a chilling prospect not worth thinking about.

Brodie picked up the first item on the ballot — a rugby league ball signed by the Australian team, which had just beaten New Zealand in the recent Anzac Day Test. An annual event held to commemorate the two nations' victories and losses in wartime, it was always an emotional and hard-fought battle. Watching the New Zealand players perform the cultural haka warrior dance always got the adrenaline pumping.

There were ten similar items on the auction list, a few autographed jerseys and balls donated by mates from other teams in the competition, a holiday to the Gold Coast with tickets for the local Seagulls game. There was even a soccer ball signed by a few of the Socceroos team, who were soon to be heading over to the World Cup. Brodie had been expecting JT to bid on that. He would have himself, if he hadn't been running the show. All items were quickly snapped up, with JT having done his best to push up the price of every single one.

Brodie had yet to speak with Caitlin. She had disappeared as soon as he'd stood up from the table. He would find her, though. She wasn't going to leave before he had a chance to talk to her, that was for sure. That was, if he could manage to speak and not just drag her into his arms and kiss that adorable mouth of hers. His angel with her heavenly voice was going to talk to him, and soon. In fact, he was going to do more than just talk to her—he was going to have her. It might take patience, but Brodie could do that. He'd use some of that 'Brodie James charm' on her.

He would have to make sure she got the message that it wasn't anything permanent. He was not the relationship type. He figured that they could have some fun, enjoy pleasuring each other, then move on. No harm, no foul. So why did the thought of Caitlin moving on have such an unsettling effect on him?

It's just my empty stomach playing up, he decided, trying hard to convince himself.

Brodie managed to finalise the payments and hand over all the purchased items to their new owners, while the remainder of the guests finished their desserts of tiramisu or crème brûlée. Brodie didn't really have a sweet tooth, but as that voice sang seductively to him as he worked, he could think of a few sweets he would like to taste right then. But he tried to rein in the fantasies. He had to finish what he was doing first—making sure the fundraising paperwork was complete.

Chapter Eight

Caitlin returned to the stage after the auction had finished and the coast had cleared. She was amazed and a little shocked at the prices some of the lots had sold at. She'd have loved to get something for Riley, as he still hadn't forgiven her for making him miss out on his chance to chat with Brodie. He wouldn't be happy about missing out on tonight either, so a souvenir would have cheered him up, but the prices of the donated items had quickly gone well out of her reach.

She and Roberto had received a few requests and were preparing to accommodate them. Van Morrison's *Moondance*, an all-time favourite, was requested so often they purposely left it off the playlist so it could be dedicated in a more intimate way. Not many nights went by without Caitlin performing the song, and it was first up.

Caitlin, as usual, quickly forgot all her troubles as she found herself getting lost in the words and music of the song. She was swaying in time with the rhythm, enjoying the feeling as she looked around the room, and her eyes stopped when they reached *him*. Caught up in the moment, she sang to Brodie, gyrating sensually in time to the music like a siren sending out her call. She had attracted the full attention of everyone in the room, men and women alike. She couldn't help herself and didn't know what had come over her. When had the heat been turned up again?

She had spoken to Angelo about the heating problems during her break, but he had looked at the sensor on the wall and informed her all was fine and just as it should be. So why was she feeling so hot again, and why was she acting so strangely? Maybe she was coming down with something. She drifted back into her song and performance.

As the song ended the applause began. People were actually standing and applauding her. She couldn't believe it and did the one thing Caitlin seemed to do best these days—she ran. Quickly, she moved off the stage and into the kitchen as the applause started to fade. She leaned both hands, palms down, against the stainless steel sink. It felt cool under her hot skin. She knew her face was burning up and she was contemplating turning on the cold tap and dunking her head right under it when a large hand clamped down on her shoulder.

Caitlin felt the electric current spark to life in her body at once. It raced from her shoulder to her very core, making her nipples pebble as the feeling continued down to curl her toes. Even before turning around, she knew the hand belonged to Brodie and that she had embarrassed him again.

The look of fire coming from his eyes, scorching her, was almost frightening. He was angry with her. Caitlin could see it in the tense way he stood in front of her, the way the square line of his jaw had tightened. She could even see the pulse throb in his neck. In musical terms, his pulse was beating *allegro*, she thought irrationally, as she tried hard to take control of her emotions.

She felt herself moving but she didn't understand why. Before she had completely realised what was happening, she found herself enclosed in his massive, strong arms. Caitlin could hardly breathe, and wasn't sure if it was due to his hold on her or her body's reaction to him. Either way, she was breathless.

Brodie held her tightly. She could feel his muscular chest pressed to her breasts, and she rubbed her nipples against him, causing more currents of electricity to spark through her body. He was cradling her head into his neck as if it had been made for her to fit there. She could feel his lips on her hair as he placed kisses repeatedly on top of her head. She wondered why he wasn't kissing her lips or breasts. That last thought shocked her. She hadn't ever imagined something like that before, but the image seemed so irresistible.

Brodie pulled her away from his neck, holding her face gently on either side with his big hands. He looked deep into her eyes and spoke in the sexiest voice Caitlin had ever heard.

"I want you."

Caitlin wanted her mind to stop spinning. She tried to focus on Brodie, on what he was saying and what he had meant. She tried to think. As she stood there, not knowing what to do, Brodie let go of her face. Caitlin immediately felt the loss of the connection — she wanted it back. Should she reach out to him and put his hands back on her face?

Chapter Nine

"I want you."

Damn it, that's not what I meant to say, he thought.

Her eyes said it all. There was a slight frown on her beautiful face and her lips were pinched shut as she continued to look at him. Innocence was written all over her. He wanted to soothe that frown line from between her eyes and run his fingers, or tongue, over those soft, plump lips. As he reached out to touch her, a voice from behind caught his attention. He turned to find Angelo, the restaurant owner, glaring at him.

"I said, Mr James, what the hell is going on here? What exactly do you want our Caitlin to do for you?" Angelo said angrily as he continued to glare at Brodie.

He realised the mess this was turning into and couldn't help smiling. Not exactly the smooth move he had been hoping for. That old James charm seemed to have deserted him for the moment.

"Sir, I assure you I do not mean any harm to this beautiful angel you have working here," he said confidently. "In fact, I have met Caitlin before and was just trying to reacquaint myself with her when you arrived." When a reply wasn't forthcoming, he continued. "Perhaps you would allow me to step outside with her for a few moments, away from prying eyes." Brodie nodded back towards the main room and added, "I was hoping to convince our angel here to come dine with me sometime."

Brodie smiled broadly at the owner, whose eyes seemed to smile back at him in return. Angelo pointed to the door off to the side of the kitchen.

"You could go out to the private car park and talk if you like," he replied. "I think you may find the night air quite refreshing, Mr James. You look like you need to cool off! Just remember, *giovane*, I will wait right here until Caitlin comes back in," the restaurateur said protectively.

Through the whole dialogue Brodie noticed Caitlin had not moved or made a sound. Her eyes were large and bright as she stared straight at him. Brodie grabbed her hand and gently tugged.

"Come outside for a few minutes, angel. I need to talk to you," he said as he started for the door. He was relieved to find no resistance from Caitlin. As he followed her, Brodie could not stop himself from checking out her butt one more time. When he'd entered the kitchen to find her leaning over the sink, her back to him, legs slightly apart, knees bent and her bottom tantalisingly jutting out at him, with her palms face down flat on the sink bench in front of her, he'd nearly lost it. The pose had been so sexual it had almost driven him mad with need. His thoughts had nearly made him blush. Angelo was right—he did need to cool off.

A rush of wind hit them as they exited the warm kitchen. Brodie felt Caitlin shiver and cursed himself for not bringing something to wrap around her. Her dress was not enough to keep her warm—although it was certainly doing it for him. He was on fire with need for her. He tried to dampen down his feelings, not wanting to scare her into running again.

Brodie guided Caitlin over to the side of his big, black car, hoping the size of the vehicle would serve as a windbreak of sorts. He caressed her gently, massaging up and down her arms, trying to warm her. She felt so soft against his rough, battered fingers, and he enjoyed the sensual feel of her skin. A picture of her—naked, hair splayed upon his pillow as he tasted her from the top of her pretty head to the tips of her toes—flashed into his mind, and his cock jerked again.

Brodie rubbed his hand over his head, raking his fingers through his close-cropped hair and massaging the back of his thick neck as he tried to get his thoughts under control, so he could actually speak words that made sense. All the time, he watched her gorgeous face for any sign of her wanting to flee.

Brodie finally spoke. "You are the most beautiful creature I've ever seen. You have the voice of an angel and the body of a temptress."

He stopped, licked his lips. Her gaze dropped to his mouth as her tongue poked out from between her sensual lips for just the briefest moment. Brodie knew he had to make it fast or he was going to come in his pants. That was something that had never happened before, and the thought did not appeal to him. What was it about this woman that affected him so deeply?

"Would you care to join me for dinner tomorrow night? You pick, I'll pick... I don't care as long as you say yes," he finished breathlessly.

Brodie watched and waited for any sign of hope from her motionless face. Terror filled him like nothing he'd felt before. What if she said no? What if he was just being an old fool? He didn't feel quite as confident of the outcome as he had a moment ago. Before he could think of another approach, she threw herself at him again. It was just as well he still had quick reflexes, or he might have dropped her as she flung her arms around his neck the way she had at the pool. She was placing sweet little kisses up and down his jawline — *my God, the woman is hot.* She was killing him.

He grabbed her thighs so he could get a better grip on her. He was not going to drop his angel, that was for sure. She weighed next to nothing, but her tight dress and the fact she couldn't wrap her legs around him was making it difficult for him to keep hold of her. He moved the dress up and hitched her hard against him as he repositioned his hands on her legs. It was then he realised he felt skin — she wasn't wearing any stockings.

"Oh, angel," Brodie groaned.

He was just holding on. Any minute now he would lose control, throw her to the ground and ravage her like a caveman. He had never felt so needy. He ground his lips down upon hers until she opened for him, then sank his tongue fully into her mouth and made a thorough exploration. She was so warm and sweet, like toffee, and he could have kissed her this way for hours. She pressed her tongue against his, at first timidly, then becoming bolder.

He had to have this woman. Brodie stroked his thumbs up her inner thighs. His hands were completely under the hem of her dress, and he could feel the edge of her underwear. Holding her cute behind with one hand, he moved her so she could sit

Donna Gallagher

on the bonnet of his car and immediately his cock throbbed at the loss of contact.

Brodie cupped her mound with his free hand. It was emitting such heat, and her panties felt moist. She stilled. It was as if a bright light flashed before his eyes, and the fog in Brodie's head cleared. He dragged his lips away from hers and gently lifted her from her perch and slid her down his aching body, brushing past his engorged and incredibly painful erection. He knew she felt it, but what could he do? It was all for her, because of her.

"Good one, Brodie, way to take it slow!" he groaned.

As Brodie set her back on her feet, he didn't break the contact between them, but continued to hold her gently by the arms. Enjoying the glazed look in her eyes and the slightly kiss-swollen look of her lips, he smiled down tenderly. "So can I take that as a yes for dinner, then?"

62

Chapter Ten

Caitlin didn't know how she managed to finish the night. As she climbed into her own vehicle she noticed the big, black car Brodie had placed her on while he'd touched and kissed her was gone. She took a moment to just sit and gather her thoughts, closing her eyes and remembering how wonderful the moment had been when she'd felt the heat of his mouth on hers. She ran her finger along her lips, imagining it was Brodie touching her.

She felt good. No, better than good. She felt alive and warm and happy. It seemed like such a long time since she had felt this carefree—a year, at least. If Brodie had been a drug, she would have truly been an addict.

It was still unbelievable to her that he had agreed to add Riley to his dinner invitation. After she'd explained that she couldn't leave him alone and had already used the sitter for tonight's event, he had happily agreed to extend the invitation. He had organised to pick them up at seven the following evening, and thoughtfully added that they didn't need to dress formally, remarking that he always felt more comfortable in jeans.

Caitlin was relieved to know the dress code was casual, as her wardrobe was limited. Riley grew inches almost overnight. She had trouble keeping him in decent clothes, but somehow she always did. She felt it was important for Riley's self-confidence that he had clean, respectable clothing to wear, even if he didn't realise some of it was second-hand from the local thrift store. Caitlin was always careful with her choices, inspecting each piece before purchase.

As she drove home, thinking of how she'd break the news to him, she realised Riley was going to go nuts. Caitlin grinned. She could already see him bouncing around the flat with excitement.

It was the thought of their flat that brought her crashing back down to reality. *My God.* What would Brodie think when he saw the old house and the little flat that had become their home? She shrugged. *Oh, well, it's our home. We own it, and that's better than some people have. Maybe we can wait out in front a little before seven.*

Caitlin parked her car on the street so as not to bother the other residents, now or in the morning, when she would need to drop Riley at squads. The noise was obvious from the moment she stepped from the car. It sounded like heavy metal music. She didn't recognise the band, but then, she didn't really listen to that genre. *It's very loud for this late at night.* As she walked down the hall to her front door, the walls were almost throbbing from the loud noise.

New tenants. She grimaced, remembering the moving van that had boxed her car in on Monday. The flat above was rented out, and tenants were always coming and going. How on earth was she going to get to sleep? Bags under her eyes from being kept awake would not be a good look for her dinner date tomorrow night. Glancing at the wall clock, she noticed it was after midnight. She corrected herself. *Make that tonight.*

That thought made her happy all over again as she folded out the sofa into her bed and quickly and efficiently added the linen. After a trip to the bathroom to wipe off the remnants of her make-up and brush her teeth, Caitlin was soon snuggled down under her pink-covered doona, and as she hugged her spare pillow she wondered what it would feel like to snuggle with Brodie instead. Caitlin fell into a deep sleep almost immediately with a little smile on her face, the loud music not annoying her at all.

* * * *

Brodie had a good training session—he was sharp and focused. JT just kept clapping him on the back and laughing at him. His teammates and the coaching staff were all in shock at the way he'd attacked the session with gusto. Brodie had not realised the extent of his malaise, but that was over. Now he felt good. Better than good—Brodie felt *young*.

He had tried not to overthink his decision to ask Caitlin and her brother out to dinner, though he did wonder why the parents couldn't look after the kid. But, hey, he didn't know their schedule. Maybe the parents worked nights or were away. Brodie managed to put a positive spin on things. The kid would be a useful chaperone. That was a good thing. He had come so close to seducing Caitlin in the car park last night that it frightened him.

Brodie James did not lose control, ever. Not even when he'd found his wife in bed with the captain of a rival team. No, Brodie had just turned on his heel and walked away. Brodie was calm, under control, and always thought things through before taking action. That was why he had captained his country for so long. He was honoured that his opinion was sought after and he was often invited to take part in forums on how to better his beloved rugby league.

Brodie led by example. Well, apart from when he'd married Lila, but that time was behind him now and he had managed to keep any gossip regarding his failed marriage out of the media. The mutual respect he and most reporters shared had helped, as did the money he'd bribed Lila with for her silence.

Having given it plenty of thought on the drive home from training, Brodie concluded that the best place to take his dinner dates was some place they'd feel most comfortable, and that place was bound to be Mia's Restaurant. It would also help him clear any bad feelings between him and the owner, Angelo, in regards to his behaviour last night. The man was not an idiot. He had seen the state of play when Caitlin and Brodie had returned, somewhat dishevelled, from their car park 'talk'.

As Brodie opened the door to his home and dropped his training bag on the floor, he smiled. Yes, he would make a booking now. Grabbing his phone, he scrolled through until he found the number he was searching for and placed the call. He had a few hours before he needed to leave, so Brodie sat at his desk and opened his laptop, checking emails before spending some time on his business portfolio.

After showering and changing into a clean, well-worn pair of jeans that fitted his large frame, Brodie pulled on a black V-neck sweater. It was woollen and soft, the feel of it pleasing against his skin. He didn't mind the way the sweater clung to his muscled torso and arms either. Why should he? Brodie had worked hard to get his body into shape, and still did. He looked at himself in the mirror, his craggy, well-worn face reflected back at him, and remembered how every scar had appeared. His was a rough sport and pretty boys didn't stay pretty for long. The crooked nose from various breaks was a little larger than he would have liked, but he knew his dark brown eyes, high cheekbones and strong, square jaw were not unattractive to women. Maybe it was the high profile that actually drew the female interest, but it didn't really matter to Brodie anymore. He was comfortable in his own skin.

He rubbed his hand over his close-cropped brown hair. He had learnt early on in his career to keep it that way. His naturally curly hair made him appear too soft for the life he led. Brodie thought about spraying on the latest fad in aftershave, supplied to him free of charge from the manufacturer, but decided against it. Brodie preferred natural. If someone didn't like his smell, they could just take a hike. He hesitated at that thought, hoping that this would not be the case with his angel.

He strode purposefully from the bathroom and pulled on his crocodile skin boots, a good purchase made whilst in the top end of Australia for an exhibition game held there some years ago. It had been to encourage Indigenous boys to turn to league instead of trouble. There were many Indigenous Australians making a name for themselves playing league, and they were always up for giving something back to their communities.

He could feel his stomach quiver with anticipation about tonight and how it would go. He was nervous, which was invigorating. Brodie felt alive.

He knew the road in Ashfield that Caitlin had given him as her address, so it was a quick trip. Ashfield was only a few suburbs away from him. As he turned his black Range Rover onto the street, Brodie noticed that he'd arrived on time for his date. Trying to catch sight of a house number so he could get his bearings, he saw two figures standing on the kerb up ahead.

"What the hell?" Brodie said, as he realised it was exactly the people he was looking for. Brodie was a little old-fashioned and had expected to collect his date from her door, but as he pulled up next to them and began to climb out of the car, both passenger doors on the left opened and his guests jumped in. Brodie was half out of the door and felt a bit comical just getting back in. This was going to be an interesting night. He turned towards Caitlin and shut his door again.

"Well, hello, angel," he said to her, with a big, goofy grin he couldn't stop from breaking out across his face.

When he turned to the rear seat passenger he was amused to see another grin—just like his own, he imagined—reflected back at him.

"You must be Riley. It's a pleasure to finally meet you," he said enthusiastically. "I'm Brodie James. Glad you could join us for dinner, mate."

He saw in the kid's eyes that he was a fan and completely awestruck. Brodie had seen this look before in young kids. Hell, he remembered feeling just like that when he'd met his hero some twenty years ago. It was quite an honour when you realised you had become a sports idol, and something Brodie never took for granted. He tried to spend as much time as he could with fans. He hated disappointing anyone.

As Caitlin and Riley fastened their seatbelts, Brodie put the car into drive and headed for the restaurant. The silence was a bit unsettling so Brodie tried to lighten the mood by informing his two dinner companions of his choice of venue. Riley whooped in the back, but a quick glance at Caitlin revealed she was biting at her bottom lip. He took her hand gently and brought it up to his mouth, kissing her knuckles.

"If you don't want to go there, that's okay, angel," Brodie whispered. "We can find somewhere else. I should have thought about it more. Of course you wouldn't want to go where you work. I'm sorry, angel. What would you like to do?"

Caitlin had trouble speaking, she was so overwhelmed. She had immediately recognised the car from last night. She was also impressed with the man's thoughtfulness and easy way of including Riley in their plans. She was relieved to be going to Mia's because she felt comfortable there. The problem was, Brodie was looking at her with such concern, and his lips sent shivers through her whole body as he kissed her hand. Finally, Caitlin managed to croak out the answer he was waiting for.

"Mia's would be wonderful."

As she sat back into the comfiest car seat ever, Caitlin finally relaxed. She was going to make the most of this night. It wasn't every day she and Riley got such a treat.

Brodie pulled the car up outside the familiar door. Caitlin went to jump out when a big hand came down onto her jeans-clad leg.

"Relax, angel. Let me come around, get the door for you. It's what a gentleman should do for a beautiful lady, and have I told you how beautiful you look tonight?"

She had never felt so special in her life. Riley was already on the kerb and looked confused as he watched Brodie walk around the car and open his sister's door, then take her arm. Caitlin heard Riley giggle. She didn't know what was so funny and would be having words with him later about good manners.

Caitlin didn't think she walked into the restaurant so much as floated in. Brodie had booked a table by the window. Angelo warmly welcomed and fussed over them.

"Ah, it is good to see you again, *giovane, bella.* Welcome—come this way. I have saved the best table for you."

Brodie pulled out a chair for her. He then seated himself next to Riley, directly opposite her.

"It's so I can gaze into your amazing emerald eyes all night," he explained, sounding so sincere she couldn't help the quiver of excitement from racing over her skin.

Riley made a gagging sound, then giggled. Caitlin sent a frown at him. It wasn't long before he was lost for words, though, because Brodie threw his arm around her brother's shoulders, giving him a manly hug and explaining how Riley would understand one day. He finished off the little talk with a 'mate' and a wink for good measure.

Caitlin thought that Riley would just explode, right then and there.

I bet he wishes some of his mates from school would walk past and see him now. She smiled lovingly at the two males facing her. She could just see Riley holding court at school, telling all his friends about the evening. She had the classic urge to pinch herself to check if this was real.

Angelo supplied some of his finest meals to their table — the freshest pasta, cooked to perfection and covered with generous helpings of aromatic sauces. She ate so much that she kept glancing at Brodie just to make sure he didn't think her a glutton, but each and every time she looked up, Brodie was smiling back at her.

She even enjoyed her first glass of champagne. Brodie had gently insisted she try the bubbly, slightly pink-coloured drink, which was sweet and very enjoyable. Riley had ordered an orange juice rather than his usual choice of Coke, to her surprise and delight. Riley was obviously trying to impress his hero by ordering a healthier alternative.

Caitlin declined dessert. She just couldn't fit it in. She sat back, delighted to watch Riley and Brodie enjoying their gelato and talking easily about football, swimming and the like. The conversation had been so easy and natural between the three of them all night.

It was good for Riley to have another male to talk with. It made Caitlin a little sad that her brother had no one, now his father was gone. It had been a year since her brother had had a father figure in his life. As if sensing her saddening mood, Brodie pushed a spoonful of lemon gelato to her lips, and without thinking Caitlin pulled the spoon into her mouth and sucked.

"Mmm," she moaned, "that's good." She licked the remnants from the spoon he held out to her.

To her surprise, Brodie reached right across the table and dragged her forward to meet his lips. There was no gelato left after Brodie had explored every inch of her mouth with his tongue. Just as abruptly, Brodie pulled away, muttering something she couldn't quite hear.

One look at Riley, and she burst into a fit of laughter. He was open-mouthed, his spoon dripping melted gelato all down his arm as he watched them, his big, green eyes nearly popping from his head. It wasn't long before the three of them were all laughing together.

Brodie was having the time of his life. He was relaxed, as the company was more enjoyable than he could have dreamed possible. His angel was breathtaking and she didn't even know it. Dressed in jeans and a simple long-sleeved black shirt, she was perfection. It appeared to Brodie that she wasn't wearing any makeup on her pretty oval face, but she didn't need to. She was stunning *au naturel*, just as he preferred. To him, nothing could outshine her — his heart was filled with her. The easy way she spoke to her brother and the love they showed towards one another made him almost jealous of the kid.

He was entranced by the sexy way she twirled strands of her thick auburn curls through her fingers when thinking about something. He had to stop himself, on more than one occasion, from reaching over and touching her hair. He knew it would feel soft. It was an incredible experience being with the Walters family, one he could get very used to — if he were the settling down type, that was, he tried to remind himself.

Of course, he had lost his head once, and who could blame him? The way Caitlin had taken the gelato from his spoon, her cheeks hollowing in as she sucked, then licked that lucky little silver spoon clean, had driven him wild. And she'd topped it off with that sensual moan! He was a man, after all, not a saint. What could he say? It had been painful with the table edge crushing his cock as he'd leaned over and engulfed her mouth almost into his. She'd tasted cool and tangy. He'd taken his time to lick all remnants of the lemon gelato from her sinful mouth. It was *his* dessert, after all, he'd mused to himself as he'd consumed her.

It had taken Brodie a few moments before he'd remembered the kid. The look on Riley's face was a worry. His eyes were wide and his mouth open, with gelato dripping down his arm. He looked a bit shocked. Brodie resolved to keep himself under tighter control in front of the boy in the future.

Caitlin's reaction had been a surprise as well. She'd burst into fits of laughter, the sound like tinkling bells in heaven to his ears. Brodie couldn't help but join in with his own bellowing laugh. He couldn't remember the last time he had laughed so heartily.

Dinner was over all too soon. Brodie paid the almost embarrassingly small bill, leaving a generous tip. He helped Caitlin back into the front passenger seat of his car by placing both hands around her hips and lifting her. In one smooth motion, he placed her gently on the soft leather seat. He wasn't ready for the evening to end just yet.

"So, Walters clan, is there any way I can tempt you into coming back to my place for a bit? The night is still young, and Riley, I think I may have a few of the movies you were talking about on DVD." Brodie knew there was nothing noble in the way he was using Riley for his own gain, but hey, he would give the kid the DVDs if it worked. *Win-win!*

"That'd be great, Brodie. Gosh, I think just being able to say I was at your place is enough. The guys at school will go ape when I tell them! Can we, sis? Ple-e-ase?"

The eager look on Riley's face left Brodie feeling of a twinge of guilt, but he just hadn't spent enough time with Caitlin so wasn't about to back down.

"Well, I guess that would be okay, but only for a short time, Riley. It's a school night so we can't stay out too late. If you're sure it's no trouble, Brodie, that would be lovely." The smile she gave him almost took his breath away, but the way she fussed over Riley sounded quite motherly.

Chapter Eleven

The trip back to Brodie's home seemed to take no time at all. Riley talked all the way there about his favourite movies and whether or not they were in Brodie's collection. Brodie was pleased to confirm he did indeed own many of the films Riley mentioned, and offered to loan them to him. All the while, Brodie greedily held on to his angel's hand. It was warm and so delicate in comparison to his. Caitlin's fingers were long and slender with short, well-groomed pink nails. Brodie just wanted to suck and lick every single one of those precious digits.

The image of doing that made Brodie groan, the sound coming out louder than he'd intended. He was truly stunned when his angel dragged his hand towards her lips and kissed each of his fingers tenderly. It was at that exact moment that Brodie knew he was a goner. Would he ever get enough of this woman? He didn't think he would, even if she was his forever. He just hoped her parents wouldn't object, or be concerned about the age difference. One thing was certain — Brodie would do everything in his power to win them over, and he already knew he had an ally in Riley.

He parked the car in the garage. Caitlin stayed in her seat and waited for him to come around and open her door. He was pleased about that. Riley, of course, had jumped from the car the moment it had stopped. The kid was a ball of energy and had taken off to look at the view outside.

Brodie lovingly lifted Caitlin from the car, brushing his lips gently and quickly over hers. He let her body slide down his, enjoying the feel of her as she made her way over his chest, hips, crotch and thighs. He took her hand and headed up the private outdoor stairway that led to his balcony and door. He was pleased to notice both Caitlin and Riley stopped to admire the spectacular view of the Parramatta River.

After a few minutes, the pair joined him inside his apartment. Riley went immediately to the large DVD cabinet that held Brodie's extensive collection, where he emitted various sounds of pleasure. Brodie took the opportunity to show off his living quarters, even feeling a tad nervous at the thought of Caitlin's impressions.

Brodie was pleased with his home and was proud at having chosen all the décor himself. The choice of modern furniture was very stylish. Large, comfy, tan leather couches were placed strategically, encouraging visitors to sit and gaze out at the busy waterway. Deep brown, lush carpet that made you want to curl your toes in it covered the floor. Co-ordinated lamps filled the room with a warm, soft glow. A large, flat-screen television was mounted on one wall, complete with the latest in media equipment neatly positioned underneath in a cabinet that matched the DVD housing. Hanging on the other wall were several accolades to Brodie's extensive and successful career.

Make no mistake, it was a man's abode, but it still had a warm and cosy feel about it. Brodie stood staring at Caitlin, wishing he could just take her in his arms and make passionate love to her all night. He wanted to pleasure her as no other man had, so no one else could ever take his place. Brodie was no fool, though. He had Riley's welfare to think of here as well, and he didn't think the boy was up for that sort of life lesson. What was more, he was sure the kid's parents would be horrified. It was okay. Brodie was a patient man. He sat down on one of the tan lounge chairs and pulled Caitlin into his lap.

Caitlin seemed to melt into his body, and she relaxed in his arms as if she had spent her life there. It pleased Brodie to know she trusted him already. He wanted to put into place a plan to meet her parents, and started to tell her so.

"Will your parents be at home when I drop you back? I'd love to meet them." Thinking of Riley and his parents had raised Brodie's curiosity — not that he overly minded sharing this first date with the kid, but he did wonder what Caitlin's parents did for a living and why they weren't around tonight.

At the mention of her parents he felt Caitlin go rigid. Even Riley, whom he'd thought was absorbed in the DVD collection, stopped and turned towards his sister. He waited for what seemed an age for her to answer him.

"What the hell is going on, Caitlin?" Brodie asked, confused and slightly angered at the lack of response from either sibling. He could only think that maybe they had something to hide. Perhaps Caitlin thought her parents might disapprove of their daughter dating a footballer, or maybe it was the age difference between him and Caitlin. Whatever it was, Brodie really needed an answer.

"I hope you don't think your parents will be put off by my career choice? I know some people think rugby league's a bit brutal, but there is a lot more to me than just my league career. I'm quite a successful businessman too..."

Brodie had never felt so insecure—couldn't believe he was spouting off a bloody résumé to convince Caitlin he was good enough for her, good enough to meet her parents. Then Brodie had another, more appealing thought. Maybe it wasn't him at all. Maybe it was her folks she was embarrassed by, and she didn't want him to judge her by parents who were hippies, or something like that.

But as he sat debating all the angles, Caitlin remained still, with tears in her eyes. Brodie's heart clenched. He had upset her.

It was then that he noticed Riley was standing in front of him. Taking his sister's hand, Riley calmly spoke. "Our mum and dad were killed in a car accident a year ago. It's just Cate and me now. If it wasn't for her I'd be in a foster home. Cate left uni and came home to take care of me," he continued, his pride and love for his sister evident.

Brodie was in shock. He didn't know what to say. She really was an angel! So much strength, loyalty and love in one gorgeous little package. He was so proud of her he could have cried. *That* definitely would have been a sight people would have paid to see. Big, tough, always-in-control Brodie James blubbering. Brodie brought his hand up to cover Riley's, connecting himself with both of these precious people.

"Well then, son," he said to Riley. "So it's only your permission I need to court your sister?"

It was a magic moment. They were all full of emotion. So much had happened in such a short time, and Brodie could not wait to become fully involved with the lives of this incredible small family. He could not wait to make them both part of his life as well. Starting tonight.

He took the time to explain his busy schedule to Caitlin and Riley. Training wasn't what took up most of Brodie's time—it was the travelling to interstate and overseas games. This weekend, the Sydney Jets were up against the Auckland side. The game was scheduled for Sunday in New Zealand, with the team leaving on Saturday morning.

"I just had a great idea," Brodie started eagerly. "The Jets are playing in Auckland this weekend. Why don't you two come over with me and watch the game? I can arrange everything. We leave Saturday morning, so Riley won't miss any school, and you can stay in the same hotel as me. My treat." He was really getting quite excited about the whole idea, his mind so busy racing off in all directions, thinking about the many things that would need to be organised, that he nearly missed Caitlin's reply.

"Not that I don't love the thought of a trip overseas, and I'm sure Riley would just love the opportunity to hang around your teammates, but I think there could be one glaring problem, Brodie. We don't have passports. Never have."

Reluctantly, Brodie had to admit defeat this time. Riley was obviously disappointed. But Brodie was not about to give up—he wanted to see that smile back on the kid's face, hated that look of sadness.

"Well, so this weekend is a no-go, but you have to at least promise to come the following weekend. We're playing at home. I can give Riley a tour of the team room before the game, then after we win," Brodie added with a wink, "you can come and join in on the celebration with the rest of the boys. What do you say, mate? Does that sound good?"

Riley beamed back at Brodie, nodding eagerly. It was all Brodie could do to stop himself from hugging the boy. Well, the fact that he still held Caitlin captive on his lap made it difficult, anyway.

It was getting late, and Brodie knew he had to get Caitlin and Riley back to their home and beds, but it was hard for him to let them go. There was so much he wanted to tell Caitlin. He wanted to explain his failed marriage, tell her about his loving parents who had property up north. He could already see himself and Riley on the quad bikes, racing around the fields of the small hobby farm he'd purchased in his parents' names. All of these things could wait. They would have plenty of time when he returned from 'over the ditch'.

Riley had selected two DVDs to borrow. Brodie was impressed by the boy's restraint in taking so few. Perhaps Riley already knew he'd have access to the others at any time soon. Brodie couldn't help but hope that was the case.

He managed a few deep, hungry kisses with Caitlin while Riley was distracted, but it was in no way enough. They made plans for him to take Riley to watch Caitlin sing the following night at Mia's, acting as chauffeur to them both. This idea seemed to make Riley very excited. Caitlin was to organise a sitter for Riley on Monday night, so she and Brodie could have some private time together. She had assured him the sitter would be free and happy to oblige, and had shaken her head at his offer to pay the sitter's fees.

She was a proud and independent woman, his angel. He loaded them into his car and started for Ashfield.

He could tell Caitlin was restless. "What's wrong, angel?" he whispered.

She just shook her head, a sad little smile on her face. "The reason we met you out on the kerb tonight, Brodie, was that I was embarrassed for you to see where we live. Even more so now, after seeing your beautiful home." Caitlin waved her arm around to encompass her surroundings as she spoke. "Your place is so wonderful. Riley and I share a little one-bedroom flat. It's tiny and run-down—shabby, really. Riley has the bedroom and I convert the sofa into a bed each night for myself. It may not be much, but at least we own it."

"Oh, angel, baby, you shouldn't have worried about stuff like that. You have nothing to be ashamed or embarrassed about. You are doing such a good job being there for your brother, I would never have judged you like that." Brodie couldn't believe what she was saying. He was so sorry that she'd believed she had to hide anything about herself.

"Brodie, I shouldn't have misjudged you, shouldn't have been embarrassed. I underestimated you, 'cause Brodie James, you are a very nice man. After spending the last few hours with you, I can see you care for us, and I know now that how I live is not an issue for you. Well, at least I hope it isn't," she added with a hesitant smile.

Brodie was afraid to speak, he was so full of emotion. He was worried that he would blurt out that what he was feeling was, in fact, a lot more than just 'caring'. But it was too soon. He needed time to figure everything out logically, the Brodie James way.

The brief kiss he planted on her warm, willing lips at the door definitely didn't do much to quell his hunger. He ran to his car and drove away quickly, to remove the temptation of returning to her home, breaking down her door and ravaging her. He spent the rest of the night tossing and turning in bed as the hunger he felt for her raged at him, until finally he took matters into his own hands again.

This time, as he stroked his length, he had memories as well as his imagination to fire his need. This time Brodie could remember how it felt to have her sitting in his lap as he'd kissed her, and although that reality had been brief, he could expand on it with his imagination. He imagined her nude in his lap, her hair falling like flames over her breasts as she moaned under the might of his kiss. Brodie could almost taste the sweet nectar of her body as he imagined kissing every inch of her bare skin until he reached his goal. The thought of licking and tasting her swollen folds was enough to finish him off. Before the image of him feasting on his sweet angel fully took shape in his mind, he felt the release of his seed in his fist, warm and sticky, the feeling shallow but enough to take the edge off, at least, so he could sleep.

* * * *

The following night, Brodie arrived earlier than he had planned. He'd had trouble keeping away from Caitlin.

His day had seemed endless, the minutes ticking by so slowly. He had changed clothes twice, not happy with his look and feeling anxious, edgy. This nervousness he experienced when thinking about Caitlin was so unfamiliar to him. Where had calm, unflappable Brodie gone?

Unable to stand the wait any longer, he was now at her door fifteen minutes ahead of schedule, a giant spray of fresh-cut farm roses in his hand. The florist had mixed in some flower called baby's breath that seemed to rattle as he held the offering up. As soon as she opened the door and he saw that beautiful smile, he relaxed, dragging her into his arms and devouring all the lipstick from her lips. The bunch of roses squashed between their two bodies created a scent that filled his nose — or was that Caitlin's sweet smell? Brodie had no idea.

* * * *

The night was really enjoyable. Brodie was feeling pleased with himself, glad he had invited JT to join them. The big man had been reluctant at first, not wanting to get in the way. Brodie knew JT would be keen to meet Caitlin, but seeing him interact with Riley was even more special. The young boy was in his element, keeping both men entertained with stories from school. He told them about his friends' reactions to his dining with Brodie and actually visiting his home the night before. Brodie was almost embarrassed by the tales, and there were more in the making. Riley had already arm-wrestled both men — winning, of course, but after a long struggle!

Caitlin had taken his breath away with her singing. She was so talented and had quite the following. Brodie realised most of the guests were obviously regulars, given the familiar way they treated her. In fact, he had felt quite annoyed by some of the male customers who'd seemed to spend a little too much time talking to her. Jealousy was not a feeling Brodie was used to dealing with.

As the time for him to take Caitlin and Riley home approached, Brodie was not sure he'd be able to leave her at her door. He was wondering if she would invite him in. He had to leave early in the morning to catch the team flight to New Zealand, so he wouldn't be able to stay too long, anyway. He was so filled with anticipation that his hands felt clammy and he was continually rubbing them on the legs of his jeans. JT noticed, of course, and couldn't let it pass without some witty retort.

"Hey, Brodes, you doing okay? You're as twitchy as a rookie before his first game of football. Need me to give you some tips on how to win with the ladies, big guy?" JT's hushed voice was low enough that only Brodie could hear his teasing tone.

"You're just ticked off 'cause she's such a beauty — but you're right about one thing, JT. I'm as jumpy as a horny kid on a first date. I just don't want to do anything to spook her before I figure out where this is all heading." Brodie, not usually one to get all deep and meaningful with the blokes, didn't hesitate to share his fear with his mate. *God help me, what's happening to me?*

As Brodie turned onto Caitlin's street, he was both surprised and relieved as Caitlin turned to him.

"Would you like to come inside for a cup of tea or something?" she asked timidly.

The shy tone of her voice touched something deep inside him. She had no idea how much she had captivated him, how much he desperately wanted nothing more than to go inside with her. But it was the 'or something' element of her offer that caused all sorts of explicit images to form in his mind. Brodie just couldn't control his thoughts around this tantalising woman.

He spent time settling Riley into bed, something he had never envisioned or had any expertise in doing before tonight. He found it surprisingly enjoyable watching the boy snuggle down under the blankets. Brodie couldn't help the chuckle that escaped his lips as he noticed Riley's Jets pyjamas and quilt cover — the kid was such a delight. But as much as he was enjoying his time with Riley, Brodie really wanted to be in the other room, the room where his angel waited for him.

Brodie returned to find Caitlin sitting stiffly on the sofa, twisting her fingers. He noticed two cups of tea on the table beside her. Brodie needed to feel this woman in his arms — now. Without a moment's hesitation, he sat next to her and pulled her onto his lap. He began with little kisses up her neck, nibbling at her ear lobe, then across her cheek, finally reaching her lips. She opened for him and their tongues seemed to dance together. Caitlin's mouth was so warm and sweet, and tasted like honey and tea.

He was fighting a losing battle — body versus mind. He knew he should be taking this slower, but his body was roaring for some action. Brodie found himself teetering on the edge of control, a very unusual place to find himself, indeed.

He placed just his fingertip on her shoulder and ran it slowly down her body, across her breast, around her hard, protruding nipple. He continued down to stroke her hips before exploring her stomach, belly button and repeating the journey in reverse up the other side of her body. Her moans and sighs urged him on as he slowly unbuttoned her top. He was going to show her so much pleasure tonight, in the short time he had with her before he had to leave. He would wait for another time to let her pleasure him. Tonight was all about his angel.

Caitlin writhed in Brodie's arms, could not control her own body. He was using just one finger, tracing it gently over her, brushing over her breast and nipple. She arched her body closer to him and his touch, wondering how he could get such a reaction from her with only one finger. She could not imagine how it would feel if he used both hands. All the while, his lips and tongue were doing more amazing things to her mouth. She was finding it hard to decide which action was more appealing as her body responded so passionately.

Yes, she would probably die, she felt. She was restless, wanting something from him to help her with this needy hunger. Her body was on fire and she didn't know how to ease the heat. Oh, but it felt exquisite. Brodie began moving his lips down her neck, nipping at her, then kissing the same spot. The sensations of pain and pleasure became one and the same to her. He dipped his head and placed his lips around her left nipple. The pleasure was so intense she almost screamed. He must have sensed her delight as he sucked at her through her blouse.

Caitlin did not know how or when it had happened, but her blouse and bra were now undone, leaving her breasts bare to his heated gaze. She loved the way he was looking at her, touching her. She had never gone this far before, and was unprepared for the intensity of her feelings. Oddly, she was not embarrassed at all to be so open to him. She wanted to touch him and tried to pull his jumper up but couldn't free him of it, so snugly did it fit over his bulging biceps and chest. Brodie pulled the wool garment over his head in one move, and she caught her breath at the sight of his muscled, masculine chest.

Curly, light brown, almost golden hair covered the upper part of his chest, and she couldn't help notice it tapering down to form a path to his pants waistline and what lay beneath. She explored his chest, getting to know the feel of it, touching the hair and twisting it, brushing her hand across and around his distended nipple. He groaned and before she had taken another shallow breath, she was lying beneath him. He had lifted her off his lap and laid her on the sofa, stretching out next to her with his leg over hers.

Caitlin was unaware of how much time had gone by. All she knew was this man. She wanted to climb right under his skin and needed to feel closer. All the while he touched her and stroked her, and the hardness of his erection pushed into her hip. She wanted to touch him, but he had both her hands held in one of his, lightly pinning them above her head. The other hand was making its way up her skirt—he touched her through her panties. She felt the lips of her vulva swell at his touch. She was so wet she could feel the seep of liquid coming from her body. Unsure, she pulled away from him a little.

"Can I touch you, angel? Feel if you're all wet for me?" Brodie whispered in her ear, the words both shocking and exciting Caitlin at the same time. "I sure hope you are wet for me. It'll make me feel so good knowing that you're as hot for me as I am for you. Trust me, angel, I won't hurt you. If I do anything that you don't like or feel comfortable with, just tell me and I'll stop." Caitlin relaxed into him, hoping it was answer enough for Brodie, not sure she could speak if she tried. For some reason, she knew she could trust this man and believed him that he would stop if she became uncomfortable. As he pulled her panties from her she lifted her bottom to help, but her movement was of little use because his leg over her pinned her down.

She wasn't scared, though he was clearly in control. He pushed a finger into her and moaned in her ear as he touched the sensitive nub of nerves just inside her folds. He began to swirl around it slowly. An uncontrollable wave of pleasure spread through her, but never quite broke over her. She panted, tossing her head from side to side as she searched for some sort of finality before she went mad.

Brodie hushed her and in a dark, sexy whisper told her, "Come for me. Let go. I'll catch you." He told her he would cover his fingers with her sweet juices, so he could lick them clean. He pinched at her little nub with magic fingers, rubbing at it until the tidal wave of sensation exploded from her with such strength she wanted to scream out from the pleasure. Brodie covered her mouth with his lips just in time to muffle the sounds of her passion.

As she lay there exhausted in his arms, she watched him lick his fingers, lapping at them like a starving lion. She wanted to make him feel how she had felt and cupped his shaft. He shook his head and removed her hand. He brought it to his chest, and Caitlin could feel the beating of his heart. She didn't know what to do and as confusion entered her mind, so did self-consciousness. She was lying topless with her skirt bunched around her hips and her panties around her ankles. She turned her head, hiding her face against Brodie's chest.

He was so tender with her afterwards, helping her straighten her clothes, and all the while telling her how beautiful she was. He eased her fears with his endearments, telling her that Monday night would be his and he would take his fill of her and make her scream his name in return. Caitlin was both thrilled and a little apprehensive about her ability to satisfy him. She supposed she was still technically a virgin after tonight, but she was looking forward to losing that label at his hands, or the erection that had felt so large and hard pressed up against her. She knew he would take her back to that intense, pleasurable place again and she could hardly wait.

Chapter Twelve

Caitlin shut the door behind Brodie and leaned against it, a contented sigh slipping from her lips. She smiled again, for what seemed to be the millionth time tonight. Her life was wonderful, and she hugged herself. If it hadn't been so late, she would have sung at the top of her lungs.

Brodie had helped her to fold out her bed without making any comments. She had been grateful not to see any pity in his eyes.

The kiss Brodie had given her before he'd left had been smouldering. Caitlin had thought she would catch fire all over again. She decided she wasn't going to fret while he was away, but look forward to his return instead. His promise of what was to come on Monday would keep her warm. She could keep herself busy with housework and her singing job, and watch the game with Riley and try to work out what was going on. Maybe she'd actually learn some of the rules.

It was silly after what they had shared tonight, but she couldn't help but be a little disappointed that

Brodie had not given her his phone number. He had programmed her home number into his iPhone the other night. Caitlin didn't bother with a mobile anymore, as it was just another expense. Riley had a pre-paid mobile that he used for emergencies only. Somehow, she felt it would have been a comfort to her knowing she could contact Brodie too, if she wanted to, though she was sure she wouldn't need to.

Caitlin curled up in her bed and tried to remember every single moment of the last two nights. It wasn't long before she was sound asleep.

* * * *

Riley was already awake and ready for squad training when Caitlin sleepily opened her eyes. She stretched and smiled at the thought of another day. It had been a while since she had started the morning in such a happy, positive mood.

Thank you, Brodie.

Even Riley was unusually motivated this morning. He had his swimming gear packed and was waiting for her when she came out from her morning shower.

"Thanks for folding away the bed, Riles," she said as she ruffled his hair. "Life is a fair bit brighter today, don't you think? Did you and Brodie plan any mischief I need to know about in your hushed conversation last night?" she continued playfully.

Riley just gave her a cheeky grin and replied, "I can't tell you, because it was man stuff and you're not a man. Ask Brodie. He told me you were his angel and that I should keep you safe until he gets back. He really likes you, Cate. I can't wait to tell the kids at school. They are going to go nuts over this."

Caitlin shook her head and cautioned her brother not to say too much just yet. She really didn't know what was going to happen in the future, but she certainly didn't want to tempt fate by wishing for too much too soon.

Just having Brodie in her life for a short time would mean so much to her, she reasoned. She'd deal with any heartbreak when it came. Heartache and tough times were no strangers to her after the events of last year. This happiness was at least going to give her hope that her future could get better.

"Come on, Riles, let's go swimming. You've got that swim meet coming up, and I think you have a real good chance of a podium finish again. You've been training really hard and the coach thinks you're in top form."

Riley did very well in competition, nearly always standing on the podium, and usually at the top. That was why Caitlin worked so hard to find the fees needed for his training. Riley's squad coach had offered her cut rates, but she didn't feel right accepting charity when so many people were worse off than them. So far she had always been able to find the money. Next term's fees were already banked thanks to the bonus from her extra singing gig on Wednesday night.

Brodie James had even been responsible for that, in a way, as he had been the one who'd booked the restaurant and entertainment. He had touched her life in so many ways already, from returning the lost bracelet that meant so much to her to his thoughtfulness and generosity when it came to Riley—he had made her brother laugh and smile. And he had helped her feel happiness again, persuaded her to open her heart, a heart that had been locked up by the pain of losing her mother. Caitlin had not realised how damaged she had been. Sure, she loved her brother, but even that love was overwhelmed by her responsibility for him. Lately, she'd just snapped or nagged at Riley instead of giving him a hug. Caitlin decided that she would try to do a better job in the future.

Maybe June had been right. She *had* needed to find a special someone to mend her heart. It had made life take on a sunnier sheen. That reminded her — she still had to speak to June regarding sitting with Riley on Monday night, so she and Brodie could spend some time alone. What was more, she was excited at the prospect of confiding a little about her wonderful man with June.

Caitlin tingled all over thinking about Monday night, wondering what was in store for her. She was shocked at the way her body came to life at the mere thought of Brodie, let alone when he actually touched her. Contact with him physically made her burn with a fever she had never felt before, a hunger she knew only he could satisfy. Here she was, with her heart racing and her nipples growing hard. For the first time, she didn't feel self-conscious about her large breasts. She finally felt like a woman.

Caitlin was feeling so alive that she decided to swim laps while Riley trained. She didn't even hesitate to leave the changing room, forgetting all about her usual insecurities with regards to her body shape. She did remember to remove her mother's bracelet, and tucked it carefully into her shoe for safekeeping. It really wasn't an expensive bracelet, but what she felt was more a sentimental attachment, and now it had even more significance with links to Brodie, as well.

Caitlin strode confidently to the pool deck, climbed onto the blocks and dove gracefully into the slightly warm water. She found a rhythm easily today and enjoyed the feel of the water as it cascaded soothingly over her body, while she powered through lap after lap.

Chapter Thirteen

Brodie sat on the bench, smiling, his legs stretched out, ankles crossed and his head resting on the wall behind him. He took a long swig of the Powerade sports drink he was holding and swallowed as he thought about the game. He had played well. He had led his team to victory and delivered a crushing defeat to the ladder leaders, Auckland. Brodie had made thirty-five tackles and nineteen hit-ups, totalling over two hundred and twenty metres. They were good figures for him. Hell, they were *great* figures! He'd probably played harder than any forward in any team this round, and he realised he still had a lot to offer his beloved game. He could outplay any prop, even the young pups coming up through the ranks.

"That will keep those retirement rumours at bay for a bit longer," he said to no one in particular.

The locker room was abuzz with noise—players slapped each other on the back as they launched into another loud and tuneless round of the club's song. Winning on the road was always a bonus, especially when the opposing team was such a strong one.

Brodie loved the bonds formed between teammates, and looked around the room to see young and older team members celebrating as one. This was what it was all about, and he couldn't wait to include Riley in one of these after-game rituals. He had never realised until now why the players who were fathers always grabbed their kids after a game. He had this mad urge to see Riley singing and jumping around with the others.

Maybe Brodie *did* want to settle down with his angel. He could already see a little version of her with green eyes and curly red hair bouncing on his knee — or maybe a big, round-headed boy, wearing a small replica of his number ten jersey. As he sat there enjoying the fantasy he was creating, he noticed JT heading towards him. Something about the expression on JT's face sent a chill down Brodie's spine. After all the years he'd known his mate, he could tell that, right now, he was bearing bad news.

Very bad news.

Brodie grabbed at his phone immediately, concerned about his ageing parents. As he switched the phone from silent, he noticed that he had a number of missed calls. Before he could see who had been ringing him, JT sat down heavily beside him.

Looking at his friend, JT spoke in a concerned voice. "Mate, you're in for a bit of a rough trot. I want you to keep it together when I tell you what's going on. At the moment there is an army of reporters demanding to be let in, but the team officials are holding them back until you decide how you want to handle this."

With that, he threw down onto Brodie's lap a copy of a weekend rugby league lift-out from the *Sydney Age*. As he took in the photo plastered all over the front page of the popular pullout, he felt sick, even before he read the headline.

Aussie Captain enjoys some light entertainment.

Brodie James, all-around good guy and poster boy for Australian League, took time away from his so-called fundraising night during the week to spend private – or should that be public? – time with a teenage waitress/entertainer.

As our photo reveals, she certainly entertained James in the car park outside the Ashfield venue.

Mrs Lila James, who had been sitting alongside the Sydney Jets and Australian captain throughout the evening, was left inside to play hostess to the guests at the event. Mrs James, a portrait of elegance, refused to comment on her husband's behaviour, but did appear shaken as she left the restaurant alone.

When will our Neanderthal sports stars learn to show some respect for women? The league's efforts to lift the image of footballers have been delivered another blow with this shameful display from one of the stars regularly held up as a role model to younger players. The only thing James was showing younger players was the age of the women they should be dating.

Brodie slowly read the damning article, cursing loudly over and over. He knew this was a body blow to his career and wondered if it was one he could recover from.

"What the fuck? Where the hell did this come from?" he snarled, thumping at the graphic photo accompanying the article. It was then he remembered the flash he'd thought had gone off in his head that night.

Had Caitlin set him up? No sooner had the thought entered his head than he brushed it away. The villain was obvious the moment he saw the name attached to the piece – the byline said 'Jack Edwards'. It was all starting to make sense, in a sick way.

Brodie didn't know what to do first. His mind raced as he tried to take in all the ramifications.

He felt some relief when he realised Caitlin's name had not appeared in the article. The photo identified him quite clearly with his hands under her dress. He could see her legs wrapped around him, but only the side of her head was visible and she was in shadow. He needed to call her.

And what was with the Lila angle they were pushing? They were divorced, for fuck's sake! Yes, he had shown poor judgement by losing control of his emotions the other night, but it had been in a private car park. God, he hadn't even slept with Caitlin yet! Well, not really. He was going to tear that dickhead Edwards apart when he got his hands on him.

It was then that JT grabbed his arm, as if reading Brodie's mind. "Mate, don't do it. It'll only cause more aggro. The son of a bitch will have you arrested, and he'll have a follow-up story." He snatched the paper back from Brodie's lap, waved it angrily in front of him and added, "Anyway, this reeks of Cruella."

Brodie was surprised at how JT had read his thoughts, but surely Lila wasn't so spiteful as to want to ruin his career? Then again, wasn't that what she had been trying to do during their entire marriage?

JT continued, putting his hand on Brodie's shoulder, "So what do we do first? I've got your back, whatever you decide. Want me to hold off the vultures for a little longer?" He nodded towards the players' tunnel, where the media were camped.

"I reckon you should give Trev a call at Channel Four and clear up some of the misinformation that is in that rag," JT said as he pointed to the offending newspaper. "And that young woman needs some reassuring too. It's obvious you're crazy for her and she's been good for you. I like her. I think I owe her some thanks," JT added with a big smirk. "You've got that James spark back and I'm sure as hell glad not to have to carry this team anymore!" Typical JT wit— never too far away.

Brodie knew JT was right. He had some good friends out there, and he sure as hell was going to need their support now. As he picked up his mobile, it started ringing. He took a deep breath and answered.

"James," he growled into the phone.

"Mate, you're in it this time," said the familiar voice of Trevor Hughes, the host of Channel Four's *Footy Forum*.

Trevor had been a good centre for the South Coast Tigers and Sydney Jets before a career-ending injury had forced him to pursue a new profession. He was a popular media figure now with a good sense of humour, solid knowledge and excellent TV ratings. Brodie had been a guest on the show many times, and knew he could count on Hughes' help with this messy problem.

Brodie gave an interview over the phone to Trevor, presenting his side of the story. He admitted to a momentary lapse in judgement, explaining they had been taking a breath of fresh air in the private car park to the rear of the restaurant when emotions had run a bit high. He pointed out he was in a relationship with the young lady who'd been photographed. Brodie could only hope Caitlin didn't mind his publicly exposing them before speaking with her.

He went on to refute any claims that he had deserted Lila, stressing she was no longer his wife and that they had, in fact, been divorced for two years. What was more, he fumed, there had been deliberate misrepresentations of the situation because Lila had arrived at the fundraiser with Jack Edwards, the reporter who'd written the article. Brodie admitted he had been surprised they had managed to get tickets, but it had slipped his mind to check out how that had happened. He didn't really care, to be honest, whose money had helped to achieve the night's goals.

"You gotta believe this will all work out, Brodie, mate. The drama will die down as soon as some other story comes along, and especially now that you've cleared up any of the contentious issues. It's got no teeth now—no one will want to run it for too long. You're a popular bloke, and your fans will stick by you." Trevor's endorsement was gratefully received by the still distraught and angry Brodie.

Once he had ended the call from Trevor, Brodie found the listing for Caitlin's number and called it, desperately trying to think of a way to make it up to her for this mess. The phone line was busy and Brodie broke the connection, frustrated. He needed to speak to her now, before the rest of the world got their hooks into her.

After a quick phone call to his parents, apologising for embarrassing them, Brodie felt a little better. On hearing the facts, his parents told him he had nothing to apologise for. His mum seemed pleased as punch that Brodie had found Caitlin, and couldn't wait to meet the young woman who'd coped with such hardship over the last year. Brodie promised to introduce them as soon as possible, adding that perhaps he could take them all to Mia's Restaurant, where Caitlin sang.

Brodie continually tried to reach Caitlin, but all he could get was a busy tone. He wondered who the hell she could be talking to for so long, and was toying with the idea of getting an operator to break into the line when the painful possibility hit him.

Had the press found her already? Oh, God – they would eat her and Riley alive. He had to get to her, now.

He took stock of the situation. He was in another country, trapped in a locker room with a mob of reporters outside baying for his blood. Brodie, still dressed in his footy gear and dirty from the game, slumped to the floor, defeated. He put his head in his hands and tried to block out the sounds of his now continuously ringing phone. He felt empty to the core.

There was nothing he could do to protect his angel, and it was entirely his fault. What if she never forgave him? What if she left him before they had a chance to begin? The thought was so agonising that Brodie roared in protest and pain.

After a few minutes spent isolated in grim thoughts, Brodie looked up. He saw all his teammates, the Jets training staff and medical crew circled around, as if protecting him. He was surrounded by people who looked concerned but focused.

"What do you need us to do?" Mitch Harris calmly asked. "We know that's not what you're like, Cap. That reporter is in for one hell of a whoopin', I'd say, and not just from your mates. Your fans know you. Everyone knows you. We've seen you watching that girl for weeks now, and that's why we gave you such a hard time about her. It took so long for you to man up and talk to her that we took bets on when you would do it. You've been like a different bloke these last few days, Cap, and I, for one, like the new soppy you." The rookie had a determined look on his face.

Brodie couldn't believe what he was seeing and hearing. Everyone was nodding in agreement. So many mates — he was blessed.

A throng of reporters, all shouting his name, broke into the room. Brodie couldn't help but grin as he watched JT and everyone in the room stand, as one, to hold them back.

Brodie held up both hands and asked everyone to calm down. He instantly had the attention of everyone in the room.

"Ladies and gentlemen, it seems I have some explaining to do, what with nearly being caught with my pants down and all," Brodie announced with a steady voice. "I believe some of you may be interested to hear all the facts, and I am willing to give them right now — on one condition."

The idea for the plan had come to him as he'd watched his teammates rally to protect him. He had to at least try to help Caitlin, even if it meant making deals with the devil.

"I have been trying to get in touch with the young lady who has been inadvertently caught up in this mess because of my inability to control my feelings for her. As you would well know, I have always been renowned for my calm. At the moment, though, I am far from calm. I'm imagining my poor angel surrounded by a pack of hungry wolves — I mean, reporters."

As a follow-up to that last line he gave one of his best Brodie James grins. He heard the gasps of surprise from everyone in the room, and looked over at JT who just smiled and nodded in approval.

"Do you think you guys could give me a hand here? Can you ring your fellow reporters and urge them to leave my girl alone? Just for long enough for me to actually confirm with her that she *is* my girl, after I've managed to embarrass her so publicly."

Brodie finished his statement by giving the room a rundown of the facts just as he had explained them a few moments earlier to Trevor Hughes, holding out his hands to the room as if pleading. It was amazing to watch nearly every journalist, cameraman and photographer in the room take out their phones and start making calls. Brodie sighed with relief. Maybe it would be okay.

Chapter Fourteen

Caitlin had been making it through the weekend quite well. Okay, the very loud heavy metal music, courtesy of her new neighbour, had made sleeping difficult last night, but that hadn't been the only reason for her restlessness. Caitlin knew that her eagerness to touch and be touched in return by that gorgeous man was the main problem. She smiled again. It seemed to be almost her default expression these days.

She had joined Riley on the sofa to watch Brodie's game, feeling excited and a little nervous at the same time. Riley had grabbed her hand and assured her it was okay, that Brodie and JT were the best props in the game — whatever that meant — and that Auckland didn't stand a chance. She'd smiled at her brother. She hadn't cared about the match so much as the chance to see Brodie, even if it was only on the television screen.

As the game had concluded, Caitlin had managed to take what felt like her first breath in over eighty long minutes. Apart from a ten-minute break halfway through, it had all been action. Caitlin had cringed every time she'd seen her sexy hunk of masculinity get slammed to the ground by up to four other large, rough-looking men.

At one point, Brodie had passed the ball on to someone else — though Caitlin didn't know how, since he'd seemed to be engulfed by the opposition — and that player had run and put the ball down for a try. Caitlin had felt a surge of pride for her wild, strong man, knowing it was because of him the team was winning. It had seemed a bit brutal to her eyes, but Riley hadn't shared her concerns. He'd jumped up and down and cheered loudly for Brodie every time he'd been involved in the action. JT had looked even bigger and scarier in football gear, and strong as he'd pounded the other team's players into the ground. It was obvious both of these men enjoyed what they did for a living.

During the game the phone rang a few times, but Caitlin hadn't been able to tear herself away from the TV so she'd let it ring out, thinking it was likely to be someone selling something she couldn't afford anyway. Her eyes had been glued to the action taking place on the little television screen.

Caitlin was brimming with energy after the game had ended. She could hardly believe that she had a date just the next evening with such a talented and obviously famous man. The voices that had commentated on the game had just kept raving on about James this and James that. She didn't know what they'd meant when they'd said he would be excused for his one blemish because he was such an inspiration to so many. She really hadn't understood much of what the voices had said throughout the whole game. Riley hadn't known what they meant about a blemish either and that had surprised her, as her brother seemed to be a wealth of information about Brodie James.

Trying to come back down from the clouds, Caitlin focused on some housework. Noticing the garbage bin was full, she asked Riley to tie up the bag and put it in one of the wheelie bins outside. As usual, Riley grumbled, but to his credit headed off to attend to the task. Caitlin had just turned on the vacuum cleaner when the phone started ringing again. Remembering that she had ignored a few calls during the game, she was starting to get a little worried that it could be important.

"Hello, Caitlin speaking."

A male voice replied but she couldn't quite make out the words he was saying.

"Just hold on a sec, I didn't quite catch what you said. Just let me stop this noise," she shouted as she stomped on the button to shut the machine off. As silence filled the room, Caitlin returned her attention to the phone and asked the caller to repeat what he had said.

"This is Jack Edwards. I'm a reporter from the *Sydney Age*. I was hoping to get a quote from you in regards to today's story on Brodie James. Were you aware of his marital status before you had relations with him, before he started fondling you in public?"

Caitlin's blood turned to ice. Her heart clenched painfully and tears rolled down her cheeks as she listened to the caller. His questions and tone were so rude—disgusting. She couldn't find her voice to answer that no, she hadn't realised Brodie James was married.

She remembered well the beautiful, blonde woman who had sat next to Brodie at the fundraising night, but had never asked him who she was. Caitlin had just assumed that the woman was with someone else after the way Brodie had kissed her out in the car park. She felt very guilty for kissing and dining with another woman's husband, making dates with him in the future and so much more.

Suddenly, it was clear to her how foolish she had been. As if a man like Brodie James would ever think she was anything more than a bit on the side. Realising she still held the phone to her ear, she slammed the handset back into its cradle. Almost as it hit the disconnect button, the phone came to life again. Caitlin reached down and pulled the phone socket from its connection in the wall, silencing the horrible bringer of such devastating news.

"My God," she cried. "How am I going to tell Riley what I've done, and why we can never see Brodie James again?"

Caitlin heard the door open and turned to see Riley standing there, just staring at her from the doorway. There was something terribly wrong with her brother. He was as white as a ghost. Slowly he lifted his arm and she realised that, in his trembling hand, he was holding some sort of newspaper.

"Sis, I hate him! I really hate him! Why did he do this to you? I thought he was a good guy, but I hate him now and I wish he would just die," Riley shouted, then broke down sobbing as tears began streaming down his face. The hand that was not holding the paper was clenched, knuckles white, by his side.

Caitlin reached for the paper Riley was still holding out to her. As she did so, she noticed June and a girl with spiky, dark hair had also entered the small flat.

As if in slow motion, Caitlin brought the paper up to read. The photo hit her first. It was a shock seeing herself in such a provocative pose. All sense of reason and reality deserted her, and she even caught herself registering how gorgeous Brodie looked — as always — in the candid shot. Caitlin remembered how being in his arms had made her feel after she had thrown herself at him for the second time. And it had been the same again the other night. Her last thought as she finished reading the article was, *I'm a slut.* Caitlin sank to the floor, sobbing as emotion and grief overwhelmed her, and covered her eyes with her hands as she tried to block out the reality that had descended on her.

When Caitlin opened her swollen eyes, she found June kneeling in front of her. June reached out and took her hand, encouraging her up from the floor and suggesting she should have a lie down on the sofa for a few moments, to recover from the shock.

"I didn't know he was married. He didn't tell me." Caitlin whimpered. "We really only kissed and stuff. I didn't make love to him all the way," she whispered, so that Riley wouldn't hear, "although I wanted to." She started crying again as the older woman hugged her.

"Don't cry, darling. It's okay. It's all going to be okay. Maybe there is an explanation for all of this," June said soothingly. "Why would anyone hurt you in this way? You're such a beautiful girl."

The dark-haired stranger was speaking, but Caitlin could not hear her clearly.

She saw Riley go over to the window and look out.

"What's going on, June?" Caitlin managed to croak. She felt sick and so tired all of a sudden.

Riley came and patted her reassuringly on the shoulder. "It's okay, sis. The reporters seem to be leaving."

This new piece of information was just too much for Caitlin to deal with.

"What reporters?" she wailed, burying her face into the back of the sofa.

* * * *

It was nice of June to stay with them in their hour of need. It seemed like hours since Caitlin's world had crashed down around her. As she sipped a cup of strong, sweet tea, Caitlin tried to pull herself together.

Life was going to go on. She still had Riley to think about. The poor kid had been cruelly delivered another harsh taste of reality. Her family appeared to be cursed by life.

She was glad it was Sunday and she didn't have her singing gig to worry about. There was no way she'd be able to sing a love song tonight without breaking down. Caitlin hoped she would be able to toughen up her heart in time for next Friday night. Maybe she'd even take a few nights off. She had already raised Riley's squad money, after all. She could afford some time off. Surely Angelo could make other arrangements to cover her shifts. Her mind had been throwing around possibilities like this for ages when a knock at the door snapped her back to harsh, current reality.

"Oh, June, I can't see anyone at the moment," Caitlin cried.

June stood purposefully, saying she would deal with the visitor as she headed for the entry.

She seemed ready to fob off the visitor and opened the door slightly, but the door was flung wide open and a tall, well-dressed, angry blonde came flouncing into the room. She pushed Caitlin's elderly neighbour aside, nearly knocking her off her feet. It was the woman from the restaurant function. The one Caitlin now knew to be Lila James, Brodie's wife. Lila stood peering down at Caitlin, who struggled into a sitting position on the sofa.

"Come, now... There, there, little girl, dry those awful red eyes. No man is worth crying over. You should feel lucky you found out so soon what a heartless bastard Brodie can be." Lila smiled patronisingly and continued, "Just thought I'd pop by and say hi. No hard feelings. I can't blame you in some ways. He is a hunk, and so satisfying between the sheets, don't you agree? He has me screaming and begging for more all the time. Pity that your name had to be dragged through the mud in this way, but maybe you will think twice in the future before getting involved with someone so clearly out of your league."

Her scornful stare ate at Caitlin's heart.

"It takes a real woman to keep someone like Brodie interested," Lila added, with a toss of her head and disdainful look around the modest flat. "He would have tired of you quickly. If I'm not even enough for him, how could a little thing like you be?" the spiteful blonde spat out, before turning on her stilettoed heel and sashaying out of the front door.

Caitlin slumped back onto the sofa with a broken heart and soul to match.

How much worse could this day get? At least she still had June and Riley for support — and, it appeared, the strange, dark-haired girl from upstairs. She was keeping Riley distracted by showing him how to play her Nintendo DS game, and glanced at Caitlin sympathetically every so often.

* * * *

Brodie finally managed to answer all of the questions the reporters asked. It seemed no one was interested in the game the Jets had just played—only his once private, now very public life. Finally he showered and dressed, but not in the team's travelling uniform. Instead he chose casual clothing—jeans, long-sleeved shirt and leather jacket—all the while trying to ignore the pain in his heart. He had tried almost constantly to reach Caitlin, but the phone was now apparently out of order. He needed to get a plane back to Sydney, and fast. After clearing his plans with the team manager, Brodie, with JT in tow, headed for Auckland International Airport.

It would be a few hours before their plane got into the air, then at least four hours before they cleared Australian immigration authorities. At least it would be a quick trip through customs with nothing to declare—they had left their bags with the rest of the team. The only declarations Brodie had to make were to his angel—the sooner, the better.

Brodie was a shell of his former self, his usually calm and collected character now impatient and fidgety. He still managed to sign a few autographs for fans, but not in his usual chatty way. JT tried to shield him as much as possible, but seemed to realise the more people that came up and showed their support for Brodie, the better things would be. Of course there were a few angry and outspoken critics who heckled him too, but that was to be expected.

After securing two business-class tickets on an outgoing Air New Zealand flight direct to Sydney, Brodie took his seat, closed his eyes and prayed.

He had time to think on the three-hour flight. He decided that he didn't care so much about losing the captaincy or even not playing again. What really scared him was going back to the solitary life he had been living. Previously, he had been unaware of how much he had cut himself off emotionally. He had just been going through the motions for so long. Training and playing, then recovering from the aches and pains of one game, just to do it all over again the next week. So many nights spent alone in his apartment or at some function for something or someone. Always busy. Always distracted.

Caitlin and Riley had shown him that there was so much more to life. They had so little, but they shared with and sacrificed for each other, and that meant they had everything he was missing. He had so much in terms of money and possessions but no one to enjoy it with. He played a game he loved but had no one to play for. There was no one to feel proud of him. He had his parents, of course, but since the disaster with Lila that relationship had been strained. Once his mum and dad had come to every game they could, but after his marriage to Lila they'd stopped. Lila had said they were relieved to hand the support role over to her and have their weekends free after so many years. It had hurt Brodie at the time, but he understood his parents had devoted almost all their free time, for so long, to running around after him as he'd pursued his league career. And, of course, Lila had a long list of friends—or, at least, people she was trying to impress—who were ready to use the tickets he'd once reserved for his mother and father.

As the plane commenced its descent into Sydney International Airport, Brodie braced himself for the full impact of his indiscretion. He knew home soil would bring an even bigger media circus. JT had sat quietly next to Brodie for the whole flight. Words had not been needed to indicate his unconditional support. What was there to say? Brodie appreciated this unflinching allegiance that could have an impact on his front row partner's career as well. He touched on this as they left the aircraft.

JT just smiled back as he replied, "We're both getting too old for this lifestyle, anyway."

Brodie couldn't help wondering if JT meant the actual football, or the fantasy lifestyle that most people assumed they lived.

At the passport counter, the officer tipped Brodie off. There was a throng of media in the terminal waiting to pounce. He offered to organise a security escort for them, strongly recommending it, not as a favour, but for safety reasons. The airport staff was keen to protect the other passengers. For Brodie, this day seemed to be getting worse by the minute. He felt the security force would just make it look more dramatic, make it seem as though he were trying to escape punishment for his actions, but what could he do? He didn't want to endanger or inconvenience the public. It seemed he didn't really have much choice.

As the men headed out, Brodie remembered they had not organised any transport.

"Great. Standing at a taxi rank, that should be fun," he muttered miserably.

JT, always able to somehow save the day, told Brodie that he had rung Trevor at Channel Four before they'd left New Zealand, and he was going to collect them and deliver them to Ashfield.

Brodie would have kissed JT if he hadn't been sure a punch in the face would be the response. JT was not the sort to kiss, or be kissed, in public and definitely would *not* appreciate being kissed by a man. Brodie ruefully considered how much better off he'd be now if he had his mate's view on public displays of affection.

Getting out of the terminal and finding Trevor went more smoothly than Brodie had expected. JT fielded most of the reporters' shouted questions with a standard response.

"James will make a statement after he goes and gets his girl." This seemed to appease the rabble. Brodie liked the way JT thought. That was exactly what he was going to do. Go and get his girl.

It had been a long day, what with the time zone differences and his body stiffening up from the game they'd played, which now felt like so long ago. Brodie was exhausted.

Night had already fallen in Sydney. It was seven p.m. and it would probably take a good thirty minutes of travel time before he arrived at Caitlin's flat in Ashfield. *Time for a few more prayers.*

Chapter Fifteen

Just as Caitlin was starting to think clearly again after the horrid, embarrassing episode with Mrs James, there was another loud knock on the door. June had gone back to her flat to rustle up some food and Mandy, the dark-haired girl, had taken Riley upstairs to find more games. Caitlin's first instinct was to ignore whomever it was, and she tried to do just that. But the knocks became louder, so Caitlin dragged herself to the door, bracing herself for more confrontation.

When she opened the door, Caitlin saw a small, grey-haired woman. Behind her stood Brodie—or what would be Brodie in thirty years or so. Were Brodie's parents here to berate her as well? To give her a piece of their minds for taking up with their married son, like some sort of harlot? Caitlin didn't think she would survive this day at all as she burst into a fresh flood of tears.

As a pair of warm arms enveloped her, Caitlin heard a cheery voice.

"Please don't cry, dear. We are here to help. I'm Ruth and this is my husband, Patrick James. We are Brodie's parents," said the grey-haired woman soothingly. "My boy told me how much he cares for you and your brother. We wanted to thank the wonderful woman who brought our son back to life and mended his heart, so we came to do that in person. Come, now, stop crying."

Caitlin was very confused. How could these people want to thank her for disgracing their son? How could they justify her adulterous behaviour?

Today had been unbearable. Not knowing what to do or say, she broke free of the small arms holding her and crossed the floor to sit back down on her sofa. It was either that or fall on the floor. Ruth and Patrick calmly entered the flat and closed the door behind them.

"Pat, go find a kettle and make some tea. Caitlin and I are going to need some girl time." Ruth spoke to her husband authoritatively.

With that she turned to Caitlin and took her by the hand. "Now, tell me why you're so upset, dear." When the only response was a shake of the head and more sobbing, the older woman continued, "Brodie will work it all out. Didn't he tell you as much when he rang? Half of Australia heard him declare you his girl, so they have already forgiven him for his little bit of exhibitionism. Don't you love my boy?" Ruth suddenly asked, after a pause.

Caitlin was stunned, shaken, bewildered.

"What about his wife?" she bleated, almost pathetically. "I promise I didn't know he was married, Mrs James. Really, I didn't. I'm not that sort of girl."

Ruth smiled calmly and patted Caitlin's hand. "My dear girl, my son would not commit adultery. He is not married—at least, not now. Thank the Lord," Ruth added, with a glance heavenwards. "That evil woman cast some sort of spell on my Brodie, but he figured her out eventually and divorced her. Cost him a packet, though. He certainly left her better off than when he found her. Considering what she did to him, I think he was far too generous."

Oh, thank God. Aside from the fact that Brodie wasn't married, Caitlin also couldn't help be relieved that Brodie's mother didn't appear to hold her ex-daughter-in-law in any high regard. As Ruth continued her personal attack on Lila, Patrick James entered the room, carrying a tray with three mugs. He chastised his wife gently.

"Now, Ruthie, that's enough gossip for today. Don't pressure the poor girl. Let Brodie have his chance to sort things out." Handing each woman a mug of tea, he continued, "Here, Caitlin, let's get this into you. Life is always better after a cuppa. I've added sugar and milk. I had this feeling it'd be how you liked it. Where is that young brother of yours? I'm looking forward to meeting him."

Caitlin could not help noting how much Mr James' voice sounded like his son's.

It didn't take long for Caitlin to find out the whole sorry story. Ruth and Patrick, having heard directly from Brodie exactly what had happened, had decided to make the two-and-a-half-hour car journey to Sydney to show their support for Caitlin until Brodie could get a flight back.

Caitlin was overwhelmed by the gesture, and by the little detail that Patrick had been on the money with the way she took her tea.

Not long afterwards, Riley returned home and met the visitors. It was at this point that he found the phone was unplugged from the wall. They plugged it back in, deciding that if it rang again Patrick would answer and take a message, or give the caller a mouthful if need be.

At first Riley was guarded towards Ruth and Patrick, but eventually he thawed a little and began talking to Brodie's dad about the match. *My, that all seems such a long time ago now – almost another lifetime ago.* She listened to their comments.

June returned and, after being updated on all she had missed, started chatting with Ruth about her pet topic, gardening. She also regaled Ruth with the details of Lila's visit earlier in the day. Caitlin heard lots of, "Oh no, she didn't?" and "Oh yes, she did!" remarks coming from their direction.

Mandy seemed slightly uncomfortable with so many people crammed into the small home. She sat quietly on the window seat, sipping one of Patrick's magic mugs of tea. Caitlin made a mental note to make the time to get to know her new neighbour when all the fuss died down. She couldn't get over how helpful and friendly Mandy had been to Riley when he'd been in such distress. And she was curious about why the girl looked so sad, and dressed in what seemed an almost scary way. And what was with the heavy, dark makeup around her unusual eyes? *Maybe she's a goth.* But that would have to wait. For the moment, there was so much more to deal with.

Caitlin, now with freshly washed and dried curls and wearing a change of clothes, was feeling slightly better. As she'd showered she had tried to remember what Ruth – as the woman had insisted Caitlin and Riley call her – had said about half of Australia knowing how Brodie felt. It was something about 'his girl'. What was that all supposed to mean? The day was such a blur and so much still didn't quite make sense, but those words had kindled a little spark of hope in her heart.

Then the phone rang. Everyone seemed to go still and silent in an instant. Everyone, that was, except for Patrick James. Casually he strode over, picked up the handset and in a very deep voice, he spoke.

"Walters residence. How can I help you?"

Caitlin watched, holding her breath, as the serious look on Patrick's face morphed into a huge grin. Caitlin saw a glint in the man's eye as he turned to her.

She thought it surely must be Brodie on the line to make his face light up like that.

Finally, on what was the second worst day of her short life, Caitlin allowed herself a small, nervous smile.

* * * *

Brodie could have put money on them getting stuck in traffic. Why not? The day had been a disaster from go to whoa.

He had programmed his phone to continually call Caitlin's number. Each time he heard the call go through he held his breath, praying for her to answer. But to no avail. The long, unbroken tone that signalled 'out of order' was all that he'd managed to get.

During the drive, Trevor had filled both Brodie and JT in on how he read the public reaction, and it didn't seem as catastrophic as they'd first feared. Many had come out and openly attacked Jack Edwards' reporting style, demanding he be shunned by the rugby league community for all his muck-raking and lies. After all, if there was a negative story around about rugby league, it was a sure thing it had come from Jack Edwards' desk.

For all Edwards' talk about his love of the game, he was actually doing the most damage, undermining the league at every opportunity. He had even been known to buy drinks for some of the rookies, with the sole objective of being around if they fell over drunk. He had a camera ready to capture an embarrassing photo of the incident, of course. The poor kids hadn't known what had hit them. Hey, how could they, if even an experienced player like Brodie could be set up?

While Brodie quietly seethed about Edwards and his methods, he was distracted and nearly didn't notice that the phone had reached Caitlin's number and was actually ringing. Brodie pressed the phone to his ear, mentally begging for someone to answer.

"Walters residence. How can I help you?" said a deep, very familiar male voice.

"Dad? What the hell? I've rung the wrong bloody number," Brodie groaned distractedly. How the hell had that happened? He looked at the display screen of his phone again. *Hang on!* It was Caitlin's number, and had his father answered with 'Walters residence'? What was going on here?

"Dad, this is going to sound weird, but are you at Caitlin's?" he asked hesitantly.

"Yes, son, and so is your mother. Where else did you expect us to be, under the circumstances?" Brodie's father asked.

JT, hearing this conversation, burst into a fit of boisterous laughter.

"We're out in front, mate. Go get her!" Trevor shouted from the driver's side.

Brodie was out of the car in a heartbeat, heading for the door.

"Don't pull a hammy, old man!" JT gave a cheeky shout as he fumbled with his seatbelt.

Without looking back or slowing his pace, Brodie gave a rude but well-known finger gesture to the men in the car. Another round of laughter ensued.

* * * *

Caitlin looked at the phone, then at Patrick, and was still wondering what to do when she heard Mandy sing out.

"It looks like the man of the moment has just arrived, and he might just run straight through the front door if nobody opens it!"

Patrick took the few steps to the door and pulled it open, just in time for Brodie to burst into the room.

As Caitlin watched the man who had made her so happy, then so miserable—all in the space of a day—look at her with so much emotion showing on his face, she knew why she had been so upset. She was in love with Brodie James. This was how it felt. And she would never love another as much as she loved him. The relief and her newfound discovery caused an unexpected reaction from her.

Chapter Sixteen

Brodie had certainly not bargained on such an odd reception committee. His mother and father, an older woman he'd assumed was June the sitter, Riley and another, angry-looking young girl were all staring at him. The look of misery on his angel's face broke his heart all over again.

But he was frozen and unable able to take the last few steps to pull her into his arms. What if she pushed him away? How would he recover? He would beg her for forgiveness—it didn't matter that all these people would see him beg. Brodie didn't care how it would look.

He heard footsteps behind him. JT and Trevor were now part of the show. As he continued to try to work up the courage to move, his angel did the most unexpected thing. She burst out laughing. She was always doing something that surprised him.

The sound didn't have the same ring to it as he had heard from her before, but it was still music to his ears. As she clamped her hand over her pretty little mouth, he moved towards her. He needed to remove that hand from her lips and replace it with his own hungry mouth.

"Well, then, now that we seem to have all the participants of today's little upset in attendance, perhaps I should make everyone a nice hot cup of tea. Any takers? Brodie? JT? What about a cuppa, then? Then we can sort out this whole misunderstanding," Brodie heard his father say.

"It's not tea that I'm wanting, Dad," he said, as he brushed past his father and dragged Caitlin into his arms.

She melted into him at once, their mouths melding as one and her arms going around his neck. Brodie moaned with pleasure. Never had he felt so relieved in his life. It felt as though he had been carrying a mountain on his back, but the pressure had now been relieved as he held his woman. He needed to be with Caitlin. He now accepted this above all else in his life.

"Ahem... Son?" Brodie heard his father clearing his throat.

Brodie had forgotten he and Caitlin had an audience, a room full of spectators. As he pulled away from his angel, he started to apologise. How could he ever make it up to her? He had embarrassed her. He wanted her forgiveness—maybe not now, but sometime in the near future. Brodie pleaded his case, telling her he wanted to be her guy, wanted her to be his woman.

Brodie wanted to tell her exactly how he felt about her but she leaned towards him and placed her finger on his lips to silence him, just as he had done to her that day at the pool, so he returned the favour and sucked that finger straight into his mouth.

"Seems you've got yourself one hell of a woman there, Brodes. Try and hang on to her... Maybe a little more privately with the groping, though." JT cheekily wiggled his eyebrows at Caitlin.

She giggled. Brodie loved that sound. JT then went over and started talking to the short, dark-haired girl by the window—who, for some reason, was now standing on the window seat, allowing her to nearly match JT's height of six foot five.

Patrick had returned with tea. Brodie didn't take any. He just held on to Caitlin. It was then that he noticed Riley, who was standing behind the circus of people, stony-faced, lips pulled so tight that they were hardly visible. The boy had red, puffy eyes, just like his sister.

Brodie realised he had more than one person to make amends with. He managed to let go of Caitlin, who looked up at him in alarm, reluctant to lose the connection. She saw where his attention had drifted, though, and nodded at him. Brodie walked slowly to the boy, stopping directly in front of the child he had hurt so much. He was concerned not only because of the damage he'd done to their budding friendship, but also because of the pain Riley clearly felt on Caitlin's behalf.

"Riley, mate. How can I make you believe how sorry I am I hurt your sister? I didn't know anything about that story being published. I really care for you both. I know I already told you that the other night when we had that talk, and I really did mean what I said. I want to be here for you, son. I want to be here for you and your sister. I want you both to become part of my life. I would have given up the footy if that's what it took. That's how much you both mean to me."

With the heartfelt speech over, Brodie held out his hand for the boy to shake.

In an amazingly similar response to that of his sister twice before, Riley jumped past Brodie's outstretched arm, throwing his arms around Brodie's shoulders and hugging him. Brodie was speechless.

Riley said, in a very shaky and emotional voice, "No way, mate. Don't give up the footy yet—you promised to take me into the sheds with you."

JT, helpful as always, chipped in. "That's okay, kid, I've got you covered. The rest of the team like me better, anyway."

The sound of laughter filling the previously tense room was music to Brodie's ears, as he stood holding the shaking Riley tightly in a bear hug. This boy had been hurt by someone's deliberately cruel actions, and Brodie was going to make that person pay if it was the last thing he ever did.

"Well, now that we have sorted out this mess, what say we organise some dinner?" June's voice caught Brodie by surprise. The older woman sounded so friendly, keen to keep the group together for a bit longer, as she continued, "You boys must be starving—you are all so big and muscley. It must be quite a job keeping enough food in your bellies. I'm sorry, but I don't think I've prepared enough for everyone. If you just give me a few minutes, I'll pop next door and see what I can find."

"June, thank you. That's a more than generous offer, but you don't have to feed us all. You've already done so much for me today just by being here," Caitlin added, her voice quavering, before JT interrupted.

"As much of a generous offer that was, Miss June, why don't you stay here and chat with Ruth and Patrick while Riley and I go pick up some takeaway pizza?"

"That is a great idea, JT. Why don't you take my car?"

"That's so funny, sis. Imagine JT trying to fit into your little car—it would be a bit squeezy!" Riley, finding his own joke extremely funny, burst out laughing.

Finally, it was Patrick who came up with a sensible solution. "JT—here. Take my keys. You can borrow my car. Pizza sounds like a splendid idea. I don't mind the odd ham and pineapple pizza."

"Thanks, Pat. C'mon, Riley, you want to come and keep me company?" JT asked as he took the keys from Patrick's hand. "Anyone else have any preferences?"

"I'd love a vegetarian pizza," Brodie heard a timid voice from the background say and realised it was Caitlin's dark-haired neighbour. Mandy, he thought her name was.

"Righty-o, then—one veggie coming up. Why don't you join me and Riley for the ride, Mandy, give us a hand?" JT added, and it wasn't long before all the orders had been taken and the three—JT, Mandy and Riley—headed off to collect the food.

"That's an interesting turn of events," Brodie murmured under his breath as he watched his big mate walk out of the door, deep in conversation with the unique-looking girl.

June also caused Brodie some amusement over her reaction to meeting Trevor, "a real TV person". Brodie even faked disappointment at her not recognising him and JT, even though they had also been on TV plenty of times.

* * * *

JT and his group returned with so many pizza boxes Brodie could hardly see his head over the top of the stack. Next to him, an exuberant Riley bragged excitedly about seeing two of the guys from school at the pizza shop and introducing them to JT. Even better, JT had told them that Riley Walters was, indeed, one of his best mates. Brodie loved that his big friend was being such a softy for the kid.

Mandy was happy to eat with them, but took off very quickly afterwards, presumably to her flat. JT definitely appeared disappointed when Mandy left and she had looked quite comfortable around JT, despite seeming ill at ease with just about everyone else.

Brodie sat with his parents and Caitlin, rage building in his gut as they filled him in on the horrors of the day. He was overwhelmed with gratitude for his loving parents, who had charged to the rescue on his behalf. His resourceful mother explained how she had contacted Mia's Restaurant and convinced Angelo to give her Caitlin's home address.

The fact that Lila had had the nerve to come to Caitlin's home and say such venomous and untrue things to Caitlin, and in front of Riley, horrified Brodie. He figured Jack Edwards must have had a hand in arranging that visit. He wasn't sure how he was going to avenge his angel, but he would.

"Caitlin, I need to return a few phone calls, thank some people for their help today. Will you be all right just for a few minutes, angel? I'd put it off if I could, but I promised I'd make a comment as soon as I knew you were okay."

"Of course, Brodie. Do what you have to do. I think I can cope for a few minutes without you." The smile Caitlin bestowed on him was the sweetest sight Brodie had seen. "I'll go chat with your mum," Caitlin added, kissing him quickly before moving the short distance to where his mother sat.

As it turned out, most papers had decided to drop the story as it was filled with so many lies, and given that the photograph had been taken without Brodie and Caitlin's knowledge on private property, most thought it unethical.

When everyone had finished their pizza, Brodie began to tidy up the remnants. He was surprised to overhear a conversation taking place between his mother and Caitlin.

"You know, darling, Patrick would love to spend some time around young Riley, and it's such a long drive home. Do you think it would be all right if we spent the night here?"

"Ruth, I'd love to invite you both to stay, but I only have this sofa bed to offer you. It's not really all that comfortable. Wouldn't you rather stay at Brodie's?" came Caitlin's reply, sounding so full of apology and embarrassment, it nearly broke his heart.

"Rubbish. Pat and I will be fine on this sofa. We can play some games with Riley before we tuck him into his bed, then in the morning Patrick and Riley can go and kick a ball around in the local park. Caitlin, it will be wonderful for Pat to have a kick with the boy."

"Well, if you're sure… I'll just change the sheets and then make up some sort of bed in Riley's room for me," Caitlin said hesitantly, as if she was trying to think of a solution to the sleeping arrangements problem.

"Well, that won't do at all, Caitlin. We can't have you sleeping on the floor. Why don't you go home with Brodie and leave us here to keep Riley company? We'll be just fine, and you and my boy can make sure you have everything all sorted out, in private. Be gentle with him, sweetheart."

Brodie nearly choked on his own sharp intake of breath. He had never realised how manipulative his mother could be, but he certainly was glad of it in this case.

Caitlin explained the plans for the night to Riley, who winked at Brodie and agreed. Patrick was quick to ask Riley if he knew somewhere they could kick a ball around a few times the next morning before school, probably thinking that would make the boy more comfortable with the arrangements. JT also volunteered to give Pat a call early on, to see where the boys were headed, adding that he'd drive Riley on to school so they had more time together. Riley bounced.

Trevor offered to drop Brodie and JT back at the team grounds to collect their cars and escorted June home to her flat, also giving Caitlin time to grab some overnight requirements. Brodie noticed Caitlin's nervousness, that 'ready to flee' look in her beautiful, emerald eyes that he had already come to know so well. So he hovered around in the doorway, just to be on the safe side, just in case she needed him or some reassurance that everything was going to be okay. He was pleased that, as she and his mum made up the pull-out bed, Caitlin glanced his way and smiled on more than one occasion. Brodie loved the picture of these two special women in his life working so well side by side.

Chapter Seventeen

Brodie finally had Caitlin in his apartment and in his arms, alone. She sat on his lap, sipping at a glass of champagne. He was trying to think of a way to ease her nerves. She seemed so jittery, it was making him nervous too.

"Now, this is better—having you here in my arms. I wasn't sure that was ever going to happen after today's debacle," Brodie said, trying to ease the tense silence that had arisen. "I'm so sorry you got mixed up in this mess, angel. I wouldn't have wanted that for the world, but unfortunately my very ex-wife is very vindictive and the more I think about it, the more I think she's behind all this drama. But I promise you it won't happen again. You are too important to me. You and Riley. I'm hoping that this, whatever this is between us, will develop into something really special, long term."

"It's okay now—now that I'm here with you. I didn't know what to think at the time, but your parents were so lovely, so wonderful to come to my rescue. All of you are so amazing. I went from feeling alone against the world—again—to being swamped with support, all in a matter of hours." Caitlin's soft voice held a tremor of nerves in it as she whispered in his ear. "But what I really need is for you to make me feel like you did the other night. It's thinking about you touching me again that has me a bundle of nerves." She giggled.

"Angel, baby, that I can help you with. Believe me, it will be a pleasure. Let me put those nerves to better use."

And with that Brodie took the champagne glass from Caitlin and placed it in the ice-bucket next to the bottle of bubbly. Taking her by the hand, he collected the ice bucket in his other and headed to the bedroom.

Brodie manoeuvred Caitlin to sit in the middle of his bed and placed the champagne on the dresser. He slowly turned towards her and smiled. He dragged his shirt off over his head, not even stopping to undo the buttons. He tossed it to the floor. Next, Brodie pulled off his boots, dropping them one by one, the sounds reverberating around the room. He could hear Caitlin's breathing getting faster, little gasps escaping her mouth. He drew his zipper down very carefully over his arousal, then slid his jeans and boxers from his body at the same time.

Brodie stood still, letting Caitlin see him—the natural him, with nothing more to show. He looked at her, filled with need and hunger and love. He knew it was love. Who would have thought he'd get to thirty before finally finding out what that meant?

Her happiness was what he craved, and her body. Her eyes were glassy, like jewels glistening at him, as he climbed onto the bed and crept on all fours towards her, like a lion claiming his mate.

She was so nervous, wanting him to make love to her, but also terrified. The night had been wonderful—everyone had been like a big family all crammed into her home, laughing and joking. She had felt like an angel floating around on a big soft cloud as the emotions just kept washing over her. Riley had been bouncing everywhere, so happy and vibrant, after being so devastated earlier in the day. She just hadn't been able to stop feeling nervous about what was to come.

Now she was sitting on his bed, and her hero was naked and so close she could reach out and touch him, if she dared. It felt like a dream.

Brodie's shaft stood erect in front of him, tangible proof of his need for her. She would be his tonight and the anticipation of this was starting to drive her crazy with need. Her mouth was dry, but her body was so wet. Caitlin had looked him in the eye as he'd stalked her, crawling towards her, seeming to take forever to reach her.

Now, he encircled her ankle with his hand and pulled her towards him, tugging at her so she fell back on the bed.

He carefully removed her shoes, massaging her insteps and kissing each of her toes. She giggled, but his passion-filled eyes silenced her as he slowly removed her jeans. She loved the way Brodie was looking at her lying there before him in her panties, and licking his lips. Caitlin couldn't stand it any longer and grabbed at her shirt, attempting to rid herself quickly of any barriers between them, but as she pulled the fabric over her head she managed to get all tangled up in it. Frustrated at her clumsy attempts, Caitlin was a little relieved that Brodie could not see her face, which was now burning hot with embarrassment.

As she struggled with her shirt, Brodie calmly removed the stubborn cloth, finally freeing her. Caitlin undid her bra and let the cups fall into her hands, leaving her breasts bare to Brodie's hungry gaze. Her nipples were already hard as she arched her back, almost as an offering.

Brodie growled. Caitlin knew that sound now — it was a good one. It made her feel powerful. She had made him growl in such a hungry way, and knowing it was the sight of her naked body making his eyes so wild built her confidence.

Caitlin noticed a drop of fluid leaking from the tip of Brodie's cock. She felt a little racy thinking of his penis as a cock, but it gave her the courage to reach out and touch the glistening tip. She couldn't help herself — she caught it up on her finger and tasted it. The salty flavour was pure Brodie.

He groaned her name and pounced on her. Almost savagely, he ground his lips down on hers. His tongue invaded her mouth, possessing it, owning it. He dragged her arms over her head and pinned them above her with one arm. She watched as he lowered his head and latched on to the left nipple, gently sucking, only to leave it tingling and go on to tantalise its neighbour.

Caitlin was making little mewling sounds, loving the slow, seductive torture this man was inflicting on her, but she wasn't sure she would survive it. He had a way of making her burn, electric sparks touching her whenever and wherever he made contact with her skin. She wanted to caress him, explore him, but her hands were trapped, pinned by his arms. She just lay back and let herself feel—feel as a woman should, enjoying the ministrations of the man she loved.

Brodie made his way down to her belly button with his lips, then had to let go of her hands. He pressed them into the mattress in a silent command for her to keep them in place. He licked, kissed and nipped all the way back down her body, her breasts, her stomach and her hips, teasing and torturing as he went. Then his hands added to the pleasure. He tweaked her nipples, pulling at them until they were firm and hard from his touch. It all felt electric. Her pussy was pulsating and wet from the onslaught.

Just when Caitlin thought she could stand no more, Brodie moved between her thighs. He spread open her aroused, swollen pink lips with his thumbs and delved in with his talented tongue. Caitlin nearly exploded off the bed—the feeling was so intense she wasn't sure if she could take it. He circled her bud and pushed his tongue quite firmly down. She experienced a surge stronger than any she had felt before, a tidal wave that overtook every nerve in her body, leaving her gasping for some release to save her sanity. Caitlin flew over the precipice into the glorious feeling of sensual completion.

Chapter Eighteen

Brodie had nearly come when she'd licked that drop of pre-cum off her finger. The touch of Caitlin's finger alone had nearly been enough. He could have gorged on her juices all night — she was like the taste of water to a parched, dying man, and her little sounds of pleasure had made him want to beat his chest with pride. What was it about Caitlin that bought out the caveman in him or, in this case, a wild animal? The need to please and protect her was so strong in him.

She lay on the bed, sated from his attentions, and he could wait no longer. Brodie grabbed a condom from his bedside drawer. Tearing the packet with his teeth, he removed the latex protection from its packet and rolled it carefully onto his cock.

He lifted Caitlin's legs, holding them up over his elbows, exposing her entrance, the place he needed to drive deep inside. As the throbbing end of his eager, hard rod prodded at her opening, he felt her body tense. Brodie whispered for her to let him in, to let him bury himself deep into her so they could be as one. He felt her relax her tight muscles and he didn't wait—he thrust into her.

Brodie felt the barrier too late, smashing through it mercilessly, his brain not sending the warning message fast enough to stop his body in time. He went as still as he could as he heard Caitlin cry out in pain.

My God, she was a virgin. Why didn't she tell me?

Brodie tried to hush her cries, kissing her tenderly over and over. He had been like an animal and had hurt Caitlin again. It was unforgivable—he should have been gentler, more patient. He eased into her slowly, letting her body become accustomed to his invasion. As he held himself there, still holding her legs up in the air, thinking he should stop and let her recover, he felt her start to move. His angel was dancing beneath him, her hips moving in a swirling motion as she moaned with pleasure.

Knowing it would only take a few thrusts to finish him, Brodie lowered one of Caitlin's legs to the bed and placed his thumb on her clit, pressing and swirling as he slowly rolled his hips. He stretched her tight pussy, not sure if she would be able to take all of him comfortably just yet, becoming part of her before retreating and repeating the measured pace again, all the time fighting against his own urge to just bury himself inside her. The friction of his movements and his finger on her clit finally made her scream his name in pleasure. Brodie thrust again, trying to wring out all he could from her, prolonging her orgasm as he exploded inside her, yelling her name to the world just before he collapsed on top of her.

Caitlin had tensed when he'd prepared to enter her, but she had been brought to such fulfilment by this man that she'd wanted to have him inside her. He had asked her to let him in. Caitlin had already let him into her heart, and this was all that was left. She just hadn't been expecting the pain to be so sharp, had tried not to cry out, but it had all happened so fast that she hadn't been able to stop herself.

When Brodie had stopped and gone so still, she'd started to cry at the frustration. She'd wanted to satisfy him and make him soar as she had. The sensations she had felt, the pleasure he had brought her after that initial stab of pain, had been so much more than she could ever have imagined.

As he lay on her now, she knew she had indeed satisfied him, could feel the rapid beat of his heart as he pressed down over her. Caitlin enjoyed the weight of her man on her body. He was heavy, but she was in a state of bliss. She was startled when he withdrew from her — her body clenched at him, trying to trap him inside her, but he continued his withdrawal. Caitlin felt the loss so intensely that unstoppable tears trickled down her face as the emotions of the day took control. She wasn't hurt or sad, just overwhelmed.

She watched as Brodie rose from the bed. It was the first time that Caitlin had seen his muscled back and firm butt close up and naked, and she took full advantage of the view as he walked away. He was the sexiest man she had ever seen. After Brodie had left the room, she could hear him moving around the adjoining bathroom and the sound of water running. Now she was alone in the bed, her tears became more like sobs as the impact of what she had just experienced sank in. Caitlin cried for her parents, that they would never meet this wonderful man, this man who had made her a woman.

Standing in the bathroom, having disposed of the used condom, Brodie tried to comprehend the magnitude of what had happened. Caitlin was his—she had slept with no other. The selfish man in him loved that exclusivity and was determined for that to never change. He wanted to be the only man she would ever want. Brodie returned to the bedroom, ready to explain the depths of his feelings for her, for the gift she had bestowed on him...only to find her sobbing.

"Angel... Caitlin, angel, please don't cry. I'm sorry I hurt you. I should have known better." Seeing her in tears was really upsetting him, and the fact that it was because of his actions just made it worse. "Oh, baby, I love you so much. It will be better next time, I promise. It only hurts the first time. Please, baby, you're killing me here."

Brodie stroked his hands up and down her back as he held her, dying a little more with every sob that racked her beautiful little body.

Caitlin sniffed loudly, the sound cutting a sob in half. "Brodie, I'm fine. It's all okay, really. It didn't hurt that much. It was more the shock than anything, and I was so worried that I wouldn't be good... You know, be able to satisfy you. I was just a bit emotional. Wait—what did you just say?"

Caitlin sat up abruptly, wiping at her eyes. She looked at him, wide-eyed and so sexy, her hair all mussed. Even her red, tear-stained face could not diminish her beauty as far as Brodie was concerned. She seemed so startled at his words, maybe a bit confused, and he felt no hesitation as he repeated his declaration of love. The woman was all about pleasing others, caring for others, worrying whether she would please him. It was amazing. She only had to be near him to make him grin like an idiot. It was time she knew.

"Caitlin, I know it's too soon, but I can't lie to you. I'm thirty years old and this is the first time anyone has ever made me feel like you do. If this isn't love, I don't know what is. Baby, you couldn't not satisfy me if you tried. One look at you, and I'm already so hard I could come without so much as a touch to my cock. I just hope that one day I can mean as much to you as you do to me." Brodie's confession was heartfelt, brutally honest. He'd never imagined putting his heart back out there again, not after Lila, but Caitlin was worth the risk.

As Brodie sat still, waiting for her reaction, he noticed the glimmer in her eye. He knew that look, knew what her next movement would be. What he didn't anticipate were the words that accompanied her actions, because as she threw herself on him and placed little kisses up and down his jaw, she whispered the words he was hoping for.

"I love you, Brodie. I love the way you make me feel so beautiful. I love the way you care for me. I love the way you have taken Riley into your life and I think you are the sexiest man I've ever seen, and I especially love the way you make my body sing."

Chapter Nineteen

Caitlin awoke to the most spectacular scenery — and the water view was nice too!

She lay in a warm bed, watching Brodie sleep. His face was relaxed, as though he was smiling at her. The creases around his closed eyelids were nearly gone. She loved the way his cheekbones were so prominent, high in his face. She couldn't help herself — she ran her fingers lovingly over those cheekbones and across his slightly crooked nose, then touched the faded lines around his eyes.

As he opened his eyes drowsily, Brodie smiled at her and took her breath away again. He was smouldering hot and he was hers. Caitlin could not believe how much her life had changed in such a short time. To be loved by someone like Brodie James, who was so accomplished, so handsome... It almost made her cry. Not to mention his friends and family. They were so caring, such nice people.

And here she was in bed, completely naked, with such a temptation within reach. Although she was feeling slightly sore from the previous night's activities, Caitlin felt her body respond at once as the naked, warm, muscular man reached out and fondled her breasts gently.

"Mmm, I love these beauties. Perhaps I should practice some of my handling techniques with them. The headlines are always going on about my handling skills."

Caitlin did not really understand the football term, but loved the way Brodie said it with a twinkle in his eye. After reassuring him that she wasn't fragile and not only wanted, but *needed* him to make love to her again, Caitlin placed her hand around his cock. He felt so warm, and the skin covering the rigid form was so soft. Caitlin ran her hand up and down, getting to know all of him. She loved the texture of the skin around the tip of the bulbous head and traced her finger around it, feeling the vein that bulged beneath the skin.

She spread the drop of liquid that seeped from him around the tip, ran her finger down the long shaft and cupped the round sacs beneath it. Brodie groaned and growled the whole time, making little jerking motions beneath her explorations. Caitlin loved those sounds he made. They reassured her that she was doing the right thing—not having had previous experience of lovemaking, she was not sure what to do. She positioned herself closer to his erection, close enough that she could run her tongue around the satiny tip, but before she could continue her sensual journey, and learn the way Brodie liked to be held and licked and sucked, she was surprised to find herself lifted and placed once again on her back.

Although disappointed to be interrupted—exploring Brodie was beginning to be one of Caitlin's favourite pastimes—she was not at all sorry at the attention he was giving her. Brodie did live up to his promise of not hurting her again—unless, of course, the torturous build-up of pleasure he managed to inflict on her, before bringing her to completion with another wave of satisfaction, could be called pain. Each of them shouted the other's name as they came.

Showering together was quite daunting to start with for Caitlin. To be standing naked in front of Brodie in broad daylight was embarrassing. Brodie was having none of it, had picked up on her shyness.

"No way should you be thinking about hiding that body from me, angel. You are a very desirable woman. Never be ashamed to show yourself to me."

"I know it's silly after all we just did..." she started to say, but was silenced by Brodie's lips.

He touched her everywhere—soaped up, lathered and washed every tiny bit of skin on her body, paying extra attention to her breasts.

"Let the shower wall take your weight and spread your legs, angel. I want to taste you, suck on your clit till I make you come all over my tongue."

Brodie's voice sounded gravelly to her ears and she melted at the heat in it. As Brodie reached her sensitive spot with his tongue and clever fingers, she saw stars.

"Oh, my! Don't stop! I'm so-o-o close. That feels so incredible," she murmured as the orgasm began to build. Her legs were shaking, and she was unsure she would be able to remain standing as the wonderful sensations hit full force. Brodie began to make stabbing motions with his tongue, massaging and probing with his fingers, and she flew. Flew over glorious mountains and sparkling rivers, swamped by the most amazing feelings she had ever experienced.

After being towelled dry so lovingly, Caitlin was almost ready for even more lovemaking at Brodie's expert hands, but unfortunately she had to admit she was feeling worn out down below. Of course, Brodie halted any further adventure, would not hear of her having even the slightest discomfort on his behalf.

* * * *

They stopped off at a local café for breakfast on the way back to see how Brodie's parents were coping with Riley's energy. Brodie assured her that all would be fine as they drank cappuccinos and ate eggs Benedict. Caitlin had never tried eggs this way and really enjoyed her breakfast, although she probably would have happily eaten sawdust on toast, just to prolong the morning with Brodie.

It was quite unbelievable the number of people who approached Brodie for autographs as he ate or, embarrassingly for Caitlin, mentioned the photograph in yesterday's paper. Had it only been yesterday? It seemed a lifetime ago that her world had nearly collapsed.

Every time someone approached them, Brodie was cheerful and happy to oblige in any way, putting down his knife and fork repeatedly. Caitlin knew his breakfast went cold while he kept the fans happy. She sighed as the full impact of this man's busy life started to become clear to her. He was always under scrutiny, people ready to complain if he ignored them, or if he somehow didn't live up to their expectations. Caitlin felt annoyed that the interruptions caused Brodie to stop eating so often. Would she be able to cope with this sort of life? With all the interruptions and scrutiny that came along with Brodie?

The thought was so terrifying that her breakfast suddenly wasn't sitting well in her stomach.

After such a fantastic start to the day, it might have been a mistake stopping for breakfast. Yesterday's news and photograph were still a hot topic. All through breakfast, Brodie had to put down his knife and fork to sign autographs or listen to well-meaning, but intrusive, fans who wanted to show support for him and Caitlin. Each comment made Caitlin shrink before his very eyes.

Brodie quickly paid the bill and was relieved to finally put her back into the privacy of his car. He knew she was upset, and he didn't know how he was going to make it any better for her. His life tended to be very public.

An uneasy feeling began to creep under Brodie's skin, chilling his heart. Brodie took both of Caitlin's hands in his. He looked into her eyes, trying to find the right words to ease her fears.

"Angel, baby, please—I need you. Don't let these people, or what I do for a living, frighten you away from me. I can't let you go now that I've just found you," Brodie begged. "I'll do what I can to protect you from the scrutiny. But if you can't cope with this life, I'll retire. Now. Today. I am not giving you up."

With the offer made, Brodie pressed his lips to Caitlin's.

Chapter Twenty

Caitlin was shocked at the emotion in Brodie's voice, the almost pleading way he'd spoken, and his offering to give up so much, just for her. She felt small and petty. This man was loved by so many, did so much good because of his celebrity status and the game he played, yet he loved her enough to give it up. Of course Caitlin didn't want that. She loved him and she would learn to live with everything that came with having Brodie in her life and heart, good or bad. She'd be fine—and anyway, Riley would disown her if she was the reason Brodie retired from the game he was so passionate about.

Caitlin pushed Brodie away from her lips. Not that she wanted to, but she needed to stop him while she still had enough control over her mind to ease his worries.

"Brodie James, my love, don't you dare use me as an excuse for retiring. If you're too old to keep playing, just admit it. I was hoping to go and see you play, sit in the grandstand and cheer for you—and JT too, of course. But I guess you can sit with me and we can cheer together," Caitlin said, giving him a cheeky grin.

She watched lovingly as his solemn expression slowly changed into that dazzling, bright smile that had captured her heart at the swimming pool, just a few eventful days before.

"I love you, Brodie. I want you to be happy too. You love rugby league and you're good at what you do. You do so much for others because of your profile. Please don't think I would ever even *consider* hearing I was the reason you stopped playing. Retire when you've had enough, and not a day before. I'll be with you until then and long after… I hope." Caitlin uttered the last two words a little nervously.

Brodie couldn't help but grin at Caitlin's words. Not only had she said she loved him, but she'd cheekily accused him of wanting to retire because he was old.

Oh, how he would make her pay for that one. He immediately imagined all the sexual ways he could 'punish' her for that comment. Perhaps he would get her aroused, then hold her on the edge of pleasure until she admitted he was still young enough at heart to keep up with her.

Caitlin really loved him. His angel was prepared to learn to live in his world, good or bad, just because he was in it. His Caitlin was so caring and selfless, so generous and trusting. He was going to make her happy.

Brodie knew he would love her forever. He couldn't believe the nervous way she spoke when she mentioned she'd be around during and after his career ended. She sounded so unsure, as if he might not always want that. Brodie was very quick to reassure her that, yes, that was what he wanted. And he wanted Riley around, too. Caitlin was Brodie's, now and forever. Always.

God help anyone who tried to change that. He would love her above all else — she was his angel.

MANDY'S
HE-MAN

Dedication

Thanks to my family and friends for their continued support and encouragement, especially Pam—your jewellery-making skills inspired Mandy's creations. Once again, I have to give thanks to the universe for my wonderful editor, Amy—thank you for bringing what was just my dream to reality.)

Chapter One

Mandy had not been expecting her ex-boyfriend to grab her by the throat, not in such a busy nightclub. When she'd noticed him heading her way, she had tried to hide her instant, mind-numbing terror by standing as tall as her short-statured body would allow. Though she'd had a little too much to drink, she'd tried not to sway as she'd planted her black boot-clad feet firmly on the ground. With her legs spread slightly apart, head up and chin stuck out defiantly, she'd done her best to portray the image of a strong woman, and not that of the vulnerable victim she had been. But the rough feel of his fingers as they'd wrapped around her throat had been something she could not have prepared herself for.

Mandy, shocked by the suddenness of his attack, feared for her life, believing that he was there to follow through on what had been a constant barrage of threats to kill her. He would do it there and then in this grungy, dark club. The sounds from the heavy metal band would be the last thing she would ever hear. The colours swirling in Mandy's head were in synch with her terror — sable and claret, violent reds and angry yellows spinning into a kind of black, angry vortex in her mind, making it hard for her to react.

Mandy always saw colours in her mind, ones that matched her emotions. She had since she was very young, not just the typical 'black means sad' and 'red means mad', but combinations that could rival any home decorator's paint charts. Depending on her mood, varying shades, tones and shimmering hues — too many to even describe — splashed and swirled throughout Mandy Magenta's head. Her mind's colours, usually a comfort to Mandy, were now doing nothing to help stabilise her emotions. She needed to get a grip on her fear, push through the angry vortex and find some shades of power to give her the courage to fight.

As Con — her biggest mistake — started dragging her by her throat towards the exit of the club, Mandy used all the strength she could muster to try to slow him down. She dug her heels ineffectively into the club's sticky carpet, hitting and scratching at the hands gripping her throat, which had delivered so much pain in the past. Her efforts brought no response from her vicious ex, so Mandy began flailing her arms wildly to try to get someone to notice what was happening and intervene.

Perhaps the doorman will help me? If I could just get his attention, she thought.

Con leaned towards her and whispered, "Amanda, you're a bad girl, hiding from me. It has taken up a lot of my time and energy to track you down. I told you what I would do to you if you made me angry again, and you know how much I enjoy our little games. It's time to play."

The familiar, threatening tone had an instant effect. A paralysing ripple of fear travelled through her body, leaving a cold fever in its wake. Mandy was unable to stop the rash of goosebumps from breaking over her skin as a heaviness formed in the pit of her stomach, accompanied by memories of pain and degradation.

Mandy was now way past frantic. She couldn't let Con take her out of the building. She had to fight harder.

I may as well die here, instead of in some back lane, probably more painfully. Fight him – kick, scream! C'mon, girl! she told herself, trying desperately to inspire some extra burst of inner strength to overcome her terror. But as she found the courage to continue her struggle, her efforts were quickly defused.

Con spat in her face. The shock of this disgusting action and the feel of the sticky glob of wetness dripping down her cheek made her gag, and she stumbled. The pain in her shoulder as Con jerked her upright again was so severe that it was all Mandy could do to stay conscious. As all hope faded, Mandy simply prayed that she would survive another of Con's brutal attacks.

Mandy wasn't sure what happened next. One second she was being choked, terrified for her life, in pain and being dragged away. The next she was standing behind a behemoth of a man and Con was in a heap on the floor.

She was crying. Big, fat tears rolled uncontrollably down her cheeks. She could not believe she had escaped from Con again. Her throat was painful and sore, but she would live.

JT had saved her.

What is he doing here? How could I have missed him in the club earlier?

The air around her usually seemed to spark when JT was near. Mandy hadn't thought this club would be the type of place he frequented—not that she really had a clue what type of place JT *did* like. She loved it there though. Because of the loud music and grungy look and feel of the place, Mandy fitted in—or at least, didn't stand out. She knew some of the regulars, fellow stallholders from the local flea markets around Sydney. Markets like Glebe and Paddington, with a trendy and slightly feral feel about them. Places Mandy could sell her art and handmade jewellery, or draw portraits.

Con had always hated these types of clubs. It was probably another positive in the club's favour, in Mandy's opinion. He had preferred chic, trendy clubs full of what she suspected were superficial people just wanting to be seen in the 'right crowd'. In fact, the more Mandy thought about her relationship with Con, the more she couldn't understand why he had even been interested in her at all. Mandy was not the 'in crowd'.

None of this thinking answered her original question, though.

What was JT doing there? Should she check and make sure that he hadn't killed Con?

Not that she was worried for her ex. It was more that Mandy knew that Brodie, her neighbour's boyfriend, would be pretty pissed off at her if he lost his Sydney Jets teammate to a jail cell.

Everything was going to be okay!

The bouncer had finally joined them and was escorting a bewildered Con out. The bouncer had probably taken JT's side in the scuffle because he looked way too big to fight. Mandy wished she could stop crying. It was embarrassing, and she hated feeling like a victim, but she had been fighting this battle with Con for so long and, up until this minute, she had been losing. So far, her life in Sydney had not reached the dizzying heights she had dreamed it would.

JT had been surprised to see Mandy at the rough inner city club. But it was a nice surprise. It had given him something to do while the boys partied hard—watch her…

He had accompanied the younger Jets players on their night out to celebrate halfback Mitch's twenty-first. He thought it was important to watch over the boys when they were in celebration mode. He could share their fun, but if anything even threatened to get out of hand, he could 'cut it off at the pass', so to speak.

Finding Mandy at the club had been an unexpected bonus. JT had been psyching himself up to go and speak to her, checking the lay of the land to see who she was with before making his move, when the drama had erupted. He had been trying to figure out just why the idea that Mandy might have a boyfriend seemed so distasteful to him when he'd picked up the troublemaker on his radar.

JT was a man with an instinct for being aware of his surroundings. He had noted the aggressive look on the guy's face as he had entered the club. But nothing could have shocked him more than seeing him grab Mandy by the throat.

At that point JT had gone into overdrive. Already angry, he had charged to Mandy's aid, and had nearly lost it completely when he'd seen the dickhead spit on her.

On reflection, that guy was lucky he hadn't copped a fist through his angry, worthless head.

Instead, JT had grabbed the guy's wrist and had twisted it so hard it could have snapped the bone. He'd shepherded Mandy safely behind him after he'd pushed her assailant to the ground.

Deep down, JT had hoped the idiot would get up again, so he'd have an excuse to inflict some more pain on the guy's worthless arse. He deserved it for laying into a woman—and not just because it was Mandy.

But the doorman had stepped in and escorted the guy away. He had gone quietly, hadn't uttered a syllable and had avoided eye contact with both JT and Mandy. *Coward.*

Gathering Mandy up in his arms and carrying her back to the Jets group was the only possible course of action in JT's mind. Her safety was paramount, and holding on to her also seemed an effective way of reining in his intense anger.

Chapter Two

His thick, muscular arm was warm under her thighs. He had gently encircled her waist with his other arm. He was carrying her towards the bar. Mandy was glad to be moving away from the little mob that had built to watch the ugly proceedings, and she dabbed at her probably smudged makeup with the hanky JT had thoughtfully given her.

When they reached the bar, Mandy finally got some answers to her questions. JT was there at the club with friends. Although JT appeared to be sober, his younger friends were all happily intoxicated, definitely intent on enjoying themselves. There were also quite a number of women surrounding the men, playing up to them and receiving plenty of attention in return.

The males of the group began cheering and backslapping JT as he rejoined them, calling him a hero. To Mandy, JT looked uncomfortable with all the fuss and attention. So, not only did he seem to not fit in at the club, he also appeared a little out of place among the half-dozen loud young men.

"Let me buy you a drink," he said with calm
authority. "I think you could use one. And then you
can fill me in on what was going on with that
arsehole."

To anyone looking on, it probably would have been
quite an amusing sight, since JT hadn't actually put
Mandy down yet. And, apparently, was not in any
hurry to do so. Oddly enough, Mandy was becoming
aware that she wasn't in any real hurry for him to
release her, either. She was enjoying the feel of JT's
warm, strong body as it enveloped her. It was as if his
touch was bringing her back to life.

Con had taken a toll on Mandy with his cruel ways.
For the first time in months, she actually felt safe. She
was just going to hold on to that feeling for a little
while longer and try not to think about the fact that
Con would be even angrier with her now.

"Thanks, I think you might be right. I need a Scotch.
And JT, thanks for what you did back there. The
arsehole was, in fact, my ex, a huge mistake that I've
been trying to erase for a while now. He... Con... My
ex just doesn't like the thought of me moving on and
isn't averse to using his fists to show me."

As Mandy admitted to her past mistake she looked
JT right in the eyes, trying to portray a look of
confidence so he wouldn't think her the weak,
pathetic type, regularly in need of rescue. For some
reason, Mandy felt that JT's opinion of her mattered.

"Dickhead needed to be taught a lesson," growled
JT. "There is no excuse for manhandling a woman.
Glad I was here, just wish I'd moved faster." JT met
her gaze, but to Mandy's relief showed no signs of
judgement or condemnation.

The end of the night turned out to be a whole lot
more fun than the beginning had been. Mandy soon

figured out that JT was acting as a babysitter, of sorts, to the group of younger team members.

"Bodyguard to all," she whispered dreamily as she sipped her Scotch and Coke, about the sixth passed her way by the happy and friendly group of men from the local rugby league side. Mandy had only managed to completely finish one of the drinks so far. As a new drink arrived, JT would swiftly remove the old drink from her, empty or not.

If she had managed to drink all the alcohol handed to her, Mandy knew she wouldn't have been able to walk. Not that this was really a problem yet, as she was still sitting comfortably on the very large lap she was becoming accustomed to. Mandy was trying not to wiggle, too much, on the incredibly hard ridge that was pressed up against her bottom, but she could not ignore the fact that it was exciting her, making her want things she hadn't wanted in a long time, such as the feel of that hardness buried deep inside her.

* * * *

As all good things must come to an end, so did her night. While the young Jets players were all being safely poured into taxi cabs by their very protective teammate, Mandy tried to flag down a taxi of her own. But JT was having none of it, and insisted that he would drive her home. He seemed convinced that if he didn't, Caitlin would have his hide. Mandy was amused at the thought of her downstairs neighbour skinning this gigantic man.

Wow, the skin would be huge. You could reupholster a houseful of furniture with a hide as big as that, she thought, and couldn't stop the giggle that was building in her chest from escaping. JT raised an eyebrow in her direction and smiled.

As Mandy walked hand in hand with JT, varying tones of soft blues and calm greens flowed through her mind. The colours travelled slowly, lazily, like a meandering river, indicating her relaxed and happily subdued state of mind, despite what had happened earlier in the evening.

JT's big, black V8 Ford GT reminded Mandy of a panther waiting to pounce. The soft leather seat she sank into was warm. With the seat-warmer and interior heating turned on, she was having trouble staying awake. It wasn't long until the excitement of the night took its toll and Mandy drifted off.

Chapter Three

JT carried Mandy's limp, little, velvet-clad body up the stairwell of the building that was so familiar to him. She had looked so peacefully asleep in the passenger seat of his car that he'd decided not to wake her. But when he reached the door to her flat he realised his mental picture of gently delivering her sleeping form into her own bed wasn't logistically possible. He had to wake her to get the key to her door.

Mandy had fitted so comfortably in his arms and on his lap earlier tonight, and now, as he held her sleeping form in his arms, he was still trying to decide what to do. He'd expected her to struggle from his grasp the minute the shock from the attack had subsided. She'd always had the air of a feisty little scrap of a thing, dressed in so much black and with all that war paint on her face. War paint that was a little smudged now, JT noticed with a smile. Something about Mandy, the handful of times he'd been around her, always brought out a protective instinct in him that he found hard to understand.

He'd been pleased that the boys had been reasonably well behaved — not giving him a hard time about her, just happily buying Mandy one drink after another. JT had thought that maybe his young team mates were plying her with alcohol for his benefit. She'd seemed to struggle with the frequency of drinks, so he had started removing the old glass from her hand as the new drink had appeared, whether she'd finished or not. The little smiles of gratitude she'd given him each time had been priceless.

The thought of just sitting down on the floor and holding her until she awoke crossed his mind. JT again looked from the locked door back to her face, but this time he found her eyes open and staring back at him.

"You have the most amazingly well-structured face I've ever seen," Mandy declared with sudden alertness. "It's so balanced. Most people have a very unbalanced face, one side out of synch with the other, but yours is so symmetrical." She reached up and drew her finger around JT's jaw line.

JT was gobsmacked. What on earth was she talking about?

"Still a wee bit tipsy, are we, Mags?"

"Urghh!" Mandy harrumphed indignantly. She struggled out of JT's hold to stand on her own two feet, then looked up into his face and spoke in a stern tone that reflected her displeasure at both his assessment of her sobriety and choice of nickname. "My name is Magenta, as in the colour, He-Man, I'm not some sort of optional extra that you put on your car. It's *mah-jen-tah!*" She enunciated the word as if speaking to a slow-learning child. "What is it about Aussie men that they have to shorten surnames into some sort of nickname? It's really not very imaginative — and I am not drunk!" she seethed.

Mandy turned her back on him and put the key in the lock, opened her front door and walked inside.

JT had felt the loss immediately when she'd struggled from his grasp, but he turned to leave. Although disappointed the night was over, he was glad the fight had come back into Mandy's amazing eyes. He was still not able to put his finger on what it was about her eyes that attracted him. Lost in his own thoughts, he was surprised to hear the challenge in her voice as she called out to him.

"Hey, He-Man, where are you going? You too chicken to come inside?"

Mandy stood back, as if to give him room to pass by and enter her home. She stood with her hands on her curvy hips and looked at him with one eyebrow raised questioningly.

"What could it hurt?" JT grinned as he stepped towards the little spitfire.

Standing just inside the door, JT looked around the room. The layout was similar to Caitlin Walters' flat on the ground floor of the same building, but the décor was nothing like it. Mandy's living room was chaos. Easels, paint and paintbrushes littered the room. Canvases of all sizes — some used and some still blank — leaned against the walls. Splashes of colour seemed to be everywhere.

It took JT a moment to realise that he was in a studio. Mandy Magenta was an artist, and judging by what he could see, she did it all — portraits, still life, landscape, abstract...it was all there. Including what looked, in JT's opinion, to be a painting of a giant penis.

Chapter Four

Mandy closed the door and waited for JT's reaction to her flat. Looking around as if through his eyes, she could see that it would appear cluttered, but she knew it was clean. Dirt and dust were not good for wet paint.

With him just standing there, his back so close, she couldn't resist any longer and had to run her hands over the well-defined muscle formation. She could see those protruding ridges stretching the lines of his shirt. He looked so powerful, so masculine. Mandy was almost drooling at the thought of copying his likeness to canvas. She was a little distracted by her own imagination, so when he spun her around and grabbed at her hands, halting their explorations over him, she jumped.

"Whoa there, wait a minute, woman. A man normally likes to take the lead in this sort of thing." JT spoke in an amused but throaty voice.

Mandy looked up at him, confused and a little annoyed. He held her hands in his, a little above her head, his grip firm but still gentle. Strangely, she did not feel even a flicker of fear.

"You have the most impressive body I've ever had the pleasure of seeing up close. I just wanted to feel every shape, ridge and roped muscle beneath my fingers," Mandy enthused. "The colours you are creating in my head are unbelievable. I want—no, *need*—to see you nude. To imprint that picture in my memory. You are the perfect specimen of everything that is male."

Although speaking earnestly, honestly, her voice came out sounding rather husky to her own ears.

JT released the hold he had on her hands. He picked her up and pushed her against the wall, his mouth closing in on Mandy's lips. JT kissed her hungrily, nipping at her bottom lip until she opened up for him.

Mandy wasn't sure what had hit her. But as that hard, hot mouth descended on hers she immediately felt the connection. The colours exploded through her mind. A kaleidoscope of vermillion reds and bright oranges combined in vibrant patterns that resembled flames licking at her. Scorching her. Her body was also on fire, fevered, the heat so intense that it was as if her skin was being stroked by hot embers. The feeling of JT's tongue consuming her mouth, invading, making a claim, seemed to wake some hidden animal within her. She threw her arms around his thick neck and wrapped her legs around his waist, finding that she was just able to lock her ankles around his massive form. She thrust her tongue into JT's mouth, trying to challenge his ownership, making her own claims in return, as she rubbed her body up against him.

"Slow down, Mags," JT said breathlessly, but she saw the wild, hungry look in his eyes that contradicted his words.

Mandy looked at JT, her confusion turning to anger. *Slow down?* The man had, without warning, pounced on her like some savage, slammed her up against the wall and kissed her senseless.

Obviously, JT had not realised it had been the artist in Mandy speaking. He had completely missed the implication that she wanted only to sketch or paint his likeness onto canvas.

But when he'd kissed her, Mandy had known that this was right. This man was what her body craved. Needed.

So why on earth did he want to slow down? She could have scratched his eyes out for heating her up so much, just to pull away. Mandy almost shouted at him as she fought her desire to pummel his chest.

"Hey, He-Man, you started this. Can't you take the heat? Not very gentlemanly of you to get a girl all fired up, just to walk away. So what *do* they call the male equivalent of a cock tease?"

Chapter Five

JT was speechless. No-one had ever spoken to him quite so passionately. Her voice, the things she'd said, had awoken in him a primal need that he hadn't felt for so long.

But he was confused by her words. He hadn't started anything. He had spent the night resisting the urge to take her in his arms and kiss her. Had worried about taking advantage, after the shock she had suffered. She had been the one spouting all that romantic stuff about his body, with that sultry look in her eye and her pouty lips biting at each other. Not to mention, it had been her hands roaming all over his back, her touch burning him in its wake. He must be going mad.

"I didn't start this, you did... All that sexy talk about me. *What* was that about?"

JT was not expecting her response. Not at all. He was shocked when she actually laughed at him. His cock would have softened, if not for the fact that her hot pussy was still pushed snugly up against it.

"I wanted to use you as a model. To sketch you, paint you. Draw every defined muscle of that amazing physique you've created. Not get down and dirty with you, He-Man. Although I think I've changed my mind on that one. I want all of you. Are you up for it?"

Mandy and JT eyed each other, standing mashed together in such a ridiculous pose—her against the wall, her legs still wrapped round him, and him snarling down at her.

They both started laughing.

"This is going well." JT chuckled. "How 'bout we start this over again? I want you, Mags! I have all night. You can probably feel just how much by what's pushing against that hot pussy of yours."

"Hmmm, I sure can," she replied before unfurling her legs from around his hips and sliding seductively down the front of him, then grabbing hold of the bulging form at the front of his jeans. "Maybe you should get rid of these, so I can get a good look at how much you want me."

She brazenly unzipped his jeans, then pushed the denim down JT's legs. Kneeling down in front of him, she took the weight of his thick, hard cock in one hand and the round, fleshy sac underneath in the other. She rubbed her thumb over the satiny tip of his rock-hard erection, spreading the pearl-like drop of fluid that had gathered around its bulbous head. Smiling up at him with a twinkle in her eye, she licked her lips.

"Careful, little girl. Don't start what you're not prepared to finish," JT growled, as he gently pushed her head back down towards his throbbing cock.

JT would have stopped, though, the second Mandy had so much as hesitated. It was an idle threat on his behalf. JT had never forced a woman, and didn't think much of men who did. But he sent a silent prayer of thanks heavenwards when Mandy opened her mouth and wrapped those pouty red lips around the head of his shaft, sucking it deep into her mouth.

The sight of her cheeks hollowing and her head bobbing up and down, let alone the feel and sound of that hot mouth swallowing him, was nearly enough to make JT spill his seed. Before that could happen, he wanted to spend some time exploring her curvaceous little body. JT, grabbing Mandy by the shoulders, encouraged her to stand. Those big, bright eyes looked up at him as his cock made a plopping sound when she released it from her wicked mouth, nearly doing in the last of his self-control.

Dragging Mandy up against his chest, JT crushed his mouth down on her very talented lips, trying to regain some semblance of control over his body.

He wanted to taste every bit of this woman, starting with her mouth, which tasted like honey and spice, warm and exotic. He nipped at her bottom lip before drawing it into his mouth to soothe it. Looking down into her eyes, he spoke, his voice a throaty, husky whisper.

"Honey, do you have a bed or should I just strip you naked and fuck you right here on the floor?"

Mandy's eyes widened at his explicit question. She licked at her lips and grabbed his hand, trying to drag him towards another destination—probably her bedroom. But Mandy had forgotten that JT still had his pants down around his ankles. JT stood his ground. As she looked back at him, eyes rounded, seemingly alarmed at his lack of movement, he calmly bent down and, with one hand, hitched up his jeans just enough that he could freely move in the direction she had indicated. He swooped her up in his free arm as he went by.

He only half noticed the décor of the room. The main piece of furniture was a huge bed. The bed's frame was some sort of metal, like a cage, that wrapped around the mattress. But he was distracted and far more interested in the private strip show going on in front of him, now that he had placed Mandy back on her feet. She was seductively removing her clothing, piece by piece. JT's mouth was watering at the sight. His hands itched to touch her, to freely explore her. Mandy's sexy, curvy feminine body was a sight JT would not easily forget.

Mandy loved the way JT was watching her strip for him—his eyes held such a wild, hungry look. It was the first time she had felt like making love in a long time. It was also the first time she'd felt like a sensual women in too long. She couldn't believe how hot and wet she was for him, feeling the cream actually leaking out from between her folds. The way he had spoken, crudely yet in a tone that had done amazing things to her already turned-on body. The fact that she was turned on at all was a surprise to Mandy.

That last time with Con, he had forced himself upon her, hitting her repeatedly and biting down on her sensitive breasts hard enough to draw blood. Even now, months later the marks were still visible, although they had faded. Her cries of pain had only seemed to arouse him more and more. Mandy liked it a bit rough, but not to the extent he had taken it. She had been scared, in pain, and Con wouldn't stop. Mandy had grabbed her clothes and run naked from his home the minute he had turned away from her. It seemed as if she had been running from him and his fists ever since.

Shaking off the shiver that ran down her spine at the memory, Mandy focused back on the magnificent male standing in front of her — focused on JT.

He would be the first man she had invited into her new bed. It was her haven, just her and the shapes she had welded lovingly into the frame work. She had formed the steelwork into snakes, inspired by Medusa. She'd made each snakehead with her own hands, embedding jewels or gemstones for eyes, giving each snake a lifelike and individual appearance.

Feeling emboldened, Mandy crawled backwards onto her bed and crooked her finger at JT wantonly, in a sign of invitation for him to join her.

JT didn't need to be asked twice, and stripped out of his clothes at a frantic pace. He reached out and pulled her back to the edge of the bed. Sitting between her splayed legs, the width of his shoulders spreading her wide, he ran his hands first over her ankles, then stroked his thumbs up the insides of her legs, up over her calf muscles, over her knees and past her now quivering thighs. Little goose bumps broke out over Mandy's skin. She should have felt embarrassed to be spread so vulnerably in front of him, but the shiver that racked her body was pure eager anticipation.

Chapter Six

JT's thumbs reached her pussy lips. He could see them glistening through her little curls. After making eye contact with Mandy, seeking approval from her to continue, JT put his head between her thighs. Opening her wide with his thumbs, he licked her from the bottom of her moist folds right up to the little hooded nub at the apex of her pussy, holding her down with his arms across her thighs, so she was trapped under his tongue's assault.

Mandy tasted like perfection. JT lapped at and feasted on her pussy like a starving man as she writhed and moaned beneath his ministrations. Every time he felt her squirming body getting closer to climax, he retreated teasingly, waiting for her to cry out his name and plead for him to bring her to release.

Mandy did start moaning JT's name, and he could wait no longer. He sucked and tongued her clit with renewed vigour as he pushed first one finger, then another, into her moist channel and pumped. It took only seconds before she exploded with such force that

JT nearly lost his grip on her—her body arched and tensed before collapsing back on the bed.

JT picked Mandy up under her armpits and gently tossed her up to the head of the bed. He manoeuvred his body into position, placing his cock against her entrance—that wet haven he had just feasted upon—and plunged in. One hard stroke and he claimed her.

It felt like heaven, tight and warm. Placing Mandy's legs above his shoulders, he thrust again, the new angle allowing him deeper access. JT wanted to be completely embedded in her.

It was then that it hit him.

No condom!

"What the fuck?" JT's loud, deep voice reverberated around the room. "I don't have a condom on. And I don't have one with me."

He groaned and withdrew his rock-hard erection from Mandy, quickly but reluctantly, still very hot and bothered.

After her initial groan of anguish as JT jerked his length from her, Mandy started making soothing, cooing sounds as she pushed at him until he rolled onto his back. She climbed over him, straddling his massive torso, and reached into her bedside drawer, her nipples brushing against his lips invitingly as she bent over him. Then she whispered into his ear, blowing an extra little breath on him, "It's okay, He-Man. I've got you covered."

After fighting to get the packet open, Mandy ripped a foil package with her teeth, then removed the condom and rolled it slowly onto his still very rigid form.

JT was trying not to blow. He looked at the ceiling, at the walls, anything, trying somehow to distract himself as this amazing woman took control again.

The touch of Mandy's fingers as she rolled that rubber onto his cock was almost torture. It was in his desperation to be distracted that he finally noticed the intricate design of her headboard. There were dozens of metal snakes, curled around as if protecting the human occupants in the bed. Those watchful eyes seemed to be blinking at him.

"Wow that's fucking awesome! I love your bed, never seen anything like it."

"That's cause it's a one-off — my design, my creation. Yours is the first erection my girls have ever seen…" Her answer faltered as she lowered herself over his rigid cock slowly. He could feel the walls of her pussy widen to accommodate his girth — the way her inner muscles tightened around him left him breathless, his eyes rolled back into his head at the pleasure she was bringing him. Then she started to rock, moving her hips up and down over him.

JT was not going to be able to hold on for much longer — watching her ride him was the biggest turn-on. Her eyes were so unique, and they burnt into his soul. It was about the time she began pulling those protruding plum-coloured nipples, her eyes boldly locked to his, that he finally became aware of the difference in the shades of her eyes, and unintentionally spoke the thought out loud.

"My God, I finally figured out what it is about those eyes of yours that have always got me so hot. Each eye is a different colour — chocolate and caramel," he stuttered, trying to think coherently while the woman straddling him did her best to blow his mind. She was winning, but JT managed one last sentence before he succumbed to his carnal desire. "Woman, you are amazing — everything about you is amazing, beautiful!"

JT grabbed hold of Mandy by the hips, taking back control. Flipping her little body over in one smooth motion, so it lay beneath his, he started pumping. He could hear the sound of his balls slapping against her bottom as she wrapped her legs around him and held on. JT, knowing he was close, but wanting to bring her apart underneath him first, reached down between their slick bodies, and using his finger, found and stroked her clit.

Chapter Seven

She loved the feel of his muscular chest under her hands and the rug of curly, black hair that covered some of that broad expanse, leading a path down to his groin and where they were joined. Her colours, so vibrant and alive, wove through her mind, a palette that even she found unusually exquisite.

The colours erupted from Mandy violently — she imagined them leaping from her, could see the picture on canvas of the many-hued lightning bolts leaving her body — as the man brought her, more than once, over the edge of the abyss into pure ecstasy. Waves climbed high, crested, rolling and tumbling around inside her head before ebbing away into sheets of shimmering hues. Mandy was sure she had heard JT cry out her name, as he'd surged into her one last time before collapsing down over her, cocooning her.

She could have happily drifted off to sleep after her orgasm, if it hadn't been for the limp, condom-covered appendage slipping from its resting place between her legs. Sighing at the loss as JT pushed himself up and away from her, she felt the cold air hit her naked skin and shivered.

"Where can I get rid of this, honey?" JT asked nonchalantly, unperturbed and unembarrassed by the things they had just done.

Mandy lifted her arm and pointed in the direction of her bathroom, and JT headed off that way. She, on the other hand, was now feeling very uncomfortable in her own nudity and wondering how awful her smudged makeup must look.

"I've got panda eyes for sure," she groaned.

God, she hadn't thought about a condom either – so not like her. She had been so aroused, just wanting to feel him inside her, filling her…and that, he certainly had. She really would need to check when her last contraception injection had been, and schedule another with her doctor.

When JT had mentioned her bed design, she had felt such a sense of pride. Now, as she thought more about it, she was surprised that JT had even noticed his surroundings. She could have been sitting on the moon and wouldn't have known, the feeling of him buried deep in her pussy had been so good. *Perhaps I didn't rock his world quite as much as he did mine*, she thought miserably.

At least I made him come – well, unless he is a very good actor, Mandy thought, trying to quell her own insecurities.

Mandy wasn't sure whether to get up and follow JT to the bathroom or stay in bed and wait. She heard the flush of the toilet and the sound of water running. Climbing under the bedding, she waited, closing her eyes.

Mandy heard JT re-enter her bedroom, and she couldn't pretend to be asleep. She needed to see him, even if it was to just watch him dress and leave. As she opened her eyes again, she had never felt so nervous in her life. She waited for his reaction to her and what had just taken place between them. Looking up into his stormy, dark eyes, Mandy knew she wanted him to stay, wanted to fall asleep in his strong, safe arms.

So, taking a chance, she smiled up at him and lifted the covers back, an invitation for him to join her again.

To Mandy's absolute relief and delight, JT made a soft, deep growling sound and climbed into the bed next to her. Dragging her body up against his, she snuggled into his chest, her head resting under his chin, and let sleep take her.

* * * *

Mandy woke slowly, savouring the feel of being safe and warm, wrapped up tightly in the arms of this strong sensuous man. She had slept so well that her mind was now a clear, fresh, minty green. She could feel the slight soreness between her legs and smiled. Taking a peek over JT's impossibly broad shoulders at her clock, she was shocked to see it was already nine a.m.. Thankfully, it was Thursday and she had no market stall to set up. She could just enjoy being where she was for a little longer. Mandy was worried, though, that maybe JT had training. She remembered some previous conversations she'd had with Caitlin about how Brodie had training nearly every day.

Caitlin and her younger brother Riley had recently become part of Mandy's life. She enjoyed spending time with both of them. Caitlin was a good friend and Mandy enjoyed having a girlfriend to chat with about life. When they'd met, Caitlin had been going through a rough spot with her boyfriend—JT's best mate, Brodie James. Mandy, happy to do anything she could to help, had spent time with cute little Riley, playing computer games to distract him. It had not been a chore at all. While all the drama between Caitlin and Brodie had been going on, she had met JT.

She'd been attracted to him from their first meeting, JT's lips, in particular, had always seemed so tempting and she had fantasised on more than one occasion about what it would be like to kiss him. Mandy smiled because now she knew for sure—absolutely wonderful. Those same lips, which now looked relaxed and inviting, were right there next to her, in her bed. Unable to resist the temptation any longer, Mandy decided to make the most of her good fortune and kissed them, licking and nibbling lightly until JT's eyes slowly drifted open. She felt the corners of his mouth curl up and knew he was smiling as he pulled her on top of his very expansive, warm chest, kissing her into oblivion again. She had to stop him to point out the time, to at least try to do the right thing even if she didn't like the thought of him leaving.

"JT, you need to know it's after nine. I don't want to keep you from anything," Mandy managed to croak out, after finally surfacing from the depths of his kiss.

"Shit…" JT groaned, still massaging Mandy's bottom sensually with one hand. "Mags, I need to get to training, but woman, I just don't want to leave it here. When can I see you again? Can we catch up tonight? I promised Riley that I'd take him to Mia's Restaurant for a while to listen to Caitlin sing. Say you'll come with me, honey."

JT waited for her answer, looking deep into Mandy's eyes, looking for a positive sign, hoping that she might want to see him again.

Needing for it to be so.

Never having wanted anything quite as much.

He was not really a confident type of guy when it came to romancing women or showing emotion. He had always been the tough guy. Certainly not a soppy man begging for a woman to see him again. He was big Jon 'JT' Thomson.

He had been embarrassed earlier on in life by his size, since he always seemed to stand out in a crowd. Rugby league had changed that, though. JT had learnt to use his big frame in a positive way and was now comfortable in his own skin. Still, he cringed a little every time he heard the same old comment—*Gee, you're so big!* As if somehow he hadn't noticed his hundred and ninety-eight centimetre frame or hundred and twenty kilogram build.

It had been one of the things that had struck him about his first meeting with Mandy—the unique young woman with her dark hair all spiked up, who'd been dressed in all-black clothing and those adorable black, army-styled boots. She had not once mentioned his size. In fact, the quirky beauty had stood on a window ledge, bringing her dramatically made-up eyes level with his. JT had liked those eyes right from the start and the way she had stuck out her tiny, delicate hand so formally to him.

JT needed to speak to his best mate, Brodie. Brodie was JT's go-to guy and right at that minute, JT was thinking he needed all the help he could get to entice this amazing woman to agree to go on a date with him—he was acting like some love-struck teenager.

JT was so distracted pondering his dilemma that he almost missed seeing Mandy smile back at him, those uniquely coloured eyes twinkling.

She said the words he had been waiting for and worrying over.

"Yes, I'd love to go out with you tonight, but on one condition, He-Man. You stop calling me Mags." She laughed, winked. "Actually, I'd go with you anyway. I think Riley is a cutie-pie and love spending time with him. You get up and dress and I'll make some coffee. You do have time for that, don't you?"

JT let out a sigh, relieved that he'd heard her say yes. He hadn't been aware he had been holding his breath until that moment. But the little vixen was telling him it was because Riley was a 'cutie-pie'.

Mandy and Riley—Caitlin's young brother—had become close friends since the fracas a few weeks back. JT had a soft spot for the boy too. Riley had lost his parents just the year before in a tragic car accident. He and his sister had been struggling through life as best they could. It had reminded him of the loss of his own mother to breast cancer at around the same age. JT had, at least, had his father around to support him through those tough years.

I will have to sort the kid out. No more cutie behaviour towards my girl, he thought jealously, then felt quite ridiculous at the overreaction. Riley was only eleven years old, for goodness' sake. He reached towards the woman who had so quickly stolen his heart, and growled.

"No time for coffee, Mandy. I won't need one. I'd rather take my fill of you!"

* * * *

JT was feeling awesome. Since leaving Mandy's warm bed earlier that morning, he'd had an abundance of energy, causing many a grumble from his fellow teammates during tackle practice as he'd crashed them repeatedly into the ground. Even Brodie—who had been acting like a happy little puppy these days, enjoying a new lease of life since Caitlin had become a part of it seemed normal in comparison.

Right from the start of JT's career, Brodie James had been there. A tough, young front-rower, Brodie had already been touted as a future star of rugby league. JT had at first been nervous when meeting Brodie, wanting to make a good impression. They had trained side by side, each pushing the other throughout the vigorous session, always keeping up and trying to outdo one another, whether they'd been weightlifting, tackling bags or running. Trying in some stupid, alpha-male bullshit way to find out who was tougher. JT had been exhausted and incredibly relieved when the coach had come over and explained that both men were needed for the game, and had requested that they not kill each other.

JT and Brodie had stood side by side on and off the field since then.

JT checked the night's arrangements with Brodie, confirming that Caitlin was to be singing at Mia's Restaurant—her regular job—and reminding Brodie that he was fine with the arrangements to look after Riley afterwards, but added he would need another seat for dinner as he was bringing a date.

"So I assume your unusually cheery mood this morning has something to do with that dark-haired friend of Cait's then?" Brodie flicked a dirty football sock at JT. "Lucky I stayed over last night, mate. If I'd turned up to take Riley to squad and seen your car at Caitlin's, I might have jumped to all sorts of wrong conclusions." He laughed a deep, chuckling laugh. "Wouldn't have worried for long, though. My angel has better taste than to hook up with a beast like you, JT. So how is Mandy, anyway?" Brodie winked and elbowed JT good-naturedly.

"Mate, she is a bloody beauty—definitely a keeper." JT smiled broadly and winked. "But that's all the information I'm giving you, Brodes. A gentleman never brags. I'll catch you later. Say hi to Caitlin and let Riley know I'm looking forward to another arm wrestle."

* * * *

With the day's training session behind him and a skip in his step, JT strode up the path to the house he shared with his father. Thinking about all that had happened the previous night brought another broad smile to his face. It had been amusing to see the young players suffering at the training session, so hung-over and ill from last night's celebration, while he was so alive, fit and raring to go.

He was happy to find his father sipping coffee in the airy, light-filled kitchen. A fresh pot had just brewed, and the comforting aroma roused his senses. JT sat down to have a chat with his old man. By the end of the pot, he had filled his father in on the previous night's adventures with Mandy. Well—not all of the adventures in detail!

JT also wanted to get some advice from the retired policeman as to how he should handle Mandy's violent ex.

Jon Senior was quick to recommend that Mandy get an AVO—Apprehended Violence Order—which would stop the violent man from coming near her. If he did, he would be arrested, JT's father explained.

"It should be easy enough to do, son, what with your eyewitness evidence. Pop on down to the station with your young lady. I'm sure Detective Morrin will help you out." JT's father was referring to a long-time friend and former co-worker. As he stood from the table, Jon Senior also had a final warning for his son. "Violent ex-partners often don't want to let go, JT. Make sure you watch out for your lady friend."

Rugby league had been taking a hiding in the press lately, but so had a lot of sports and sportsmen. That was why JT and Brodie kept a close eye on their younger teammates, trying to keep them on the right path while they got used to the lifestyle and flickering, fickle limelight. "Yeah, okay, some young upstarts should be given one on the chin for the way they act, disrespecting the public in displays of uncouth behaviour—but hey, people are not all angels. Just 'cause you can play sport doesn't make you a nice bloke or good role model, just sporty," JT had often commented. It wasn't only high-profile types that knocked their missus or kids around. Those lowlife types existed in all walks of life, and JT despised them all. If JT ever saw that dirtbag who had hurt Mandy again, he hated to think what he might do.

He had always tried to be a good role model, but then, that was more to do with his father and the way he had been raised than anything to do with playing rugby league. He despised men like Mandy's ex-boyfriend, who were able to knock a women around but always ran scared when it was someone more their size. JT was not going to let anything happen to

Mandy, that was for sure, and he was going to discuss his father's advice with her later tonight.

Recently JT's life had been a solitary one when it came to women—a celibate life, what with training, travelling to and from games, playing then recovering. Throw in sponsor commitments and public appearances for charity or fundraising, and it was a busy schedule. He'd given up trying to form any sort of relationship, and was sick of the meaningless one-night stands. Representing Australia—standing proudly beside his best mate and captain as the sounds of the national anthem of Australia rang throughout the stadium—had been enough. That was, until now.

Until Mandy.

Now he wanted more than just footy.

Chapter Eight

Mandy had spent the morning lazily soaking in a bath, the fragrance of the lavender oil she'd added to soothe her deliciously aching body wafting in the air and the feel of the warm water lapping against her skin.

She had replayed, in minute detail, every precious moment of the night before—her time with JT. Her mind had been full of a mix of relaxing, soft and comforting pastel hues.

What a man! she'd thought dreamily, her eyelids closed as she had been consumed by images of JT. He was utterly gorgeous, and had such a talented mouth. He had drunk her incredibly dry, milking several orgasms from her before pounding his thick cock into her again and again.

"Who would have thought Mandy Magenta would be awestruck over a He-Man footballer?" She'd giggled out loud, the sound of her voice bouncing around the quiet bathroom.

But knowing there was still a lot to do in preparation for the next day's markets, before she could prepare for tonight's date with JT, Mandy had reluctantly dragged herself from the tepid bathwater.

She needed to stock up on more of her earring designs, having mostly sold out of her products at the last market stall.

It was an unusually relaxed, contented Mandy who set to work on designing more of the intricate and original earrings she created, humming away continuously. She heated the tinted glass rods and twirled them to create the unusual patterns and shapes, often using the colours in her mind as the blueprints.

Needless to say, the designs in progress heavily featured pretty, romantic hues and flowing whimsical shapes. Mandy had not even bothered to turn on the heavy metal music that usually accompanied her creative process. Up until now, more often than not, Mandy—unable to sleep as nightmares of Con had invaded her dreams—had worked throughout the night with the music blaring in her ears.

As the day grew into late afternoon, Mandy was buzzing with excitement, couldn't refrain from looking at the clock every few minutes. She had made some good headway with her jewellery designs but could not settle. Thinking that a nice, girly chat with her new best friend might help make the time pass more quickly and bring with it JT's return—not to mention the fact she was bursting with the need to fill Caitlin in on her night's adventures—Mandy made her way downstairs.

Mandy had, on many occasions, listened to Caitlin discussing her new but intense relationship with Brodie. It had not had an easy beginning and Mandy had been impressed at the level-headed attitude of the twenty-year-old with regards to the relationship. To

Mandy, it seemed that Brodie had been going full steam ahead, wanting everything at once. But Caitlin had stayed resolute, wanting to take it slow, to not rush into living together since she wanted to keep her own place for a little while longer.

Caitlin had also spoken of her affection for June, their elderly neighbour, and didn't want to move away and leave her yet. June had taken on an unofficial grandmotherly role towards Riley, and because of Caitlin's and her brother's tragic past, it was an important role. Caitlin had also mentioned her blossoming friendship with Mandy being an important factor as well. Mandy had to admit the sentiment had made her feel a little teary.

"Plenty of time to live together in the near future," Caitlin had apparently promised Brodie, when he had asked her to move in with him.

Mandy had understood her friend's explanation completely, of course. With Brodie often away, playing games interstate and in New Zealand, Caitlin would feel more comfortable, happier, in her own home. After they'd spent some time together in the off season, Mandy believed Caitlin would feel more at home in the very stylish and spacious waterfront apartment she'd heard Brodie owned.

Now that conversation with Caitlin held a more personal meaning for Mandy, as she realised it meant that JT would also often be away from home, playing rugby league.

As she hurried towards her friend's front door with a skip in her step, Mandy decided that her recent interactions with rugby league players had left her with the opinion that they were decent men. Decent, very hot and sexy men!

Caitlin Walters was quick to answer the door to Mandy, as if she had been expecting a visit. A big smile brimmed on the auburn-haired woman's face.

"Well, I was wondering when you would show, Miss Mandy!" Caitlin said, as she grabbed Mandy by the arm and dragged her inside. "I've just got off the phone from Brodie and he had some interesting gossip for me. I've got to tell you, Mandy, Brodie is sick with glee that he knew about this before I did."

Caitlin sat on the sofa and pulled a startled — and now slightly embarrassed — Mandy down next to her.

"Spill! So what *did* happen between you and JT? And don't spare the details, my friend!"

"Oh, Cait, it was wonderful... Well, actually, it was really frightening then wonderful," Mandy clarified. "I was at this new club, just catching some music and minding my own business when the next thing you know Con has me by the throat..."

"Are you all right, Mandy? Did he hurt you? My God, when is he going to leave you alone? Maybe I should get Brodie to have a word with him..."

Caitlin's worried expression tugged at Mandy's heart. To know that she had someone in her corner, someone who worried about her, was a nice feeling. Though it was quite foreign to Mandy — she had been looking after herself for so long.

"It's all good, Cait, no need for Brodie to get involved, not after what JT did. You didn't let me finish my story. Anyway, just when I thought I was done for, at the mercy of Con's vicious temper once again, I found myself free from Con's grasp and standing behind this mammoth back. JT's gorgeous, wide, wonderfully sculptured back. JT had come like a shining white knight to my rescue. Con was all but crying on the floor after JT got through with him."

"Gosh, Mandy, thank goodness for JT. But a white knight? I picture him as more of a *black* knight when it comes to riding in to save you, what with you all gothic and dark-looking. I think it fits better." Caitlin gave a little, romantic, wistful sigh. "So how did he end up staying all night? Brodie saw his car here this morning."

"Well, after spending time with the other guys he was at the club with, some of his teammates, JT put them all into cabs and sent them home. But he insisted on driving me home personally. In fact, he blamed you, Cait, saying if he didn't you would skin him alive."

"Well, I would have been disappointed in him if he hadn't, but the thought of skinning him… Yuck!" Caitlin laughed.

"Yeah, that's exactly what I thought…anyway, after a bit of a misunderstanding at first, one thing led to another and the rest of the story is pure ecstasy," Mandy said, grinning from ear to ear, her face feeling a bit flushed and hot at the memory of her night with JT.

"*Oooh*, look at your face! I'm so happy for you, Mandy," Caitlin squealed, clapping her hands together in glee. "And I hear that you're coming out to Mia's with us tonight. So do you think this could become serious? How nice would it be if you and JT became an item? We spend so much time with him— Brodie, Riley and me—that it would be nice to have you with us too."

"I'm not sure… It's a bit soon to make any plans. But I do know that I am just bursting over the need to see him again. He just makes me feel… I don't know… Sexy, feminine, hot… *Whole*," Mandy said after a while, trying to put her feelings for JT into words, but at the same time trying to keep some sort of grip on her own emotions and protect herself from any future heartbreak. *If that painting hasn't already been finished and hung!* she thought.

* * * *

Having eaten off the previous layers of her lipstick due to nerves, Mandy re-applied yet another coat of her favourite red lipstick and waited impatiently for JT to arrive. In the end, she went to stand out on the veranda that overlooked the front of the old, majestic house she lived in, to keep watch. Mandy's flat had a set of beautiful French doors that opened onto a spacious veranda. Sometimes she moved her easel out into a sunny spot to paint. Caitlin's flat, underneath Mandy's, had a small garden that she shared with the other ground floor tenant, June. June was, more often than not, to be found pottering around the garden. Mandy loved the way the flowers, the grevillea and native fuchsias, bloomed in such a variety of shades, even now in the colder winter months. June definitely had a green thumb.

Mandy's own colours, flitting around her mind, didn't help ease her nervousness. She felt like a hyperactive child. The hues were changing so rapidly, the strobe effects like disco lights—she could hardly keep up with them. Combining them and her ever-changing emotions with the anticipation of what lay before her this evening was nearly enough to drive Mandy insane.

Chapter Nine

JT had tried to not look as if he was dressing up especially for Mandy, although ironing his jeans was not a regular occurrence. His father had looked on, chuckling at him in amusement.

JT had never thought he was an overly attractive bloke, with his square-shaped head, solid jaw and nose that was amazingly straight, given the amount of hits it had taken. Add in his extra-large body, big shoulders and hips, plus thighs that had been described more than once as looking like tree trunks, and JT was just one big unit.

Now he was freshly showered, shaved and dressed, ready to collect Mandy. His hands were already sweating from nervous anticipation. With an on-the-fly comment about not being sure if he would be home that night, JT bade farewell to his father before all but sprinting to his car – the big man was not really known for his speed!

The drive, one that JT was familiar with – but had never undertaken quite as enthusiastically before – seemed to take a little longer this time, as if life were drawing out the suspense. Finally, JT pulled into the small private parking area beside the old house, stopping beside Caitlin's funny little green car. The other two cars parked were a red van with signage that read 'Artworx by Magenta', and Brodie's black Range Rover.

"Full house tonight, then!" He grinned to his reflection in the rear view mirror.

Noticing that Mandy was watching him from her veranda above, as if waiting for him, pleased JT. As he headed inside, the impatient anticipation of touching her again quickened his step. Unfortunately, as JT entered the downstairs hallway, Riley came shooting out of his flat and bounced around him. The kid began chatting happily away about school, his day and other things young boys found interesting.

JT, so caught up with his thoughts of Mandy, had forgotten he was taking Riley to Mia's tonight as well, then bringing the boy home early and sitting with him, leaving Brodie free to stay behind until Caitlin finished her singing gig. Riley had school the next morning, so couldn't have a very late night. When the arrangements had been made, JT, loving nothing better than spending some boy time with Brodie and Riley, had not expected to be taking a date.

JT was wondering how to broach the subject when Riley smiled at him, the grin broad and honest. Then in a hushed voice, the tone laced with a taint of conspiracy, Riley gave him some advice.

"I'll give you a tip, JT. You had better head up and get Mandy. She's been pacing around all afternoon. I'm worried she's gonna wear out a hole in her floor and end up in our place." The cheeky but astute boy — in JT's opinion — added, "I don't get what all the fuss is about, JT? Of course you would love Mandy. She is so cool—who wouldn't? Can't see why she's so worked up over it."

JT ruffled the boy's ginger hair affectionately.

"Thanks for the advice, young Romeo. I might just do that, mate. I'll go and collect Mandy and bring her down to your place, using the stairs," he said, and added a wink, "and we can all walk to Mia's together."

As JT took the stairs three at a time, he couldn't believe his luck that Mandy might be just as eager to see him as he was her. As he reached the landing he almost barrelled into her. Mandy had been coming to him. JT caught her and hugged her close. The smell of her hair alone was enough to make him instantly hard and needy.

She smelt like spring—fresh and clean. Her spiky black hair pointed every which way, tickling his chin. She had a rose-red velvet top on over a skintight, long, black velvet skirt with shiny black boots peeking out from below the hem. She wasn't showing an inch of indecent skin, but to JT, Mandy was the most incredibly sexy woman he had ever set eyes on.

JT grabbed her delicious backside in both hands, enjoying how the soft globes felt as they were hugged tight by her skirt. The fabric was almost sinful in its texture, as he rubbed his hands up, down and around those two plump mounds. He loved this bountiful backside.

JT could feel Mandy's breasts pushed up against his body and his mind quickly filled with images of what he would like to do to those inviting swells—images of himself drawing each, in turn, into his mouth and devoting hours to just lavishing attention on them alone. *My God, this woman makes me hot!* He needed to stop thinking like that. They needed to get to dinner, and to behave in front of Riley. JT wasn't sure he could pull it off and couldn't resist a little taste of her mouth, just to see him through the start of the evening. He kissed her long and tenderly, savouring every moment.

Chapter Ten

When JT had arrived, Mandy had nearly been knocked over — the man had been charging so fast towards her, like an out-of-control freight train. He looked stunning.

And massive!

His chest, hugged by a blue sweater, felt like a rock shelf as she slammed up against it. From the V-neck of the clingy top, he was showing just a hint of chest hair, which begged to be stroked and petted. As JT hugged her close, all the anxiety of the last few hours flew away. She was home in his strong arms, and the kiss was sensational. Not all hot and hard like last night, but soft and tender. Sexy as hell! If they hadn't been going out with Riley, she would have dragged him into her apartment and bonked him stupid.

Riley was going to get it for telling JT she had been pacing — little tattle-tale. She had been listening, mortified, as the boy had squealed her secrets.

Eventually, Mandy pulled away from JT. She took his hand and they headed back downstairs, and farther away from her tempting bed. Riley was standing at the bottom step with a big smile. Mandy playfully punched him in the arm and called him a traitor as she dragged JT past him and entered Caitlin's flat. Riley giggled, saying something about men having to stick together, as they went past.

Mandy pushed JT down on the sofa next to Brodie, then placed a loud smack of a kiss on his lips and informed the men she was going to talk to Caitlin.

Mandy found Caitlin in the bathroom, adding finishing touches to her stage makeup. Again, she marvelled at Caitlin's transformation from the cute girl-next-door to super-hot, sexy singer. Her looks were so different when she was wearing her stage clothes and makeup. Mandy thought it remarkable that her friend was unaware of how stunning she was.

"Hey, sex goddess, I see your hunky hero is out there already waiting for you. How does he manage to get through a game without seeing you?" Mandy teased Caitlin. "Games go for – what? Like two hours, don't they?"

"Yeah, Mandy, let's just see who's talking when everyone starts tripping over JT's big body all the time."

"I can't see myself complaining about that. I'm quite partial to JT's size. It's quite in proportion, really…big everywhere, if you get my meaning, Cait."

"Oh, you are such a bad girl, Mandy! Thanks for that mental picture. Definitely falls into the TMI category. But just so you know, Brodie doesn't have any reason to feel inadequate either. Must be a front-row forward thing – they are built big!" Caitlin's quick reply had both women giggling like schoolgirls.

Mandy had created a pair of drop earrings for Caitlin. The crimson stones complemented the colour of Caitlin's hair perfectly, twinkling as they fell from her small delicate earlobes.

"Oh! Mandy, they are *beautiful!*" Caitlin exclaimed, teary-eyed.

Mandy was touched by her friend's reaction to the gift and reached out to her. As they hugged each other, Brodie entered the bathroom. He seemed a little embarrassed at the emotional scene. Mr Dependable was so big and serious all the time that Mandy couldn't resist the temptation to tease Brodie, telling him that she and Caitlin had decided to become lovers, and so Caitlin was breaking up with him.

"Ha, figured the big unit was lousy in bed. One night with him, Mandy, and you've given up men! Can't fault your taste in women, though." Brodie laughed back at her.

The conversation was all starting to get a bit ridiculous when JT squeezed into the little room, bellowing that it wasn't his fault. "Hey, don't go laying that sort of blame on me Brodes. Mags didn't seem to be complaining last night…"

"JT, shush!" Mandy said, embarrassed but thoroughly enjoying the moment, the bonds of friendships being strengthened, as the four erupted into howls of laughter. The raucous sounds even enticed Riley into the room, wondering what was so funny.

"What's wrong with you guys? Geez, can't we just go and eat? I'm starving," Riley whined, shaking his ginger head in frustration at the continued laughter filling the small bathroom. "What are you all doing in here, anyway?"

"It's okay, Riles," Brodie said, rubbing the boy's head affectionately. "The girls were just trying to decide which one of us was the hottest."

"Yuck... I do not need to hear this conversation at all." Riley covered his ears and made 'la-la-la' noises, obviously trying to block out the conversation, much to everyone's delight.

Mandy felt settled, as if she belonged in this small group. They were a family of sorts—something she hadn't realised she had been missing. A group of special people who didn't judge her or try to make her act *more normal*. Mandy didn't need to change for them—they seemed to be happy with her the way she was.

Looking forward to the night, everyone headed out. Brodie was holding Caitlin's hand, and had an arm around Riley's shoulders affectionately. Mandy was fitted snugly under JT's arm, as if her body had been made for that area alone. She thought she would burst, hardly able to contain the emotions that she was feeling. Mandy's mind was a volcano erupting with colour—hot and heavy, passionate reds and purples, which were quickly replaced by calm, safe, flowing greens and browns, then turned into a rainbow of happy pinks and yellows.

* * * *

Mia's Restaurant was crowded. More and more customers were coming to enjoy not only the food and entertainment, but also the opportunity to dine with the local sports stars who seemed to be regulars these days. Caitlin had told Mandy that many of Brodie's and JT's friends had made the restaurant their regular, dining in quite often. Mandy was introduced to the restaurant's owner, Angelo Donetto, who greeted Brodie and JT as if they were royalty. He personally showed the party to their table. Angelo's profits had definitely taken a turn for the better since his first meeting with Brodie, a few months before.

Mandy enjoyed listening to the light-hearted banter around the table, as the three males devoured their plates of pasta and garlic bread. She had ordered a generous helping of pesto linguine, which was scrumptious. The colour of the green sauce, made from basil leaves, appealed to her artist's persona.

Throughout the meal, Mandy had to learn how to twirl and eat her pasta one-handed. JT would not give up possession of her right hand, holding it in his and occasionally brushing little kisses over her knuckles, or just stroking her fingers with his thumb. Luckily, being left-handed made the task of eating a whole lot easier for Mandy, although the sparks from JT's touches were making her hungry for something that was not on the menu at Mia's.

Caitlin sang beautifully, as usual. Mandy enjoyed seeing the look of adoration on Brodie's face as he was mesmerised by his woman's voice. He really loved Caitlin. It was obvious to anyone who watched the man. Mandy glanced over at JT, who was in the middle of another arm wrestle with Riley, and wondered if he would ever look at her that way.

Riley was a cheeky monkey all night, teasing Mandy about her liking JT. Mandy threatened revenge on Riley when he least expected it, which brought another round of laughter from the happy table.

As JT, Mandy and Riley walked home, Mandy found it hard to fathom how, after so many years of feeling as if she didn't really belong anywhere, she could now feel so much a part of this world. And all due to the man who was walking beside her.

* * * *

It had taken a while, but finally Riley was asleep. Mandy and JT were cuddled up together on Caitlin's sofa-bed, which was still in its sofa position. It was as if they were teenagers, not game to go too far and risk getting caught by their parents — or in this case, Caitlin and Brodie. JT's kisses were like a drug. Mandy was addicted — she couldn't get enough of them. His mouth tasted like vanilla and spice with just a hint of garlic, and all male.

"If you knew the things I've been thinking, the images of what I want to do to your body. How hard it was to sit at that table with my cock rock-hard and hold a civilised conversation with Riley…"

"Really, is that so?" Mandy purred against the side of JT's neck, delivering little kisses repeatedly. She was so hot for him, her nipples hard and her breasts full as they ached for the touch of his mouth. She could feel his solid length pressing against her, and just wanted to be filled by it. "Let me see if I can guess. Would you have been thinking about stripping me bare, spreading me out on the bed, fully open to you — on display, hiding nothing from you, my body wet and glistening, ready for your cock, the cock that I can feel pressed hard against me now…?"

"Mags…"

"What's the matter, JT? Worried that you aren't going to make it?" She stroked his erection through his jeans, gently applying a little pressure. "You're not going to go off before Caitlin comes home. That would be a waste, especially when you could be inside me, all warm and wet… Or, better yet, maybe I feel like a bit of dessert. Maybe I could use that nice, hot rod of yours like an ice cream. Lick and suck on it till I get some cream."

Mandy could not believe the words spilling from her mouth—they were downright dirty! But they sure were having the right effect on JT, who moaned and growled in her ear, finally cutting off any more of her provocative words by covering her mouth with his.

His kiss was deep, desperate and so, so very hot. Mandy was sizzling.

JT pulled away from her.

"You're not playing nice, woman. I'm so hot for you right now, it's bordering on painful, my dick is so hard. I love the way you talk, but just so you know, you will not be involved in any licking or sucking anytime soon, because for the first good long while after we're relieved of this babysitting torment, I will be doing all the sucking, touching and licking. I'm looking forward to devouring that sweet-tasting pussy of yours. I'm thinking of a number—a very high number—of orgasms you will have to endure before you get anywhere near my cock."

* * * *

The time it took for Caitlin and Brodie to return after Riley had gone to bed was the longest, most torturous and yet most pleasurable hour Mandy had ever experienced, as she and JT each took turns trying to outdo the other in describing the ways they intended to pleasure each other.

At the sound of the key turning in the door's lock, JT jumped up. He scooped Mandy into his arms and headed for her upstairs flat, not even stopping to speak to Caitlin and Brodie in the doorway on the way out. Mandy just heard the sounds of their laughter behind her, as her He-Man carried her away to ravage her—she hoped!

Unlocking and opening the door while still in JT's arms was an easy task for Mandy. He walked them through the door with his mouth attached once again to her lips, and with his heel he kicked the door closed behind them. Both were so hot from their time spent petting that it took only seconds before they were both naked, still standing only a few feet from the doorway.

Mandy ran her hands over JT's sculpted, hard chest, moaning and panting as the feel of him under her hands aroused her uncontrollably. She kissed his flat, dark nipples, as they were on a level she could easily access with her mouth, and grabbed his shaft in one hand, loving the feel of it—hot and throbbing because of her. Mandy heard JT moan as he grabbed at her and turned her around, so she was facing away from him.

"My God, Mags, I can't wait. I need you now. Bend over the table and spread those pretty legs wide for me. I'm going to ram my cock so far into that sweet, hot pussy of yours, you're going to feel like I've become a part of you."

Mandy could not have been any more excited by the way he pushed her down onto the worktable, his voice sounding so gravelly and needy. She all but came apart at the sound. Even though JT was acting dominant, she was not the least bit concerned. She knew he would not hurt her—he was nothing like Con.

Her aroused nipples pushed against the cold table and puckered even more as she waited for him to finally fill her. Using his feet, JT spread her legs even wider apart, and she felt the end of his cock part her swollen and wet lips from behind. Expecting him to plunge in, Mandy was surprised at his breathtakingly slow entrance. Impatient, she tried to wiggle back onto him, but he held her still as he inched his cock home.

Ever so slowly.

Mandy could feel her inner muscles at first trying to repel him, before opening and welcoming him in, holding him tight as he slowly stretched her womanly core. When finally she thought she could take no more of this exquisite torment, JT pulled back, nearly retreating all the way out of her, only to repeat the entry process again, even more slowly. Mandy was actually begging him, surprised to hear the sounds of her own voice sobbing and pleading for him to fuck her hard and fast. She was relieved when JT did just that.

At the sounds of her begging, JT seemed to lose control, slamming in and out of her relentlessly. She was lucky the table didn't break apart under the force. Mandy could do nothing more than hold on as she took this man fully into her body and soul. The orgasm hit Mandy hard, the feeling so intense that she seemed to hover for minutes in pure ecstasy. Streaks of silver exploded like stars in her mind, before liquefying to form a lake of melted silver ore — pure perfection. She felt JT empty himself into her, shooting hot wads into the inner depths of her pussy.

Mandy said nothing, not wanting to mention to him that they had forgotten a condom.

Her body trembled underneath JT's weight, not because of it but because her whole body was like warm, mushy jelly. JT had not mentioned the lack of protection either.

As he picked her up around the waist, her bottom against his stomach, she felt like a ragdoll. He just seemed to carry her around so easily. Which was an added bonus, as Mandy was not sure she could have made her legs function anyway. They headed towards the bedroom. JT, still holding on to Mandy, managed to crawl under the covers, laying them both down and pulling her even closer to him. She fit so well beneath his chin and with her bottom tucked up against his groin.

Mandy was so sleepy and satisfied, her body humming with pleasure.

* * * *

When she woke, again held tightly in warm, strong arms, she couldn't help but smile. How complete she felt when she was with JT. It was as if she had found her other half—the half that made her whole, happy and content. The sound of his husky morning voice was so hot and arousing.

"Hey, my sexy woman… How did you sleep?"

"Mmmm… Like a baby," she replied. It was then that she remembered the night before and the lack of protection. "JT, we didn't use protection last night," Mandy whispered, almost scared of what his reply might be. "I'm so sorry. I should have stopped you, but I just forgot all about a condom. It's okay—I'm clean. I got tested just recently, and I'm pretty sure there is nothing to worry about, but I won't hold you responsible…"

Before she could finish, JT had flipped her on her back and was staring down angrily at her. Mandy was not scared of him, not like she was of Con. She knew somehow deep inside her that JT wouldn't physically hurt her. Emotionally, he could devastate her—but that wasn't his fault. She had to take full responsibility for falling so fast.

"What do you mean, not hold me responsible?" JT's voice was both powerful and direct. "It was as much my fault as yours and I can't ever remember forgetting a rubber before. I sure as hell wouldn't walk away from the responsibility. Fathering a baby is something that I wouldn't mind considering in the future."

After holding her gaze for a time, the serious expression on his face plain for Mandy to see, JT kissed her roughly, possessively, not giving Mandy any time to react to his words. The passion in his kiss was so intense the sparks could have lit up the room. Mandy felt swallowed up by JT's mouth as he started to move down her body inch by inch, taking ownership of her senses. Kissing and licking. Biting and soothing. Setting every nerve on fire. She would never get enough of him.

He was a dominant male, yet she didn't feel trapped or pressured. She felt cherished, adored.

Mandy knew this was meant to be. The colours inside her mind were almost fading away as they seemed to reach for JT. It was as if they were telling her they were not needed anymore. It was his turn to be inside her head, to inspire, soothe and ultimately love her. Well, she hoped that JT would grow to love her, because she — Amanda 'Mandy Magenta' Smith — ignoring any sense of self preservation, was fully, without any doubt, in love with him.

Chapter Eleven

JT was calm. He had left Mandy's bed knowing, in his mind, that she was his. He knew it to be fact—just as the sun would come up tomorrow, it was understood. Mandy was, and always would be, his woman. Now all he had to do was convince her of that, without coming off as some kind of controlling nut-job, like her ex. No wonder his father had never dated again after his mother had died—if his father had felt about his mum as JT did about Mandy, what would have been the point? No one could compare.

JT had to attend a training session, then he was taking Mandy over to meet the old man. He wasn't worried—he knew his father would love her. How could he not?

Mandy had said she had some work to finish first. She had a market stall on Saturday to prepare for, and had told him she needed to make some more bits and pieces of jewellery to sell. He didn't know much about women and fashion, but even with his limited knowledge JT knew one thing for sure—Mandy's designs were good. Good enough that he would purchase something from her if he was looking for a gift.

JT wanted to be with Mandy every free moment they had, but he had already promised young Riley that he would go and watch the boy compete in a swimming carnival. So he had made Mandy promise that she would go with him to the league game that Saturday night, offering to seat her next to Caitlin and Riley so she wouldn't be alone. The thought of her sitting in the stands, watching him, made him smile. It would be a good feeling to play for her, knowing she was cheering for him.

JT was in love and he wanted the world to know. The fact that Brodie and JT had both met their true loves around the same time, living in the same building, was not lost on JT.

"Good things come to those who wait." JT laughed.

But first he had tonight with Mandy, and was looking forward to showing her his family home – and his bed!

* * * *

Mandy, at first incredibly nervous about meeting JT's father, had ended up having a wonderful night. Jon Senior was adorable, just a bigger, older version of JT.

"Who would have thought anyone could be bigger than JT?" she had told them.

Dinner was relaxed and JT appeared happy and loving. He didn't seem to care that his father was around as he kissed her, often, and pulled her into his lap at every opportunity. Mandy loved the way she could sit so comfortably in JT's lap.

"You are like my own private, portable chair," she teased him, earning another smouldering kiss in response.

Mandy looked at photographs of JT and his mother, Elaina. She was beautiful, although she looked so fragile in the candid shots, standing in between her giant men like a porcelain doll with long, black hair, blue eyes and such pale skin. Mandy was sad she would never get to meet the mother of this wonderful man. The thought brought tears to her eyes, for not only JT's lost mother but the mother Mandy did have, who was not part of her life either, but for different reasons.

* * * *

Later that evening, when they were alone, Mandy felt the need to tell JT about her colours, wanted him to be privy to the secrets that made her who she was, but she was apprehensive. In her past experience, those few times when she had opened up and had tried to explain her gift, most had thought her a little strange because of the way her mind filled with colour in a parallel to the emotion she was feeling at the time. Mandy was never quite sure whether her mood caused her mind to react that way, or if it was the other way around.

Mandy Magenta had not always been her name. No, in her boring life back in an unremarkable suburb of Perth, boring Amanda Mary Smith had lived with her boring parents. Her mother, Ann Smith, had been a homemaker and church groupie who had spent all her free time doing one thing or another for the parish. Mandy's father had been an accountant—yes, unimaginative William Smith continued the pattern that had made up their boring life. Chops for tea on Monday, sausages on Tuesday, Wednesday was chicken, roast on Sunday. Routine was the Smith household way.

Young Mandy — or Amanda back then — had found it hard to breathe. Her mind had been filled with only grey and white. It was at school that Mandy had found her reason for living. When she'd picked up that first crayon, way back in kindy, her world had become bright. Colours had begun to fill her mind.

Although she had been praised and acclaimed throughout her school years as a talented artist, Mandy's parents had discouraged what they'd seen as frivolous behaviour. Ann and William had always been afraid for Mandy — they'd worried that her different-coloured eyes were an indicator of something evil. Often using this phenomenon as a reason to explain her strange and unconventional behaviour, they'd told her repeatedly that cooking or sewing and Bible study was the right path for a proper young girl to follow.

"No future to be had in drawings," her father had repeated, over and over.

Her parents' attempts to quell her desires had only managed to inflame them. As a rebellious teen, Mandy had dyed her hair continuously — bright pink, indigo, even cyan blue. Anything just to be different. Not boring.

Mandy loved her eyes. One iris was a dark, chocolate brown and the other was a light caramel. They made her feel unique. Mandy had discovered that the phenomenon even had a medical name — heterochromia.

Mandy had painted or sketched anything and everything. Her pièce de résistance and final act of betrayal, in the eyes of her parents, had been her painting of a giant, engorged penis. Or what Mandy had assumed one would look like. At that stage, she had only seen images of them in books. She could still see the look on her mother's prudish face, eyes bulging in shock and horror, as she'd sputtered verses from religious texts to rid her of her evil spawn. And so Amanda had left and Mandy's life had begun, for better or worse.

JT listened intently to her, holding her a little more tightly when she mentioned her parents, obviously trying to support her as she spoke of her unhappy childhood but his smile grew wide, with a hint of mischief showing in his eyes, as she described the flame-like effects and splashes of vibrant hues that often filled her mind when they were intimate. The way the colour reflected the heat and intensity of her responses to JT's body.

"So, what you're telling me, babe, is that I set your world on fire... Is that it?" He grinned smugly at her.

"Yes, He-Man, there is that. But I've also never felt such calming green tones as when I'm with you. You seem to evoke the most amazing rainbow in my head."

"So...what sort of colour does—let me see—me nibbling on your scrumptious nipples evoke? Is it the good kind? What about if I pinch them like this? Mmm... I think we should experiment a little and see if we can conjure up something truly unique, what do you think, you gorgeous, remarkable woman? Let me inspire the artist in you and create our own masterpiece."

Mandy loved the way JT was touching her and the way he understood her, believed in her. She tried to interpret the shades he was inspiring, describe them in words that he could understand, but before too long Mandy could not concentrate on her mind — it was her body that was exploding with sensations, every nerve end tingling under JT's undivided attention.

* * * *

They had stayed in JT's room all night. Mandy had loved the scent of JT on his sheets and pillows, but had been a little embarrassed at the sounds of their passion, knowing Jon Senior was just down the hall. It certainly hadn't seemed to worry JT at all, as he'd moaned her name loudly more than once.

Finding both men wandering companionably around the spacious kitchen the next morning filled her heart, made her smile. As she stood watching these two mammoth men — JT wearing only pyjama bottoms, his chest bare to match his feet, while Jon Senior wore, more modestly, PJs, robe and slippers — Mandy wished her life could have been as easy with her parents. Sensing her gaze, JT turned and smiled. The warmth of that smile alone was enough to cause those now familiar fluttery feelings — needy feelings — to wash over Mandy. She was surprised by her body's immediate response. JT had already satisfied her more than once, the last time just minutes ago.

"Hey, woman, bacon and eggs sound okay?" JT questioned Mandy, as Jon Senior pulled out a chair for her so she could sit down.

"Well, now! A good morning to you, Mandy. We've never had a female guest stay over before. I hope you slept well?" the older man said with a cheeky wink.

Mandy didn't know whether to be embarrassed by the wink or delighted by his statement about her being the first woman to stay the night with JT.

It wasn't long before Mandy was happily digging into the first breakfast any man had ever made for her, chatting away easily as if she had been there at the table with these two men her whole life.

The day ahead was busy for both Mandy and JT. She had a stall to set up, and JT was off to watch Riley compete in a swimming carnival before preparing for tonight's game. JT dropped her off at home, leaving her to get on with her plans after a delivering a few more scorching, no-holds-barred kisses. She was comforted by the knowledge that they would see each other again in only a few hours.

* * * *

Since she had already packed and stored her newly-made jewellery safely in readiness for transport the day before, it didn't take her long to get moving. Mandy pondered that being happy obviously made her very productive. Climbing into her little red van, she headed out to the markets, still able to smell JT's scent on her skin. His lovemaking early that morning had been as satisfying as ever. She had joked with him about the rumour that sportsmen abstained from sex before a game, but JT had said that was only for the wimps. "My woman makes me stronger, harder...more manly," he had bragged, then had proceeded to show her how hard he was, the memory of his actions alone causing her to blush. Her temperature soared so hot that Mandy was forced to turn the car air-conditioning on – and it was winter.

Mandy knew she wouldn't have achieved much at all today if JT had been around, distracting her. She was looking forward to going to watch the Jets play tonight, joining Caitlin and Riley for the game. If

Mandy was honest with herself, she was also a little terrified at the whole idea of watching her first game. After hearing from Riley what exactly JT did, it had all sounded a bit brutal to her. Mandy was also worried she wouldn't fit in with these types of people. She was used to attracting stares with her unique appearance, but Mandy didn't want to embarrass JT.

In a well-practiced routine, it didn't take long for her to set up the display table full of her original and interesting designs. Metal and glass beads of all shapes and colours, intricate patterns or chunky, hand-painted enamels. All of Mandy's jewellery was very popular. Mandy loved the idea that her designs, little pieces of her, were scattered all over the city, maybe even the country. Mandy also displayed some of her canvases. Most of her paintings were dark and haunting, and seemed to invoke strong emotions from all who looked upon them. People either loved the despair and sadness that were created in her work, or found it far too depressing to hang.

Mandy enjoyed chatting with the fellow market stallholders about a variety of subjects. Climate change, carbon tax, conservation or politics, and even the weather were among the many topics up for discussion. Mandy was in agreement with the consensus that the day should be a busy one, as people came out and enjoyed the winter sunshine.

Mandy had always felt as if she fitted in with this mix of people. Although lately, surprisingly, she was finding other groups just as easy to get along with. These particular markets in Glebe attracted a mixture of visitors. Some had plenty of money to splash around, while others were looking for a bargain or maybe that special gift.

Mandy hoped she would sell out quickly so she could prepare for the night ahead. She wanted a good chat with Caitlin to calm her nerves. She was worrying about what she should wear and thinking that maybe she should tone down the almost masklike, very black, dramatic eye makeup she usually preferred.

When her stall table started to shake, Mandy — still slightly distracted by her own thoughts — took a moment before she finally realised something was wrong. She looked up.

Con was standing in front of her stall.

As though she was frozen in time, her mind stilled.

Went grey.

She watched in a trancelike state, unable to move as Con smashed her pretty little designs. Earrings and other pieces went flying through the air. An earring hit her on the cheek, causing a stinging sensation. But Mandy did not move.

He was yelling at her. Calling her all sorts of horrible names and blaming her for him being hurt the other night.

Threatening her...again.

"Bitch, you are so going to regret making a fool of me. This time *you* will be the one in a world of hurt, I promise you." Con started towards her.

Mandy knew she should run, but she couldn't seem to move. The happiness of the last few days now shattered like a mirror, jagged and splintered. She stood helplessly, quivering in fear...again.

The way to protect herself was unfathomable...

Out of the corner of her eye, Mandy noticed a young man approach. He seemed to be with an older lady — perhaps his mother — she wondered why they had stopped. Couldn't they see that her goods were all ruined? She had nothing left to sell.

As these thoughts whirled through Mandy's head, she saw the familiar-looking young man speaking to Con.

"Oh, no!" she cried out. The boy, even though he looked fit and healthy, was still slight compared to Con. He was going to get hurt. The horrible thought that the unsuspecting boy could be harmed finally dragged Mandy back into reality. As she stepped forward to warn the boy and his mother, and to confront her ex, Con fell to the ground.

It was the birthday boy from the other night.

JT's friend.

And he had flattened Con in one quick jab.

What was his name? *Rookie, or something?* Mandy tried to remember.

The woman accompanying Rookie started towards her, arms outstretched, as if about to comfort Mandy.

"What have I done?" Mandy cried.

The woman put her arms around Mandy's shoulders and, in a soothing voice, spoke. "There, there, you haven't done anything. My name is Laura Harris. That is my son Mitchell, the one who put that oaf on his behind. Are you okay, sweetie? Did he hurt you?"

Mandy couldn't help it. Her body was going into shock and she started to shake. She was sobbing uncontrollably by the time the police arrived on the scene.

Finally, managing to pull herself together a little, Mandy started rambling to the caring stranger. Words tumbled from her mouth fast and confusingly, almost irrationally.

"I'm so sorry... Your son... Oh, no, look—the police are here, why are they are arresting him? It's all my fault. He was my ex-boyfriend. JT is going to be so upset." Mandy sobbed through each garbled statement. "What about tonight's game? How will Mitchell play if he is in jail? How will you ever forgive me? He shouldn't have got involved...although I'm thankful he did. I'm so scared of Con. I try not to be, but he's hurt me so much. I need to talk to them...tell them not to arrest him... Your son, I mean."

"Hush now, dear..." Laura Harris spoke to Mandy in a soft, soothing voice, all the while rubbing Mandy's back in small, circular movements. "It will be okay. You know big Jon Thomson, do you? Hmm, I see. Are you the girl from the other night? You poor thing. How awful! My boy told me all about what that brute did to you. I'm glad Mitch thumped him. He deserved a lot more, manhandling a woman like that. I'm proud of my son standing up for you...so don't you worry about the police. I'm sure everything will be okay when they hear what that man has been doing to you."

Laura continued as she started picking up Mandy's wares, "Look at these pretty little pieces — some seemed to be unharmed. I'll help you straighten things up while everything else gets sorted out."

Mandy finally managed to calm down enough to give her version of events to the policewoman investigating the fracas. The policewoman confirmed to Mandy that Con wanted to press charges against Mitchell, but that it was highly unlikely the charges would hold up, given recent events. Mandy gave the officer details of the incident at the club, as well as today's confrontation, and also a brief description of what her life had been like with Con. Mandy couldn't really answer the policewoman's question as to why she hadn't pressed charges over the previous assaults.

Mandy had found JT, and had tried to forget about Con and how he had turned her into a victim.

* * * *

JT had been sitting with Brodie — watching Riley winning yet another race and thinking the kid was like a fish, he moved so fast through the water — when Brodie's cell phone started to ring. The expression on Brodie's face alone was enough to set warning bells off in JT's mind. He immediately moved in closer to the phone, and as Brodie switched it to loudspeaker, he heard the familiar sound of Rookie's voice.

"Yeah... I know, Cap, I'm a mama's boy, but she loves those markets and it's a way to pass the time before the game. Anyway, there was a bit of a scuffle at one of the stalls. When I went to take a better look, I recognised that bloke from the other night. You know — the one giving JT's girl a hard time."

JT nearly jumped out of his skin. Brodie put his hand on his arm, as if to hold JT down, as he spoke into the phone.

"Okay, Rookie, hold on. JT is listening. Is this going to end up bad? Should he hear the rest?"

JT growled angrily at Brodie, "As if you could stop me!" but was cut off by Rookie's voice once again coming through the phone's speaker.

"Hey, JT. It's all good — well, apart from me getting arrested for decking the scumbag. One punch and he hit the deck like a sack of spuds. Your girl's with Mum, still back at the markets, packing up. She's a bit shaken, but I didn't let him touch her."

JT had heard enough. Filled with concern for Mandy's wellbeing, as well as murderous rage towards her ex, he jumped to his feet and started running towards the exit. He wanted — no, *needed* — to see with his own eyes that Mandy was okay. Until he had her safe and in his arms, he could think of little else.

* * * *

JT made it to the area the markets where being held in record time. When he spotted Mandy standing with Laura Harris, he ignored the 'No Entry' signs and drove his car right up beside her. The tyres gave a loud screech as he slammed his foot on the brake and put the car into park, seconds before he threw open the door and jumped out.

JT didn't give Mandy a chance to say anything — he just wrapped his arms around her and held on to her for dear life. He was fighting a losing battle, trying to conceal from her the overwhelming rage and fear that had consumed him as he'd raced to be by her side. JT's anger was a living thing still simmering under his skin, ready to explode at the slightest provocation.

Laura Harris, after managing to get JT to let go of Mandy for long enough that she could wish the girl good luck, went to find out what was happening with her son. She left the couple as they joined together again in a kiss that left little doubt as to their smouldering attraction.

When JT had pulled her into his arms she'd been able to feel the shaking. It had taken her a while before she'd realised it wasn't her body trembling anymore — it was JT's. She'd lifted her tearstained face to look at him. His jaw had been so clenched she'd thought his teeth might break. It had been as if JT was vibrating. His eyes had been glassed over, his nostrils flared.

Mandy had felt him breathing in and out at a rapid pace. Her man was angry because of her.

She put her arms around his head and pulled his face down towards hers. As she pressed her lips to his, she felt the tension in them. His lips felt flint-hard and cold. It took Mandy a few seconds of gentle coaxing, by nipping at his bottom lip, before JT opened his mouth. Mandy thrust her tongue inside in an effort to distract him.

Hoping she could make him forgive her for causing such a scene.

Mandy felt the power surge through JT as he began to return her kiss, at first slowly, then with more urgency, until he was almost devouring her right there on the street. She knew people were probably looking at them but didn't care, and started to smile under the kiss, thinking of the picture they must make standing on this busy street.

JT felt Mandy's lips form a smile under his, and pulled his mouth from hers, wondering what on earth she was smiling about. He had forgotten they were out in full view of the passing public. *Well, so much for me not being big on public displays of affection*, he thought, or perhaps even said out loud.

He didn't care — he had been so angry with himself for not being with Mandy. He had forgotten to talk to her about getting an AVO, leaving her open for this man to hurt her. Thank God Rookie had been there. He owed the kid big time. JT pulled out his cell and rang his father, speaking the moment his father answered.

"Dad, there's been some trouble. Mitch Harris has been arrested."

Jon Senior cut his son off mid-sentence. "Son, slow down. Mitch is getting out. Brodie and I are heading to the station to get him now. No charges have been laid, but the press did get wind something is up, so I don't know how long before the full story is out. How is Mandy?"

JT was a lucky man and he knew it. He had good people around him. A strong, dependable father and loyal mates—people who could be counted on in a crisis.

"Shaken, but okay. Thanks, Dad. I'm going to take her home, but I don't have long before I need to get ready for tonight's game. Hopefully Caitlin or Riley will be home to look after her. Before all this happened they were supposed to be going to the game, but I don't want Mandy to be alone."

"Well, son, if she doesn't feel up to going out after such an ordeal, maybe I could come over and keep her company, or she could come and watch the game on the TV with me. Keep it in mind. Good luck with tonight's game, Jon. Play strong. I'll be watching," Jon Senior offered before JT ended the call.

Chapter Twelve

Mandy's thoughts had been interrupted by the sound of JT's phone ringing. The one-sided conversation that had followed had made her realise the trouble she had brought to JT's life.

She pulled herself free from his embrace and moved slightly away from the warmth and security of his body. She needed to get moving, had to get home so that JT could focus on the upcoming game. She had caused enough disruption to the Jets team already today.

It took Mandy a few minutes to convince JT that she was able to drive her van. He could follow her – she wanted her vehicle at home so she could go through her stock and see what was salvageable and what needed replacing.

Finally, JT reluctantly agreed with her and they both drove off towards Mandy's home. It was strange to look in her rear-view mirror and see the big, panther-like car stalking her little van, but Mandy felt comforted knowing JT was there.

She parked in her usual spot, and had started to lift her plastic tubs of stock from the rear of the van when a set of big arms encircled her and lifted her, roughly, to the side. JT was growling at her, but not the sexy growl Mandy had grown to love.

"Mandy, will you leave this to me? I am about the only one who has not been able to do anything for you today—at least let me take care of this grunt work. That's all I seem to be good for."

With the last remark almost snarled, JT lifted all the tubs out of the van in one move, slammed the door closed with his broad shoulder and stalked inside.

Mandy was a bit shocked at his tone and wasn't sure what JT had meant by it.

He was still angry at her because of all the drama? *Why wouldn't he be*? she thought. He definitely had been very angry when he'd first arrived. This was not the day he had planned, she knew that. He should have been with Riley. He certainly would not have expected to have half the team running around because of her. Remembering the phone call JT had made to his father, who had also been involved, and the comment about hoping Caitlin was home, Mandy couldn't blame JT for wanting to get away fast.

Even though she felt her heart breaking, Mandy knew she had to let him go quietly. Her problems had caused so much drama in JT's life already. She could not expect him to uphold any promises he'd made in the heat of passion. As Mandy headed inside, she tried to put on a brave face, but wasn't sure how she would be strong enough to send him away and out of her tumultuous life—one he didn't need to be involved in. Mandy knew she had to do what was right. She was already in love with the man, but she believed that he deserved better than her. This was what she deserved, after all. It had been her mistake to get involved with a man like Con. She had always disappointed the ones closest to her. Her parents, Con—why else would he hold such hatred towards her?—and now JT.

JT was waiting patiently at the door, his arms full. The picture of the gorgeous man holding all her precious designs, his arms bulging with muscle, his shoulders straight and broad, that huge backside firm and delicious in a pair of tight, black denim jeans, was an unforgettable sight. How right it looked—him at her door holding onto her art. The picture would stay in her mind forever.

"It doesn't matter. I'm no good for him," she whispered quietly to herself. Mandy took one last look, cementing the scene to her memory bank, before going inside her flat. "Just put everything down over there," she said, and pointed to a spot on the floor. "Then you'd better go," Mandy managed to add quickly, before the emotion showed in her voice.

JT just stood rooted to the spot, staring at her, his eyes like black coal, his gaze hard and unforgiving. He didn't move a muscle.

"I am not going anywhere!" Although his body was rigid, which made Mandy believe he was angry, the words he spoke were filled with emotion. He sounded hurt, upset. "I'm sorry I let this happen to you, Mandy. If I could turn back time, I would. It was stupid of me not to have made more of an effort to protect you. We should have taken an AVO out on that bastard, had him charged the other night, but I forgot about it. I'll kill him myself if he ever comes near you again. I was so wrapped up in my feelings…so happy because of the way you filled my life. I just didn't think. My God, woman, you have to forgive me. I don't want to lose you. I can't lose you. Please let me stay."

The last few words sounded choked as the pure, heartfelt, emotional words poured from JT.

Mandy was stunned, speechless. She didn't know what to say. He wasn't angry at her — JT was angry at himself. As if this was his fault, somehow. She didn't understand how he could blame himself for what her ex had done.

She went to JT and took the tubs from him one by one, placing them at his feet. All the while JT watched her, standing like some giant statue, unmoving. He looked so fierce, so hard, so beautiful. After she transferred the last box from JT's arms to the floor, Mandy replaced it with her body.

She reached up and linked her hands behind JT's thick neck, once again pulling his face down to her level. She could see the pulse beating in the vein on the side of his throat. Looking deeply into JT's eyes, wanting to communicate directly to his soul, she spoke clearly and slowly so he would be under no confusion.

"He-Man, I thought you were angry at me. I'm the one who is sorry — my drama has involved your friends, your father, interrupted your life. You can't blame yourself. How is any of what Con did your fault? My heart breaks at the thought of you walking out my door. But what could I do but let you go, if that was what you wanted? Jonathon Thomson, I love you. I would do anything to make you happy, even if what that took was to give you up. I am not good enough for you. You deserve so much more, more than what I have to offer you — a victimised, financially struggling, weirdo artist."

With her heart now open and vulnerable to being ripped apart, Mandy waited, nervously watching JT's face, searching and hoping for a sign.

Any sign.

JT closed his eyes for what seemed like minutes to Mandy, but was probably only a second. He was breathing heavily, his chest rising and falling quite noticeably. As he finally opened his eyes, Mandy was relieved to see the hard look of a moment ago had been replaced with a softer, almost watery gaze.

He put his arms around her, squeezing her so tightly she could hardly breathe.

"Did you say what I thought you said?" JT asked. His voice sounded tentative, but tinged with constrained excitement. "Tell me again. I want to hear you tell me you love me again. Need to hear it. Oh, honey, my woman, I love you. Think I have from the moment I saw you. Just as well we finally got on the same page. So let me hear you say the words again." JT, with Mandy in his arms, began to spin around in circles, like some big tornado building up steam.

"I love you, JT... I love you!" Mandy squealed joyfully, over and over again as the room went spinning by.

Mandy and JT were so focused on their declarations of love that they didn't notice that they had drawn an audience until an amused, masculine voice—and other various giggling voices—interrupted their spinning.

"Well, that's fantastic to hear! But maybe you two could stop spinning. We're all getting a bit motion sick, watching you two whirling round the room like some out-of-control juggernaut."

Chapter Thirteen

Mandy and JT froze, then turned simultaneously, both looking in the direction the sound of the voice had originated, hardly believing that they had made such private declarations so publicly. Much to the couple's horror and embarrassment, standing in the very open doorway to Mandy's flat — all wearing big, toothy grins — were Brodie, Caitlin, Riley, Rookie, Jon Senior and June.

"Just shut the door on them, Mandy, the no-good eavesdropping bunch," JT groaned.

"Don't be like that, JT. I'm so happy that you love me — me, of all people — I don't care who knows. In fact, I'm thinking of painting a mural to show the world."

Mandy's pledge to inform the world caused even more roars of laughter from the delighted onlookers.

Brodie had apparently come to collect JT for the game, and Rookie had wanted to see if Mandy was okay. It gave Mandy the chance to thank the young man for his help, and she offered him some jewellery pieces she thought his wonderful, caring mother would like.

"All the guys could get presents for their girls from Mandy—how popular would all the blokes be then, eh?" Rookie said. The statement brought even more laughter as the strain of the day's events finally started to wane, leaving even stronger bonds of friendship in its wake.

Mandy would have loved more time with JT, but he had to leave, as did Brodie and Rookie. Caitlin decided to stay to help Mandy decide what to wear. An excited Riley headed off with the men, so the girls were left alone. Mandy didn't really know what had happened to JT's dad and June, but they must have left at the same time as the others. It had been another rollercoaster of a day, but Mandy felt deliciously happy now. JT loved her.

Mandy took in what Caitlin was wearing—black jeans, an aqua green sweater, mid-length boots and a long, black wool coat. She noticed also that Caitlin was wearing the earrings Mandy had made, and they twinkled through her friend's long, auburn tresses.

"What on earth will I wear?" Mandy groaned as she started hauling clothes from her wardrobe and throwing them haphazardly onto her bed in a growing mountain of garments. "I've got nothing normal enough...everything is so out there. Black, black and more black! Caitlin, what am I going to do? I won't fit in with a sporty crowd. Look at you and what you're wearing. You look so nice, so normal...and I look like some angry panda bear, all spiky and black. God, what was I thinking? I can't go to a game and sit with JT's people. I'll embarrass him."

Mandy sat down in the middle of her bedroom floor and held her head in her hands, just moments away from a complete meltdown. Tears threatened to flow as she struggled to deal with her fears, and she was enveloped in a growing bout of low self-esteem and crippling self-doubt.

She sensed Caitlin sit down next to her, felt her friend put a comforting arm around her shoulders.

"Oh, Mandy, why would you even think such things? Did you not hear JT profess his love for you, just minutes ago? I certainly did. And nowhere in his declaration of love did he mention that he did not like the way you looked, or dressed, or acted. Normal, you say? I'm almost offended. I don't want to be normal. I want to be me. And Mandy, you should want to be you—the amazingly talented artist that JT has fallen head over heels for."

Caitlin stood and started rummaging through the avalanche of clothing Mandy had emptied from her wardrobe.

"This is lovely, Mandy. I've always loved this crushed velvet skirt and it will be warm. It gets a bit chilly in the stands at night. This shirt and jacket will fit perfectly. C'mon put this all on."

Mandy stood and took the skirt out of her dear friend's outstretched hand, loving the texture of the fabric.

"You think so, Caitlin?" Mandy's voice hitched a little with emotion.

"I know so. Let's get you fixed up and head off to the game. If you think you are upset now, just wait till you see what those boys do in a game... It's scary as."

Spiking her hair and putting on her makeup, as usual—including doing her eyes as dark as always with plenty of kohl pencil—Mandy looked at her reflection nervously. She had never before cared what people thought of her look. The approval of others had not been a concern until today, but she let Caitlin's encouraging words ease her fears.

Wearing her favourite pendant design around her neck made Mandy feel a little more confident. It was a large, flat black-and-gold flaked, handmade glass bead on a black leather rope. The gold swirled inside the black in the most spectacular way, as if perpetually moving. She added matching earrings — smaller glass beads with similar gold flake swirls. She'd never questioned her own talent or her designs.

* * * *

Mandy sensed that Caitlin was as nervous as she was, quite jittery and unsettled. They parked in the private parking area at the football stadium, reserved for families of the team members. Finding their seats had not been a problem, since Caitlin had watched the Jets play before and knew her way around. She introduced Mandy to some of the women already seated around them. The group of women consisted of other players' wives and girlfriends. Mandy noticed that the group was varied. Some women looked as if they had just stepped off a model's catwalk, while others were more homely-looking.

No one seemed to show any overt surprise or criticism towards Mandy or her appearance. Some remarked that they were pleased to meet the woman who could tame JT, and laughed. Mandy recognised Laura Harris, the woman from the market, and had quite a long conversation with her about the day, her jewellery designs and life. Laura Harris sure could get a person to spill their guts — Mandy was surprised at how easily she had told this virtual stranger almost everything about her life, except her colours, of course. Mandy hadn't even told Caitlin about her gift—just JT.

It wasn't long before the crowd began to get noisy, cheering and shouting as the Jets players—led out by Brodie—took to the field. Mandy caught her breath at the sight of her man running onto the grassy playing arena. JT looked gigantic, his wide shoulders and thick chest so prominent in the tight-fitting, black-and-gold number eight jersey.

Mandy sat with her hands fisted in her lap, grimacing every time JT took off like a torpedo to grab a player from the other team. If that hadn't been bad enough, Mandy also winced when JT, while carrying the football, was jumped on by as many as four men who tried to drag him to the ground and stop his momentum.

She noticed Caitlin in much the same state of discomfort she was when Brodie, wearing the number ten on his back, repeated JT's actions, and she understood Caitlin's earlier comments about feeling upset over 'what the boys did'. Riley, on the other hand—who had now taken his seat next to Caitlin—was cheering and shouting his obvious approval at the way the Jets were playing. By half-time, when the bedraggled-looking men left the field for a well-deserved break, Mandy was exhausted. Looking around at the other women, she wondered how they could all look so calm.

Mandy also spoke to an attractive, smiling woman named Jenny, whose husband was the number nine. Jenny told Mandy not to worry, assuring her that she would get used to the brutal game eventually. She also explained to Mandy that JT was one of the best props around and trained hard so his body could take the punishment it did. She joked that JT would probably be 'too sore' to take out the garbage bin if Mandy asked him to, laughing that her husband always was.

Jenny and a few of the other women commented on Mandy's jewellery, expressing their views on how talented she was to be able to make such beautiful pieces. Caitlin proudly showed off her earrings, which then led to Laura Harris showing the ring and pendant that her son Mitchell—or Rookie, as he was known by most—had given her just before the game on Mandy's behalf. Mandy was a little overwhelmed with all the fuss, and was almost glad when the game started again—that was, until the first time JT got slammed to the ground. He bounced straight back up every time as if nothing had happened, thankfully, or Mandy wouldn't have made it all the way to the full-time siren.

Riley was very happy—the Jets had won. Mandy had been so focused on JT, watching him wherever he was on the field at any given moment, that she'd missed most of the action, so had not known the outcome of the game. Of course, she could have looked at the scoreboard but the thought of the Jets winning or losing had not been uppermost in her mind—JT had. She was just relieved that he and Brodie had made it through the battle in one piece. The group of family and friends surrounding Mandy seemed full of cheer as they talked about whether or not they were heading back to the club for dinner and a few drinks. Mandy wasn't sure what she was supposed to do now. After the drama earlier, she hadn't really sorted out any final arrangements with JT.

She must have looked a little lost. Mandy felt Caitlin take her hand.

"Let's head downstairs, Mandy, to wait for JT and Brodie while they shower and change back into civvies. We're all going back to the club for the after-game celebration. It's expected the players will attend," Caitlin told Mandy, adding cheekily, "I think JT is keen to show you off. Hey, I had to go through show and tell with Brodie. Now it's your turn. At least you already know me—I was on my own."

Mandy shook her head and smiled wanly. She and Caitlin had so much in common, each such a novice when it came to this strange brutal game, but in love with two of the game's most popular players.

Riley was bouncing up and down, wanting to get down to the sheds. Brodie had given him a pass to gain access, so he ran off ahead as Caitlin and Mandy trailed after the other wives and family also headed down to wait for the conquering heroes.

Mandy was impatient—she wanted to see JT, to make sure he was okay. It seemed to take forever before players started to trickle out through the door leading from the dressing area. Mandy recognised Rookie as he came out the door. He was quickly surrounded by many eager fans wanting his autograph, but she was surprised when he headed straight towards her, followed closely by his adoring mob.

"Great game, wasn't it?" Rookie said to Mandy. "You okay now? You're certainly looking fine!"

Mandy didn't know what to say to the heroic, polite young man. She was about to answer him and thank him, again, for earlier when she heard a familiar, loud growl.

"Rookie, get away from my woman. Just 'cause you scored a couple of tries doesn't mean I won't kick your butt," JT shouted above the crowd as he headed over to Mandy. In less than a heartbeat, Mandy's mouth was being crushed under JT's, and they were serenaded by the whirring and clicking sound of cameras as journalists swooped to take photographs of the couple.

"Aww! Come on, JT… Can't help a guy for trying. Mandy deserves someone better-looking than you, and I certainly fit that bill," the cheeky—and obviously tired of living—younger man said, accompanied by mutters of agreement and laughter from his adoring fan club.

"Rookie, don't push your luck, mate. Although I don't think JT is even listening anymore. He seems a little distracted. About as distracted as I'm about to be." Brodie, arm around Riley's shoulders, had come out just behind JT. He took Caitlin in his arms and kissed her just as soundly as JT had kissed Mandy—obviously not wanting to be outdone!

Rookie, feigning a bored look, turned to Riley. "Hey, Riley, my little mate, let's leave these old folks to smooch while we go get some food at the club. What do you say? Want a lift?"

Riley looked to be overjoyed at the thought of hanging out with Rookie. He had told Mandy enough times that Rookie was his favourite player, not counting Brodie and JT, of course. Mandy was happy for him when Caitlin nodded in approval, smiling as the boy bounced happily away.

Elated at finally being able to touch JT, Mandy didn't want to let go of him. Unfortunately, some of his fans weren't too keen on that idea as they badgered him for autographs. A few reporters also hung around, still after quotes about the game. Mandy and Caitlin stood patiently off to one side, watching their men conversing with the fans, old and young.

Caitlin reassured Mandy that this was normal and eventually people would get all they wanted and leave. A few young women seemed to be giving Mandy and Caitlin very unfriendly stares. Mandy just tried to ignore their unmasked animosity.

Finally, JT grabbed her hand, apologising to the last of the fans and saying it was time for him to get to the club. He and Mandy headed towards the car park, leaving Brodie and Caitlin behind. Mandy was going to mention the fact, but before she could JT explained the plan for the night.

"Brodie will stand there all night. He's going in Caitlin's car and I'm taking his. I need to spend time with you now, woman. So, what did you think of the Jets' number eight? Sexy enough for you?"

"Oh, Jon, you were amazing," Mandy gushed. "I was so worried for you. It's such a rough game. How can you still be walking? I am going to have to inspect every inch of you *thoroughly* when we get home, just to satisfy myself that you're really okay."

The wanton look Mandy directed at JT was full of promise. She heard JT growl again before he devoured her mouth in yet another smouldering kiss, leaving her panting and wanting more. As her panties grew wet and her nipples hardened, she rubbed her body, almost feline-like, against the bulge in JT's suit trousers until he lifted his mouth from hers.

"Enough… You're killing me, woman! We have places to be, but hold onto that thought. I will definitely be making you scream my name long into the night as I feast on that warm, tasty pussy. I can just imagine how wet those folds are for me right now. Are you wet for me, Mandy? I'm going for some serious deep purples and crimsons tonight—strong and passionate colours... Are you on board with that?"

The rumbling tones of JT's low voice caressed Mandy like a warm wind, making her feel even hotter. She squirmed and squeezed her legs together, trying to ease the ache of her needy pussy.

Yes... She was very wet for her man.

Chapter Fourteen

Mandy didn't know how she would make it through the night—she was so hot and horny. But the evening flew by and proved quite enjoyable. A large group of players and their partners dined together. JT possessively held on to Mandy all night, with either his arm around her or holding her hand throughout the dinner. Mandy was getting very adept at eating one-handed. As the evening drew to a close, Mandy once again found herself in JT's lap, enjoying the feel of his erection against her, a promise of what the night would bring her if she was patient.

During the night, Brodie made a few speeches to the sponsors, club directors and members of the Jets supporters club. It amazed Mandy that playing rugby league was more than just the game on the field—it was also about making public appearances and saying the right things to the right people. It really was quite an experience for Mandy. She was selfishly glad JT didn't have to be as busy as Brodie, the team's captain. Caitlin seemed to handle it all okay, though, and

Brodie managed to keep her close by throughout the night.

The friendship and camaraderie between the players was evident to Mandy. Also evident was the high esteem in which the rest of the team held both Brodie and JT. Mandy was effortlessly fitting into this small community. All were shocked to hear of her problems with Con — many of the fit, tough men offered their services to even the score on her behalf. She made them all promise not to do anything that would get them into trouble, reminding them about Rookie having been arrested because of her. The many masculine voices were quick to expunge her of any blame, saying any one of them would have done the same thing. Mandy couldn't help but feel as if she had somehow lessened Rookie's heroic deed.

* * * *

As she and JT walked up the stairs that led to her apartment, finally home from the long day, Mandy felt an incredible rush of hormones. Her body was anxious for the touch of the man beside her. JT seemed tired, though, and Mandy remembered the rough abuse his body had endured earlier. After she had closed the door to her flat behind them, she took his hand and led him to the bathroom.

"I'm going to run you a hot bath, JT. I want to massage your body," Mandy said as she started to undress him, "as a reward for all its hard work today."

She had expected an argument from JT, so Mandy was relieved when he sat on the edge of the bath and waited while she ran and tested the water for him. The antique claw-foot tub was just big enough for JT to sit and recline with his legs outstretched. The sight of JT filling her bath was so sensual and erotic that Mandy had the urge to sketch him. It would give her the ability to savour the scene long after. She not only loved him, he made her so damn hot, and he was all hers. But she decided she was too *hungry* to sketch.

After lathering her hands with soap, she began to massage JT's broad shoulders, loving the feel of his shapely muscles under her fingers as she imagined drawing every sinew, tendon and hard mound. As she slowly moved her hands down to his pectoral muscles, the broad, raised shelf of his chest, she circled his nipples, stroking her fingers over the tight, flat buttons, feeling them harden. JT jerked and water splashed over the edge of the bath.

Deciding she didn't want her clothes getting wet, Mandy removed them quickly. Completely naked, she knelt back down to continue her journey, all the time ignoring the hungry look in JT's eyes as he watched her every move, like a large predator about to attack.

She continued running her hands and fingers over JT's abdominal muscles. He had more than a six pack—more like eight well-defined, separate ridges. Each ridge got harder, almost flexing under her touch, as Mandy stroked and rubbed. Then, ignoring JT's growl of disapproval, she changed course and moved to the end of the bath, rubbed her palm up one hard foot and over his thick ankle, felt the coarse hair that covered his shin, then travelled past his knee and up his rock-hard thighs before repeating the action on the other leg.

JT was breathing heavily, the sound clearly audible in the quiet room, mixed with the sounds of water lapping against the bath. Mandy finally gave up on her slow, deliberate torture and took JT's thick, hard cock in both hands, the tip bobbing out of the water. She massaged that warm, silky-smooth appendage with one hand after the other, sliding up and down from the base to the rounded head. JT bucked in time with her movements. Mandy felt moisture weep from her folds as her nipples, puckered and hard, bumped the cold side of the bath. She moaned.

She was so hot. She climbed into the water, sliding her sopping wet entrance over JT's engorged penis, and sat, engulfing him completely, her legs folded on either side of him. JT reached for her but she knocked his hand away, whispering, as she began to rock up and down on him, "This is my time, He-Man... You just lie back, watch and feel."

Mandy studied JT's face intently, looking for clues as to what was the best motion to pleasure him. She was so close to orgasm herself that she decided to help along her own release, so she could concentrate fully on JT's needs. Mandy sat back a little and pushed two fingers in past her wet, swollen lips in search of her clit, and began to swirl her fingers over the sensitive nub. With her free hand, she squeezed one of her nipples. Rocking and moaning, she brought herself over the precipice.

Before the wave of pleasure had dissolved, JT began thrusting up into her. It took him only seconds to reach his own climax.

Getting out of the bath, Mandy could not help but feel satisfaction with her seduction technique— pleasuring JT was so very fulfilling and exceptionally rewarding. As was the sight of JT as he stood with water dripping from his body. It was like seeing water falling from a statue, or from the body of a mythical god. Her man was awesome in the nude.

She rubbed at him with a towel, drying him off, until he picked her up and walked with her to the bedroom.

Chapter Fifteen

Their lovemaking had been monumental, a feast of pleasure so fulfilling it took all that was left of JT's energy to gather Mandy to his chest and stumble to her bed. Holding Mandy tightly, JT whispered for her to sleep. She looked so beautiful in her slumber. JT felt the sense of protectiveness grow stronger as he gazed lovingly at his woman. She was so small, yet so vibrant and alive. JT would never in a million years understand how anyone could cause her harm.

"I'll never let anyone hurt you again. You are safe now. I'll protect you," JT whispered to her sleeping form. He lightly kissed Mandy's cheek and pulled her in close, wrapping his arms around her body. His mind drifted back to the pleasure she had just given him. He had been enthralled, had never experienced anything as intimate or as erotic as what he had just experienced with Mandy.

JT was hard again—hard as a post. All his reminiscing and the feel of Mandy's warm backside against him had his cock full and ready for action. He should let her sleep, though. God, the woman certainly deserved the rest after what she had been through just that day.

You're a selfish prick. Forget about your dick and go to sleep, JT cursed himself.

He distracted himself by thinking about the following morning's training run, therefore managing to find a semblance of control, enough to try to sleep. Just as JT had settled down, he heard a whimpering sound. Confused, he tried to figure out where the noise was coming from. It took him a moment to realise that the pitiful sound was actually coming from Mandy.

She was crying in her sleep. She moaned, then cried out, "No!" and "Please, stop!"

She was having a nightmare, JT finally realised. He shook her shoulders gently.

"Baby, Mandy, wake up. It's just a bad dream. I've got you… Shhh…"

It broke his heart to watch the fear cloud Mandy's eyes as she sat up abruptly, her arms flailing out wildly. A scream tore from her throat as she scrambled from the bed to tumble onto the floor.

"Mandy, stop, you'll hurt yourself. It's me, JT… You're safe. Come here, baby, come back to me."

JT crouched down in front of her, his anger simmering under his skin at the sight of the woman he loved so distraught. He gently gathered her into his arms, then stood and carried her back to bed. She had curled her body into his. JT could feel her tears on his bare skin.

"Hush now, you're okay." He stroked her back, feeling so inadequate over his inability to calm her, to take her fears away. He was like a giant oaf, certainly unable to find the words or deeds to comfort someone as precious as Mandy.

After what seemed an eternity, Mandy finally raised her tearstained face to his and kissed him. It took JT by surprise as he felt her lips on his, but too quickly they were gone again.

"JT, I'm so sorry. I was having a nightmare. I didn't mean to disturb you. I have them all the time. I usually don't sleep very well and spend most nights working on my designs to keep the dreams at bay. This is the first one I've had since we've shared a bed—I feel so safe held in your arms. It must be because of what happened today. God, was that only today? He's really worked me over, has turned me into a basket-case. I just can't seem to shake the fear off. I want to... I feel so helpless and I hate it. But the things he did to me—I should have fought more, left him after the first time...but I didn't." Mandy shivered, and another throaty sob tore from her mouth.

"You have me now. I love you, Mandy, and no-one will hurt you again, least of all that lowlife scum. If I even catch sight of him in the same suburb as you, I'll make him wish he had never been born." JT growled, the sound low in his throat. He was trying not to scare her any more than she already was, but he was so filled with absolute rage, the need, desire to rip Con apart with his bare hands was all but overwhelming him.

"Just hold me, JT. I feel safe with you. I can see the warm, safe colours now. They are washing away the fear. You do that for me—bring me peace. Just like you saved me physically at the club, you can also save me mentally... Hold me tight."

"Always, Mags, always. Whatever you need, I'm there for you." JT held her tightly, afraid he might be causing her pain because his grip was so strong, but his need to hold Mandy was just as strong as her need to be held.

* * * *

JT jerked awake. He hadn't thought he would be able to fall asleep after Mandy's nightmare, but he obviously had. He looked over at the clock on the bedside table—it was nearly eight, and Brodie would soon be waiting downstairs for him to go to the recovery session. JT was opposed to the thought of leaving this warm bed, and was still concerned for Mandy. He hoped she was feeling better, because he'd have to go. He did have time to remind Mandy she was his, though…

"Hey, gorgeous. As much as I hate the thought, I have to leave for a while, but before I go, come for me," JT whispered into Mandy's ear.

JT pulled Mandy's bottom against his erection and pushed his finger into her pussy. He stroked and plunged one, then another into her tight channel, feeling the moisture build. To his delight, Mandy's body started to move, to dance in response to his intimate caress. JT drew his fingers from her warmth and licked the juices that covered them, before returning them inside her hot, wet and throbbing pussy. He speared in and out while he pushed the knuckle of his thumb on her clit.

"Come for me now," JT demanded as he nipped at Mandy's earlobe.

And she did, pushing hard into his hand and crying out his name.

"That was a small token of my thanks for giving me such a special night last night. I love you, Mandy. Go back to sleep—it's still early. I'll be back in a few hours."

JT reluctantly left the bed and the warmth of her body before taking one last look at her, curled up and surrounded by the many snakes that made up the intricate features of her bed's frame. The eyes glittered at him, as if in confirmation that the snakes were protecting their sleepy queen.

* * * *

Mandy snuggled back into the warm bed. She could still smell JT and the musky odour of sex on her sheets. She smiled up at her snakes happily, the horrors of her nightmare having been lessened by the light of day and the sated feel of her body, thanks to JT.

"Girls, what do you think? Am I one lucky woman, or what?" She spoke as if the snakes would answer her, before shutting her eyes and falling back into a deep and restful sleep. She dreamt of JT and how wonderful her life was turning out to be.

Mandy could hear a banging sound, and she slowly opened her eyes, still half asleep, wishing the sound would go away.

Someone was knocking on her door. Loudly.

"I'm coming... Just give me a sec." She squealed when it finally dawned on her that it was JT, back after training, and immediately jumped into action. She ran for the door, shrugging into her robe on the way, trying not to trip over the fabric in her haste.

JT didn't have a key. She would be sorting that problem out immediately, she thought as she threw open the door to reveal the breathtaking sight of a smiling JT. He was holding take-away coffee cups and a brown paper bag.

"I'm sorry, Jon," Mandy said as she dragged him inside. "I was still asleep. Someone gave me a new type of sleeping medication, and it worked—nothing like a good orgasm to relax you, I always say," she added with a cheeky grin. "Mmmm... Is that coffee?"

JT had bought croissants as well, so Mandy placed all the food out on her worktable, the memory of how she and JT had used it only nights ago making her blush. As if reading her mind, JT mentioned something about preferring the spread from a few days ago as he parted her robe and stroked her bare leg.

"Could life get any better?" Mandy happily asked.

Unfortunately, that happiness was quickly shadowed, as JT explained the team was leaving on Wednesday and travelling to Townsville for the game on Friday night. They would not be returning until Saturday. He didn't want to leave Mandy alone. He wanted to go with her today and organise the AVO against Con. He even asked her to travel to Townsville and meet him up there.

Mandy was happy JT was concerned for her safety, and agreed to go to the police station, but not to meeting up with him in Townsville. As much as she might have liked to visit the North Queensland tropical township, she had to sell her jewellery at the markets. It was what she did for a living, she explained to an unhappy JT, who had even offered to buy all her stock just so she would go with him. Mandy tried to explain to JT how much she loved what she did, just as he loved what he did, and was a bit shocked when he mumbled something about not loving it quite as much as her.

"Don't you do this, JT. You go and play. I will be watching the game, probably with Riley and Caitlin—you play for me, make me proud. If you're good I'll make it worth your while, He-Man," Mandy said, trying to sound cheery.

JT stood and dragged her into his arms, holding her close for a long time before he agreed, somewhat reluctantly.

* * * *

Mandy and JT had spent every spare minute together. Mandy had still managed to make plenty of new pieces of jewellery and had even started a sketch of JT—a nude, naturally. Although she never seemed to get very far, since every time she ran her hands over him—for the sake of her art, of course—she was distracted by another round of intense, fulfilling lovemaking, or just good, old-fashioned down-and-dirty sex, depending on the mood.

JT was easy to be around. He had happily worked at something on his laptop or made phone calls while she'd worked. He and Brodie had trained every day for hours on end, and Caitlin and Mandy had caught up at those times. They had made plans for Mandy to sit with Riley on Friday and watch the game. Caitlin would be singing at Mia's, so Mandy was going to text the details of the game to Caitlin's new mobile, courtesy of Brodie. Both she and Caitlin were feeling a bit down at the thought of their men being away, but both had agreed that it was a comfort that they'd have each other for company.

Mandy kept herself busy after JT left, trying not to worry about his worrying about her. She restocked her plastic tubs with new jewellery pieces ready to sell on the Friday and Saturday markets. She tidied her flat, changed her bedding, even cleaned the glass in the French doors.

Sleeping in a bed without JT seemed too hard, so on Wednesday night Mandy just worked through.

On Thursday morning, she fell into bed, exhausted…

* * * *

On Friday, Mandy was up early to repack her van with products for the day ahead. She hoped it would go fast, already excited about the thought of seeing JT, even if it was just on the television.

Mandy was missing JT so much she was shocked at how her body ached for him. No other person in her life had impacted on her as he had. Mandy didn't even want to think about the other occasions he would be away. Every time her phone rang, Mandy prayed it would be JT just so she could hear his voice. True to his word, JT rang her often during the day.

That night, Mandy sat with Riley in front of the television, nervously waiting for the action to begin. Mandy recognised the sports commentator Trevor Hughes—she had met him right in this very flat, during that terrible, drama-filled period for Brodie and Caitlin. He had seemed nice enough and was obviously a friend of JT's. Trevor was talking about the Jets team being favourites to win the game. She listened, interested to hear what he was saying.

"Jets' stalwart props, James and Thomson, are in the best form in years. It seems as if they have found a new lease of life. The Townsville forward pack should be prepared for a hard encounter if they plan on stopping the Jets' momentum."

Mandy smiled, wondering a little smugly if she and Caitlin might be to thank for Brodie's and JT's 'new lease of life'.

"The Jets' halfback, Mitchell Harris," the commentator continued, "is really maturing as a player and young man under the guidance of the Jets' coaching staff and strong mentors like James and Thomson. In fact, I have been informed by a reliable source that a few days ago, Harris went to the aid of a young woman who was being assaulted."

Mandy's stomach dropped when she heard Trevor comment about what had happened to her and Rookie. She was not really happy that it was now public.

"At least my name wasn't used, though," she murmured at the television screen, relieved.

The game was harder for Mandy to watch than she had expected. She had thought seeing a game live at the ground was bad, not realising that the close-up shots of the action would make the play look even more brutal, not to mention the slow-motion replays that showed every tackle, hit and knock. Mandy could even hear the sounds of impact as bodies slammed together. The North Queensland team remained in the lead for most of the game.

Mandy nearly fell off the sofa when a very close-up shot of JT showed blood streaming down his face.

"Oh, my God!" she cried out as the image was displayed on the television screen. Riley—bless his heart—took her hand and told her it was all part of the game, and that JT had bled many times. Riley's words didn't really help Mandy all that much. She could not imagine how, if it had been Brodie bleeding the way JT was, she'd be able to describe that, over the phone, to Caitlin in her promised match update.

The game went right down to the last minute, when a player accurately nicknamed 'the Flash' scooted away and scored what ended up being the winning try. The siren sounded soon after, ending the game. The Jets had won.

Mandy was jumping around the room, high-fiving with Riley, looking like some sort of madwoman, when Riley stopped and pointed to the image of JT on the television screen. Mandy listened to her man's deep voice as he answered questions about the game — he sounded so sexy.

Mandy's heart skipped a beat when she heard JT ask if he could send a shout out to his woman at home. "Love you, Mags. See you and Riley soon, gorgeous."

Riley bounced around the room, going on and on about everyone hearing JT saying his name on national TV. Mandy felt exactly the same — she didn't even mind that JT had called her Mags.

* * * *

The month of July saw Mandy and JT settle into a familiar pattern — Mandy working while JT went to training, him accompanying her to sell her art at the various markets around Sydney when he could, and Mandy to the league games played at the Jets' home ground. The happy couple socialised with Brodie, Caitlin and young Riley at least once a week. They ate dinner with JT's father regularly, and the odd breakfast.

Riley had stayed over with them one night so Brodie could have a special night out with Caitlin. JT had a 'cat that swallowed the canary' look about him all night long. He definitely was a shocker at keeping secrets, Mandy had decided. With all the fuss and secrecy involved, she'd guessed that maybe there was a wedding proposal in Caitlin's future.

Just as Mandy had surmised, after a romantic dinner at one of the finest restaurants in Sydney, Brodie had in fact proposed to Caitlin — down on one knee with a pink, heart-shaped, diamond solitaire gold ring held out on offer, Brodie had vowed to look after Caitlin and Riley forever, if she would have him. When an excited, squealing Caitlin had rung to give the good news that she had — of course — said yes, describing the night and Brodie's promises, Mandy had become so emotional she'd begun to cry with happiness.

Mandy and JT remained incredibly passionate. A single touch or look made her melt, and her mind usually erupted like a volcano, spewing colour like molten lava. Mandy's breasts, so used to being aroused, just remained full and almost painful to touch these days. JT always appeared to be hard and ready for her, his appetite insatiable. The busy schedule did take a toll on Mandy, though. By the first week of August, she just couldn't shake off a tiredness that was draining most of her energy.

JT had travelled away for two games over the last month, but Mandy was getting better at dealing with his absences. Caitlin and Riley kept her company. One night, when the Jets were away, some of the players' partners got together at Mia's to enjoy dinner and Caitlin's singing. Mandy, although not hungry, as food seem to unsettle her sensitive stomach, did enjoy the company. She felt more and more like a part of JT's rugby league life, and often wondered how she had managed before JT.

Unconsciously, Mandy was changing. She didn't hide behind so many layers of makeup now, preferring to spend the time she used to take to create her dramatic image in bed with JT. Her all-black clothing was slowly being replaced with more feminine-looking shirts, and even a pair of jeans. Mandy had thought her large bottom was not suitable for jeans, but JT's enthusiastic encouragement and continued caresses of her denim-clad bottom convinced her otherwise.

Her artwork was also changing. The dark, brooding images that had often appeared in her paintings had now morphed into softer, happier lines and colours — vibrant sunsets and shimmering moonlit scenes were among her new work. Her jewellery line now consisted of romantic, swirling fine designs, as opposed to the chunky harsh lines of the pieces that used to make up her sales inventory.

Chapter Sixteen

JT was worried about Mandy. She seemed to be pale and tired all the time. He knew he was asking too much of her sexually, and every night he promised himself that he would just cuddle her and let her get a good night's sleep. But then JT would see Mandy's sexy, curvy body, and he would forget any promises he had silently made. Mandy never needed any coercion — she was always hot, wet and eager for him, and often the aggressor. Those nights were particularly popular memories for JT.

It was Mandy's twenty-sixth birthday in a little over a week, and luckily for JT, it fell on the day of a home game. He was going to make the day one that Mandy would never forget. He had arranged that he and Mandy would arrive earlier than necessary to the ground, and as they headed inside, the electronic score board would be programmed with the words to ask Mandy the big question, while JT knelt down on one knee in front of her.

He had it all planned. His father had given him his mother's engagement ring. It was perfect for Mandy, the rose gold ring's antique design very different to today's modern rings. It was a large and unusual chocolate-coloured diamond, surrounded by small, brilliant diamonds. The larger diamond's hue reminded JT of one of Mandy's uniquely pigmented eyes.

JT had known he wanted to marry Mandy from the first night they'd spent together. But he was now nervous that she was becoming ill and might not be up to such a public proposal. Unsure of what to do and thinking that maybe he needed a woman's view, JT decided a chat with Caitlin might help him to soothe some of his fears.

He knocked on the downstairs door first, hoping Brodie would not arrive for a few minutes so he could have a little privacy. JT was already feeling slightly embarrassed at the thought of speaking about Mandy and his plans at all, let alone to another woman – and he certainly didn't need Brodie making fun at his expense.

He explained his concerns over Mandy's continual tiredness to Caitlin, even overcoming his embarrassment and mentioning Mandy's unusually tender breasts. He also spoke of his hopes to propose to Mandy on the Sunday of her birthday.

JT was a bit annoyed at the wide grin forming on Caitlin's face – she seemed to not be taking JT's worries seriously. He was about to tell Caitlin to forget anything he had said and walk away when the pretty, young redhead finally stopped grinning and spoke.

"JT, you look so fierce. I'm not laughing at you, sweetie, I'm just happy." She patted JT's bulging, tense biceps and continued, "Mandy has become very dear to me, and I really wasn't looking forward to leaving her when Brodie and I get married. For some reason, Brodie doesn't want to live here," she said, laughing. Then, looking more serious and slightly uncomfortable, Caitlin asked JT a direct and very personal question, adding her own diagnosis of what was ailing Mandy.

"JT, honey, do you and Mandy use...ummm...any protection when you, you know, make love? Could Mandy be pregnant? She hasn't said anything to me, but I have noticed she isn't eating and does seem tired all the time. At first I thought maybe you two were just too nocturnal, but now I think it's more." Caitlin quickly looked away, seeming embarrassed to look at JT directly.

She could have knocked JT over with a feather. *Could that be it? Could Mandy be carrying our child? Does she know? Why didn't she tell me?* he thought in a rush of questions, but with no clear answers.

"I don't know, Cait. I think she has an injection or something. I stopped using condoms and Mandy didn't say anything about it. Do you really think she could be...?"

After more discussion, JT and Caitlin decided it was best to give Mandy more time, let her tell them when she felt more comfortable. JT wasn't sure how long he would be able to keep quiet and under control, and hoped she would tell him soon. Although, he hoped he had time to propose first, so she wouldn't confuse his reasons for wanting to marry her. JT loved Mandy more than anything else and he wanted her to be his in every way possible, including legally.

It was going to be a very long week.

* * * *

JT did manage to keep from asking Mandy about the possibility of her being pregnant, but he tried to make her rest more, even complaining he needed to catch up on sleep as a cover. Her little disappointed face nearly broke his resolve, but he pulled her close and held her all night, hand splayed protectively over her abdomen. Hoping.

Finally, the Sunday of Mandy's birthday arrived. JT was awake early, watching for the first signs of her waking. As her eyes sleepily opened, he pounced on her mouth, licking at her lips with his tongue until they opened for him. JT kissed her passionately, thinking of what the day would bring. The promise he hoped she would make him.

As they started exploring each other more intimately, a loud knocking started at the door to Mandy's flat. JT, grouching about lousy timing, went to see what was so urgent as to disturb them so early, pulling on sweat pants over his very prominent erection, on the way.

Standing in the doorway were Caitlin and Brodie, with Riley trailing behind, each carrying wrapped gifts and what smelt, to JT, like breakfast.

"Didn't interrupt anything, I hope, mate? We all want to wish Mandy a happy birthday! Where is the birthday girl?" Brodie chuckled heartily, poking his head around JT as he spoke.

"Yeah, right, laugh it up—you're a funny man, Brodes. You know exactly what you're interrupting and if young Riley wasn't here I'd make you sorry for the intrusion..." Behind the grumbling, unhappy JT, a robed Mandy arrived. She was probably worried that he would just shut the door in their friends' smiling faces, and he contemplated the idea of doing just that very thing so he could take her back to bed.

Mandy started to say something, and JT turned his attention towards her.

"Hey, you guys are the best friends ever..." But she stopped suddenly.

Something must have happened to her, because the next thing JT knew, Mandy was sprinting off in the direction of the bathroom, leaving him, Brodie, Caitlin and Riley standing stunned and motionless in the doorway, watching her flee.

Chapter Seventeen

Mandy had wanted to say more in welcome, but as a waft of the food's aroma had reached her, her stomach had rolled over. She'd known she was about to vomit, and she'd had to hurry to the bathroom so as not to make a disgusting mess in front of her friends.

She sat, feeling miserable, on the cold tiles of the bathroom floor, her head hanging over the toilet bowl as she threw up for the second time. This was the third day in a row that she had been physically ill, and she was starting to get worried, thinking a trip to the doctor was probably needed, when there was a soft rap on the door.

"Mandy, it's me, Caitlin. Can I come in?"

"Yeah, if you're game. I think I'm finished puking up." Mandy watched as Caitlin entered the room. A huge, bright smile was covering her friend's face, and Mandy groaned at the look of happiness her friend exuded. "What's the hero done to make you so happy?" she said, referring to Caitlin's nickname for Brodie.

"Oh, Mandy, don't you realise what's going on? Goodness, didn't your parents tell you about the birds and the bees? What makes a woman tired, her breasts feel tender and full...and makes her vomit at the smell of food? Doh! Think about it, girl!" Mandy could feel Caitlin stroke her back tenderly, obviously waiting for the proverbial shoe to drop.

"Oh, my *God!*" was all Mandy managed to get out before she threw up again, the retching sounds cutting off any more exclamations.

It was at about the same time that the door banged open and JT stormed in, looking fiercer than ever before.

"Enough! It's time you finally told me, Mandy. I'm big, not stupid. I know what's going on here, and I'm a bit pissed you haven't told me yet." JT was standing down at Mandy. She could see the disappointment and maybe a little anger in his expression. "I want to yell to the world that we are having a baby. I want to hold you when you're sick. I want to share this wonderful blessing with you, woman. Not stand on the sidelines as if I've been benched. I love you. Why are you keeping such good news from me?"

"Settle down, JT. I think I'll leave you both to it. Be gentle, big boy—it's not you chucking up," Caitlin joked as she squeezed by the huge mass of a man. "I think you guys need some privacy, and Brodie and Riley must be wondering what in goodness is going on."

"He-Man, just hold up..." Mandy tried to stand. She wobbled a little and had to take JT's hand, grateful for his assistance. She rinsed her mouth under running tap water, then turned to him.

"Firstly, I am well aware that you are, in fact, extremely above average in the intelligence department. In fact, maybe you could have clued me in on what was happening to me, seeing as I seem to be last to know." She giggled nervously as she continued, "Maybe I'm just small and stupid, Jon. I didn't even think about being pregnant, not until Caitlin just mentioned it. I've had the contraceptive injection. It was a while ago, but I thought I was still safe... This shouldn't be happening."

Mandy, after taking a deep breath and grabbing hold of JT's big hands in her smaller, quite clammy ones, asked him the all-important question.

"So... How *do* you feel about the chance I might be pregnant? That you might be a father?"

"Mags, baby," JT said without a moment's hesitation as he pulled her into his embrace, lifting her feet from the ground, his strong arms holding her to his chest, "if you have our baby growing inside you, my life will be almost complete." Although Mandy was not sure what he had meant by 'almost complete', she was surprised by the tears her strong man was shedding, feeling them wet against her skin.

"I think I need some weak tea and toast," Mandy said, in an effort to try to get them out of the bathroom and back to their friends. "Maybe you should go to the chemist, JT, and get me a pregnancy test so we can confirm our news, and then you can blab to the world. But first, you need to put me down, He-Man."

"That, you gorgeous woman, is a fantastic idea. Let's go gently persuade Caitlin to make the tea so I can shoot off and get those tests," JT happily replied as he carried Mandy out to see the others, who were still waiting patiently to wish her a happy birthday.

Mandy and JT had cleared some of the art studio to make a little living area, complete with a small, two-seat sofa and matching chair with a coffee table in between. JT had fixed a small television to the wall so he could keep himself amused while Mandy worked. As JT carefully placed Mandy on the sofa, brushing a confused Riley out of the way, he grabbed Brodie by the arm.

"C'mon, mate, I don't think I can drive. We need to go pick up some things. Hey, Caitlin, could you make Mandy some tea and toast while we're gone?"

As a confused and slightly worried-looking Brodie and Riley left with a smiling JT, Mandy sighed.

"Could my life be any better?" She rubbed her hand lovingly over her possibly pregnant tummy and daydreamed about being a mum, envisioning her baby as a little version of JT, with black hair and dark eyes, or maybe a curly, dark-haired girl with Mandy's unusual eye-colouring.

Mandy daydreamed the time away while waiting for the tea and toast Caitlin had offered to make, and it wasn't long before the two men and Riley returned from their shopping expedition. JT had purchased five different varieties of pregnancy test. A laughing Mandy went off to the bathroom to do some serious 'peeing on sticks', as she called it.

"Thanks for the mental picture, Mandy—I really could have lived without it!" Riley, obviously embarrassed by the image, groaned behind her as she left the room. "Yuck! Girls say the most disgusting things. I'll never understand why you guys get so gushy around them," he grunted, obviously speaking to JT and Brodie.

Mandy used three tests, and placed the sticks carefully on the vanity top. She called for JT to join her. JT sat on the closed toilet with Mandy in his lap as they waited the required length of time for the results to show. Time seemed to slow, and the anticipation built as the minutes ticked past.

"Okay, Mags, time's up. Are you going to look?"

"No, I'm too nervous! Jon, can you do it, please?" Mandy begged.

"If you're sure, honey." JT lifted Mandy gently and stood up. He picked up the first stick.

"It says positive."

He placed it back down and picked up the second stick. "This one's showing two pink lines in the little window…"

JT picked up the third…

The next thing she knew, Mandy was being showered with kisses by an enthusiastically cheering JT. Before long, the bathroom was crowded—her friends were also there to congratulate them, hugging and just being happy for her and JT in their special moment.

* * * *

JT had seemed particularly nervous before today's game, Mandy had noticed, and wondered if it was under the weight of the news about the baby. She was deliriously happy, her mind so bright with colour that she wished she could wear some sort of mind sunglasses to turn down the light. She giggled aloud at the thought. JT looked over to her from the driver's seat of his panther-like car, raising an eyebrow in question.

As usual, JT parked in the team's reserved parking area. He jumped from the car and after grabbing his bag from the boot, he insisted on helping her from the vehicle, then took Mandy's hand in his, leading her towards the entrance to the grandstand.

Mandy was floating along, happily touching her tummy all the time in wonder. She hadn't even noticed that they had stopped. The sound of cheering and clapping had Mandy looking around wondering what was going on. Finally, she noticed the giant scoreboard—her name was lit up brightly in huge, neon lettering. Mandy read the words written alongside her name.

'Mandy, love of my life

Make me the happiest man alive

Agree to be my wife

I love you

Jonathon 'JT' Thomson'

Mandy looked back to JT, who was now kneeling in front of her and holding out a ring. Even kneeling, JT was still almost at eye level with her.

Mandy didn't mean to wait, but it took a minute for her brain to catch up before she threw her arms around the love of her life and agreed wholeheartedly to be his wife. The sound of cameras clicking and people cheering were almost muted by her happiness and desire for her man.

After placing the ring on her finger, JT escorted Mandy to her seat next to a teary-eyed Caitlin. Brodie, having used Mandy's seat to watch the show, stood and clapped JT on the back in congratulations. Mandy was amazed to see the stand nearly full of people who had arrived early, just to see JT's proposal.

"Pretty confident there, He-Man. What would you have done if I'd said no?" Mandy asked JT teasingly.

Looking down at her with a deadly serious expression, he replied in a slow, sure tone. "Died a million deaths, Mandy. I couldn't imagine life without you. You are the love of my life."

Tears threatened to spill from Mandy's eyes as her man gently kissed her goodbye and went to prepare for the game. His words had been so heartfelt, they'd caused a shiver to run up her spine and goosebumps to erupt over her skin. She would never forget that simple statement, or the look on his face as JT had answered her.

Watching the game was getting no easier for Mandy. She still cringed every time JT was involved in any part of the action, only managing to breathe normally at the times he was off the field. Players were often substituted during a match — a fresh player could have an impact in a game as others became tired.

Mandy was starting to understand a lot more about what JT's role was in the Jets team. With JT being so strong, it often took many of the opposition players, all working together, to wrestle him to the ground. Even then, JT was often still able to run many metres first. If he passed the ball on to one of his teammates before he went to ground, they could often find a space to run, given the fact that so many of the other team's players were already distracted by JT. He was also very good at stopping the opposition from running when they had the ball, slamming players hard into the ground before they could get very far.

Even with her little experience of the game, Mandy could see how talented JT was. No player on the opposite team gave the Jets the amount of trouble that JT gave in return. It was good to have Riley explaining the rules and finer points of the game to her. Mandy was impressed with the boy's knowledge. She couldn't say she actually enjoyed the game, but did appreciate the skill involved.

JT's and Brodie's Jets team won again. They were being touted as the team to beat in the finals. The

regular season was coming to a close in a few weeks —
then the top teams would play for a chance to compete
in the grand final and ultimately win the title of
Premiers. The Grand Final Week — Mandy had been
told by the other wives — was very exciting, usually
involving a fanfare of events and media attention
hyping up the excitement levels for players and fans
alike. She wasn't sure her nerves could cope with any
of that, so just concentrated on the normal games
ahead, trying to survive those first.

As the usual group of family and friends gathered
outside the door to the changing rooms, Mandy
absorbed her surroundings. So many fans were
waiting excitedly for the chance to see their favourite
players, and kids were dressed as little versions of
their heroes. Men and women were dressed in the
team's colours of black and gold, wearing scarves and
hats, waving flags. Reporters and photographers
milled around, waiting for a comment or photo that
would give them a story to print, which would justify
their employment. Seeing everyone so happy now
their team had won, Mandy realised what a huge
responsibility the team of Jets players carried onto the
field.

Chapter Eighteen

It had been a good victory.

JT sat next to Brodie, watching as his fellow teammates, team officials and staff rowdily sang the team song—a tradition after a win. People were thumping their hands on the walls or cupboards, anything to make more noise as they jubilantly celebrated the outcome. JT couldn't help smiling at the way Riley was enthusiastically joining in, enjoying his life, deserving to after having to survive the loss of his parents while so very young.

"Love seeing the kid so happy…better feeling than the win, really," JT spoke quietly. "You and I are lucky bastards. Great women prepared to put up with us forever, the kid over there and me with one on the way, your parents, my father, people that we can count on, not to mention some loyal friends. All of it—all this—makes a bloke feel real grateful. We've certainly come a long way this year, Brodes! I got a feeling that this is our year, big fella!"

"Yep, you got that right, mate." Brodie took a long swallow of the sports drink he was holding. "Pinch myself every day at my luck in finding Cait and young Riley. Can't imagine my life without them, now. Wouldn't want to. Mandy's a winner for sure, couldn't be happier for you JT. Hope the kid takes after her, though!" He grinned. "What do you say we get cleaned up and out to our women, pronto? Don't know 'bout you, but I need to taste some sweet lips, and real soon."

JT couldn't have agreed more with Brodie, so he dragged his tired, stiff and sore body up from the bench and headed for the showers.

* * * *

JT was appreciative of all the fuss being made over him and Mandy back at the after game function. Sponsors and club directors wished them well, buying champagne and insisting on toasting to them and their future. He noticed that Mandy was only having a token sip before making the champagne glass disappear, as if by magic. JT was aware that alcohol was not good for a developing baby, and was so proud of her. He knew she was going to be a wonderful mother. He was also relieved to watch as Mandy cleaned her plate at dinner, glad that her stomach must have settled down since the morning.

He really wanted to tell his father, in person, the good news that Mandy had agreed to marry him, and so had called earlier and invited his dad to come and join them at the club. He was also looking forward to breaking the good news about the baby. JT had been pondering what his father would want to be called — maybe 'Pop' or 'Pa'. 'Granddad' sounded way too formal. The impending conversation brought a smile to his face as he imagined his father's delight at the news.

Chapter Nineteen

Mandy noticed Jon Senior and June — her downstairs neighbour — arriving together, and elbowed Caitlin.

"Well, would you look at that, Caitlin? Did you know those two were friends?"

"No, I didn't," her friend replied, obviously surprised by the sight as well. "Although, now I think about it... Remember the night the boys were away, and you and Riley watched the game? June declined Riley's invitation to join you, which was really funny — she loves watching the footy with Riles. Anyway, she said she had something else to do. That night, when I came home after work, I thought I saw JT's dad's car in the street. I mentioned it to Brodie, but he just said plenty of cars looked like Jon Senior's." Caitlin shrugged. "So I forgot all about it."

Mandy and Caitlin decided to not mention anything about the older couple to anyone, and in the future to just be a bit more observant. The two young women giggled conspiratorially together over the whole idea.

Mandy was pleased at JT's father's reaction to both the engagement and pregnancy. Mandy had worried the man might think the engagement was forced as a result of the pregnancy, but he really didn't seem to be worried at all. Mandy was reduced to tears, again, when told of the emotional history of the engagement ring she now wore, and how Jon Senior had offered the ring that had belonged to his deceased wife — JT's mother — when told of his son's plans. He assured Mandy he couldn't be more pleased than to see the ring on someone as lovely as her. She was touched, lost for words as the true sentimental value of the beautiful jewellery became apparent.

June was 'tickled pink', as she put it, hinting unabashedly to both Caitlin and Mandy how much she loved weddings, and how she was just about to splash out and make herself two new outfits, hoping she might have some occasion to wear them. Mandy thought that June did look happy, and wondered if the weddings were the only things lifting the retiree's spirits.

Riley spent most of the night with a young, athletic-looking girl who he introduced as Phillipa, the coach's daughter. He explained that everyone called her Pipsqueak. It didn't look, to Mandy, as if she actually enjoyed her nickname, though. Phillipa — whom Mandy guessed to be in her mid-teens — was quite focused on Mitch 'Rookie' Harris, as most of the young girls her age seemed to be.

* * * *

Mandy and JT finally managed to escape the night's activities at around ten p.m., and headed back to the flat. JT insisted on carrying Mandy up the stairs — he reminded her that he had done the exact same thing on the first night they had made love. Mandy didn't complain. She was tired and loved being in her man's arms.

This time there was no special bath for JT—the couple were both emotionally and physically drained from the long and life-altering day. As they lay in each other's arms, JT whispered to Mandy, "Happy birthday, Mags. Hope you've had a day to remember."

"Oh, He-Man, the best ever. But it's still my birthday and I want another present. It amazes me how something so hard can feel so soft to touch..." Mandy gave a sultry purr as she wrapped her palm around JT's erection. "My favourite part is this raised bit, just here," Mandy teased as her finger rimmed the mushroom-shaped head of JT's penis, stopping at the slight join of flesh at the top. JT could only moan and growl in response as she wrapped her soft hand around his steel-hard cock.

Mandy lowered her head and blew gently on the enormous length that stood erect before her, then ran the tip of her tongue slowly over the same path that her finger had taken before it, loving the way JT jerked in response. She took him into her mouth slowly, pressing her lips together tightly to create just enough friction as she sucked his warm cock all the way into her mouth, until the head bumped the back of her throat.

Mandy tried to relax her throat even more, so she could take all of him, moving her mouth up and down. She grazed her teeth gently along the rigid shaft as she pumped her hand in a complementary rhythm.

She was enjoying herself, totally absorbed in her endeavours. She could feel the moisture building between her thighs and squeezed them together to try to ease the ache. Now she was so in tune with JT's body, Mandy knew he was getting close. When he tried to pull her mouth away from his almost exploding cock, she shook her head and sucked harder.

"Woman, I'm coming in your mouth if you don't let go. I can't hold on any longer," JT groaned.

It was exactly what Mandy had intended, and as she felt the warm, salty fluid hit the back of her throat she slurped it down greedily, not wanting to waste a drop of JT's essence. When she was certain she had milked him dry she rested her head on his thigh and looked up at him coyly, licking her lips.

"Mmmm! You taste *so* good," she said.

JT was on her in seconds, caressing and stroking, pinching and tugging, making her cry out in pleasure.

JT licked and nibbled first at one nipple, then the next, bringing them both to hard protruding buds. He placed kisses over every inch of her, first light and gentle, then hard and possessive — she could feel him leaving his mark all over her body. The pain was so pleasurable that Mandy reached a climax even before JT paid any attention to her moist folds. But when he did reach that hot and swollen place...oh, how he made her explode.

The intensity of Mandy's orgasm was so strong that she rode it for what seemed an eternity. Finally, as she shuddered, the wave nearing its completion, JT entered her. His thick cock was hard once again, filling her as her inner muscles clenched at him eagerly. The pleasure began to build again instantly as JT pumped and thrust into her. Mandy wrapped her legs around him and locked her ankles as she clung to him bonelessly, unable to do anything more than ride another tidal wave of desire to its conclusion.

Just like all the times they had made love before, Mandy was astounded at the colour explosions in her mind, never the same, but always breathtaking in their combination. Recalling the pattern of swirling shades could always give Mandy plenty of inspiration for her art and jewellery designs.

Needless to say, she would never be short of an idea!

Chapter Twenty

The last game of the season—before the finals series—was on the coming Friday night. The game was scheduled to be held in Brisbane. JT, Brodie and the Jets team were flying up on the Thursday morning to prepare for the important game. If the Jets won, they would go into the finals series in first spot, giving them an extra bonus—a week off. At this time of the year, a week off would be of great value to any team, since it there'd be time for any niggling injuries to heal. The first spot also meant two chances to reach the Grand Final. Plenty of nervous energy was flowing around the local area, with expectations high for a Jets premiership.

Mandy was overjoyed that her morning sickness had abated, often wondering why it was called that, when nausea seemed to have stricken her at various times of the day. Once, while enjoying an intimate moment with JT, with him in between her legs, his mouth doing amazing things to her little nub, she had been forced to push him away and race to the toilet, only just making it in time before emptying her stomach, which had quickly dampened any further sexual desires that night.

Mandy and Caitlin had made the decision not to travel to the Brisbane game, knowing that JT and Brodie would need to be totally focused on their jobs. Instead, both girls would remain home and go about business as usual, Mandy selling her wares at the markets during the day and Caitlin doing her usual Friday night gig at Mia's Restaurant. Mandy and Riley would watch the game together and send updates to Caitlin. The two women put on brave, confident faces as they sent their respective men off early on Thursday morning, Riley even missed swimming squad training to say his farewells and wish Brodie and JT good luck.

* * * *

JT had rung her three times during the day of the game. He'd seemed happy, but eager to get the game underway, so they—the team—could begin to focus on the end prize. Mandy had thought that maybe he should just take one step at a time, but had kept the thought to herself. She had reminded him that she would be proudly watching the game and telling their 'little peanut' how well Daddy was playing, which had brought forth a gush of romantic endearments from the other end of the line before JT, reluctantly, had had to end the call.

Mandy, weary from a busy, profitable day, was glad to be home and after unpacking her van of the few remaining unsold items, she treated herself to a long soak in the bath. Relaxing and enjoying the warm water that was easing her muscles, Mandy couldn't resist rubbing her hand over the slight rise of her abdomen, where the baby was growing. She enjoyed having one-sided conversations with her tummy, telling the growing bump how much he or she was loved and what was happening during the day. JT also spoke into her belly button quite often, adding stories of his day and future plans for his son or daughter when the baby finally arrived.

She was trying not to think about the birth too much — plenty of time to worry about that in the parenting and childbirth lessons. They had been for the first antenatal appointment. An ultrasound that showed the excited parents-to-be the first glimpse of their baby had made it all seem more real. Upon seeing what had appeared to be a big head and long body, Mandy had thought the baby had looked more like a peanut. She had proudly displayed the photo image in a frame by her bed.

Now warm after her bath, Mandy pulled on one of JT's big sweat tops and her own new sweat bottoms, a present from JT. She had never worn this sort of clothing before, but really liked the comfy feel of the material against her skin. Wearing JT's oversized top was also a way to feel closer to her absent man, his scent still part of the soft fabric.

Now hungry — a state Mandy was finding increasingly common these days — she thought pizza would be a nice treat for her and Riley, and her stomach growled in agreement. Mandy pulled the door to her flat closed and headed downstairs, not even bothering to make up her face. Gone were the days when she had applied layers of makeup. Mandy did not feel the need anymore for a barrier to protect herself from the world.

Riley was always interested in food of any kind, so Mandy phoned the local pizzeria and ordered a home delivery. The order—for two large, deep-dish pizzas, one ham and pineapple and the other vegetarian, plus a serving of garlic bread—was promised within thirty minutes, so thankfully for her complaining tummy, it wasn't long before she and Riley were greedily munching away on their delicious but not-so-wholesome dinner, anxiously waiting for the telecast of the game to begin.

Riley, his mouth full of pizza, told Mandy that he'd invited June to join them but that she had been busy again, not telling him why. Mandy was worried that maybe she had pushed in on June's territory, taking up Riley's regular time with June, and decided she would speak to her elderly friend about it very soon.

The telecast began with a camera shot of the Jets team in the dressing shed. Mandy's breath caught in her throat at the sight of JT wearing only a pair of the team's shorts.

"Oh, my..." was all the reaction she could manage verbally. Her nipples responded at once, becoming hard pebbles, and poked against the fabric of JT's shirt. Mandy couldn't help admire JT's amazing body, but felt a little pang of jealousy that the whole television audience had got to see him that way as well. Riley was laughing at her, asking her which shirtless chest she had been looking at—as if she'd actually noticed anyone else.

The camera shot changed to the Brisbane dressing room, and the commentators spoke of the hard game ahead. Mandy was still trying to settle her raging hormones at the sight of JT when the two teams ran down the players' tunnel and onto the field. The game kicked off. It was a physical match, with neither team able to post any points before half-time. JT and Brodie were looking battered and weary as they left the field for the half-time break.

Mandy dutifully texted Caitlin details of the nil-all scoreboard, and that Brodie was okay. Even the always-bouncing, exuberant Riley was quiet for a change.

The second half of the game was just as tough, neither team making the most of its opportunities, or so the commentator said. Mandy didn't really understand what that meant. She watched as JT, reaching out over the line to score a try, dropped the ball. As camera replays from every angle repeated the dropped ball, Riley wailed his disappointment, actually berating JT. Mandy was very shocked at the outburst. She felt so sorry for JT—he had looked so dejected when the camera had showed a close-up shot of the face she had grown to love so much.

With less than five minutes to go, the Jets team were in possession of the football. JT made a barnstorming run, eating up the field. Once JT's forward momentum was stopped he placed the ball on the ground at his feet and rolled it backwards, so the next runner could pick it up. Brodie was that player and he made as much ground, struggling against the force of his opponents as JT had before he was tackled. Brodie, jumping quickly to his feet despite the attempts by the defence to slow him down, played the ball, rolling it between his feet to the teammate standing directly behind him. The Jets were so near the try line that it looked as if JT, now standing close by, was going to be passed the ball, take another run and crash his body over the line in an attempt to score. The Jets player holding the ball pretended to pass to JT, and the Brisbane players headed en masse to stop JT, expecting him to receive the pass. They left a space, and the player still holding the footy used the distraction to dive over the try line and score.

Mandy and Riley jumped up and down and cheered loudly. The Jets now led with only minutes to go.

As Mandy and Riley sat perched on the edge of their seats, clutching each other, praying the Jets would hold on to the win, Mandy heard a crashing sound come from above. It sounded as if something had fallen in her flat. Quieting Riley, she stood, trying to listen. It sounded as though someone was in her home. Not really thinking about the possible danger of her actions, Mandy shouted to Riley as she ran out of the door, "Stay here, Riles, I'm just going to check my place is okay. I'll be right back."

Mandy raced up the stairs to discover her front door slightly ajar. As she stormed inside her home, angry at the thought that someone had been inside, Mandy realised at once that she had made what could end up being a fatal mistake.

Standing in amongst the rubble of what had been her studio stood Con. The look on his face was enough to make Mandy's blood instantly run cold.

Chapter Twenty-One

"Well, what do you know... The big hero didn't take you with him to Brisbane after all? When you weren't home I thought maybe he had." Con's voice was full of malice. He grabbed Mandy by her arm, dragging her closer to him, close enough that she could feel his breath on her cheek.

"This is a pleasant surprise, Amanda, although you are looking a bit different these days." Con's gaze roamed over her body. Just the feel of him looking at her made Mandy nauseous.

"Look at how you're dressed, Amanda. You really have let yourself go. You're looking like quite the slob. Still, it won't matter to me. I know how to make it so you will arouse me, and I promise it will hurt—a lot. You owe me some pain after all you've put me through. I did warn you."

Con's voice was creating continuous shivers of fear that rippled along Mandy's spine. She tried to struggle out of his grasp, striking out at her cruel captor, slashing at his face with her fingernails and drawing blood as they found their target.

But her fight just angered Con even more, resulting in him backhanding her hard across the cheek, the force rattling her teeth and knocking her to the ground. Mandy fell hard, desperately trying to protect her stomach with her arms as she hit the floor, her cheek burning with pain. *I have to stay calm*, Mandy thought, as she tried to fight off the paralysing fear beginning to overwhelm her. Thinking that maybe, if she gave Con what he wanted, he would eventually let her go and maybe her baby would survive.

Let us live through this, she silently prayed.

Con grabbed her by the hair, using his grip on it to roughly pull her back to her feet. Just as Mandy managed to steady herself, he punched her.

Hard.

In the stomach.

"You think I can't read? You fucking slut. Do you think I like seeing your photo plastered everywhere I look…and with that ox? Are you trying to make me look stupid, like I wasn't man enough for you? I'm going to hurt you, Amanda. Use you in every way, until I'm completely satisfied. Then, and only then — after I've used you all up — I am going to kill both you and that maggot growing inside you, leave you here for that fucking interfering ox to find you. You were all mine, Amanda, and if I can't have you, sure as I'm standing here, no one else will." The anger, hatred and obvious insanity were very clear in Con's voice.

His intent was plain. He was there to kill her.

Mandy lost her colours, becoming strangely calm as her mind went pure white. An image of JT's face filled the once vibrant space. She was going to die and so was her baby, JT's baby. Mandy, so truly sorry for the man she loved, knew JT would be devastated because of her reckless behaviour. JT, having already lost his mother when he was so young, was now never going to get the opportunity to meet his child. And it was all her fault. Mandy, completely disassociated from reality, didn't even register the pain as Con kicked her with his metal-toed boots, shattering the bones in the arm that she'd wrapped around her abdomen in an effort to protect her unborn child.

She could not give up! She had to fight. She had so much to live for and some insane arsehole was *not* going to take that away from her. With a stunning moment of clarity, devoid of the pain from her shattered arm, Mandy spotted the glass bottle of turpentine on the floor not far from where she lay. She carefully inched her hand closer to the bottle, trying to mask the movement as best she could, never once taking her eyes off Con. Mandy's fingers finally reached their destination and she wrapped them round the cool body of the bottle.

As he lunged for her hair, ready to grab a handful and inflict another torturous blow, Mandy struck. With all the strength she could muster, she slammed the bottle straight into Con's face, resulting in a direct upward hit to his nose.

Mandy heard the crack as something broke, then felt the rush of cool liquid splash down her arm. The strong scent of the turpentine was familiar, surprisingly comforting.

She heard the agonised, high-pitched wail from Con as the strong, alcohol-based cleaning astringent splashed into his eyes and shattered nose.

"You stupid bitch, I'm gonna make you pay for this. Just wait till I get my hands on you," Con groaned.

As the fog settled into her brain, Mandy thought she heard another male voice, "Well, boy, I guess I'd better make sure that doesn't happen, although from what I can make out, Mandy seems to have saved me the trouble. But please, you worthless piece of shit, don't hesitate to try to get up. I really would like the opportunity to pound your face some as well. That's it, boy — get to your feet. Try taking on someone your own size."

Mandy heard a crack and a thump as Con fell to the floor beside her. His swollen, inflamed red eyes rolled back in his head while blood gushed from his flattened nose. Mandy heard the male voice again and tried to put a name to the familiar sound. Her mind was so muddled she was finding it hard to think.

"Riley, call an ambulance. June, help Mandy while I try and get this lowlife to wake up so I can hit him again before the police arrive. Oh, and let me apologise for my use of profanity before."

Mandy was finally able to put a name and face to the voice. It was JT's father. It was Jon Senior.

She could sense that June was sitting beside her, could feel the sensations of June's hands stroking her shoulders, could hear the sounds of June's positive, reassuring murmuring, the actual words just beyond her comprehension. The whoop-whoop sounds of sirens became louder, but Mandy just wanted to sleep. She was so tired.

* * * *

Jon Senior had nearly had a stroke when young Riley had knocked on June's door, worried that Mandy had gone alone to her apartment with an intruder possibly inside. What the hell had his future daughter-in-law been thinking, putting herself in such danger? He just could not understand it. Jonathon Thomson Senior was full of remorse. He had been enjoying June's company so much he had been distracted and had not heard Con break into the upstairs flat — or Mandy go to investigate.

"Must be losing my touch," the grief-stricken man said to no one in particular as he sat vigil beside Mandy. It was his fault the poor girl was lying broken and bruised in the hospital bed, crying in her sleep. He was beside himself with worry, not knowing what he should do to help her.

Remembering the sense of desperation in his son's voice as he'd tried to explain what had happened, how the love of JT's life had been so brutally attacked and hurt before Jon Senior had been able to intervene, was heartbreaking.

Jon Senior had let his son down, and in a big way. JT had asked him to watch over Mandy, but he had let her be hurt. The hours it had taken to confirm the continued pregnancy and health of the unborn child — his grandchild — had been a nightmare. The only other time that Jon Senior had felt this helpless was the time before the death of his beloved Elaina. Having to watch her waste away and not being able to do a damn thing to help her had been a different kind of nightmare.

Jon Senior was grateful his son had been saved from that despair — no thanks to his efforts, though.

Chapter Twenty-Two

JT was furious, beyond furious and frustrated. No plane was available until the morning, not even a private charter. Sydney airport was closed for the night due to the noise curfew — the airport was close to the inner city and highly populated housing areas. How ironic that a government decision that JT had once applauded — because it allowed him to get a good night's sleep without the constant drone of planes above — now worked against him. It would take too long to drive, at least eleven hours — better to wait for the airport to reopen, he'd been advised.

He paced back and forth in the suffocating hotel room, feeling as if he would explode. His skin felt too tightly stretched over his body, and every nerve was on edge. His jaw was so tight it ached, but the pain was nothing compared to what he felt in his heart. Mandy was hurt and he was trapped in another state. He hadn't even been able to speak with her — had been told she was sedated from surgery, then during a later attempt, asleep. But JT couldn't help but wonder whether Mandy was refusing to talk with him. He had, after all, let her down again. All his empty promises to keep her safe, and he hadn't made good on any of them.

"Fuck…" he said for what was probably around the hundredth time, as he dragged his fingers over his face in exasperation.

Brodie was sitting watching him, his face grim, but he stayed silent, as if knowing no words would help. JT's friend had booked them on the six a.m. flight, which would arrive in Sydney at around seven-twenty a.m., but the flight was still two hours away.

All of JT's fellow team mates and the Jets staff had been in and out of the room, getting updates on Mandy and the baby's condition. It had been unbearable for JT to not have the answer to that question for so long. Seeing the pity in the eyes of his well-meaning mates was more than he could stand. Everyone seemed numb with the shock of what had happened to one of their own.

When his father had confirmed that all was okay with the baby, the feeling of relief had been so overwhelming that JT had fallen to his knees and wept. Mandy was hurt, though, and that was impossible for him to live with. JT hated himself—and rugby league for taking him away from her and the baby. It was over. He was retired, as of now. No way was he ever leaving Mandy's side again.

Thank God JT and his father had come up with the plan to watch over Mandy. If Jon Senior had not been in June's flat, as had become usual for JT's away games, JT hated to think what the outcome would have been. The mere thought brought another wave of fury crashing down over him as he clenched and unclenched his fists, trying to vent the built-up anger without putting his fist through something.

Brodie, clearly seeing the restlessness in JT, tried to distract him.

"Jon, mate — thirty minutes. Just hang in for thirty minutes and we can head for the airport."

It was unusual for Brodie to use JT's given name, and the significance was not lost on JT.

"Shit, mate, I'm trying, really I am, but I just feel so useless. I can't leave her ever again. You know that, don't you? I'm finished with all this." He waved his arm around the room, referring to the game he had once loved, his voice full of emotion. "She means more to me than I can put into words. I just hope she can forgive me, forgive me for putting all of this before her safety."

One minute, the world had been bright and loud, full of celebration. The Jets team had finally done enough to win in what JT had felt was one of the toughest games of his career. He'd been concerned at not being able to reach Mandy on her mobile, had wanted to share with Mandy how good he'd felt about the win, and had needed to hear her voice. He had been confused when the phone had gone to voicemail again.

So he had rung Caitlin's flat, looking forward to hearing Riley screaming at him with excitement, as well. When that phone had rung out, unanswered, he had asked Brodie to ring Caitlin.

"Maybe she's trying to ring me at the same time. How long should I wait before trying again?" JT had muttered at the phone impatiently, as if waiting for it to answer him. As he'd stood staring at the phone, debating, the device had started to vibrate, indicating an incoming call. The caller ID had informed JT that it was his father. Really wanting the call to have been from Mandy, JT had answered in a clipped, impatient tone, wanting to clear the line quickly.

Then the bottom had fallen out of his world.

* * * *

JT sat aboard the plane, ready to snap, having replayed the scene over and over in his head like a bad movie stuck on repeat. Remembering first the complete and utter desolation as he heard the news about Mandy's vicious beating, and then the overwhelming relief, as finally the second call had come confirming mother and baby—his future family—were both safe.

It took forever, or so it seemed to JT, for the aircraft to taxi to the terminal. JT was up and out of the door first, impatiently helping the startled stewardess to open it in the process. He could hear Brodie's footsteps trailing him and knew he didn't need to wait for his mate to catch up. Just knowing Brodie had his back was a small comfort to JT. He was thankful the ever-dependable Brodie had taken control and made all the arrangements for him.

Caitlin sat waiting in her little green car, parked in a 'no stopping' zone, as he and Brodie charged through the exit doors. They swapped seats quickly, and Caitlin handed the keys to Brodie so that he could drive, while the big men squeezed into her little car.

JT couldn't speak, but just stared out of the back seat's window as the world whizzed by. A world that thankfully still contained Mandy.

* * * *

Mandy slept fitfully. Her arm ached, but she was happy to feel the pain as she woke from a nightmare, one with a different outcome of the night. One where the baby had been lost and an angry JT had blamed her for her stupidity, calling her nothing more than a murderess and evil. Mandy welcomed the unpleasant sensations stemming from her battered body, as it reinforced that she had been dreaming and that, in reality, JT's baby was alive and safe. No thanks to her.

The few hours after Mandy's attack had been a blur of faces, medical tests and discomfort. Mandy had shuddered, remembering the look on poor Riley's worried face, and felt guilty that she had upset the poor boy. Riley had lived through so much already.

At the memory of June's caring, teary-eyed expression and the fierce look on Jon Senior's face — scarier than anything she had ever seen on JT — Mandy was devastated that so many people had now been affected by her past mistakes.

Caitlin had come to the hospital and had held Mandy as she'd cried again. Some tears had been in response to the agony that racked her body, some as a result of being terrorised once more by Con, and other tears had been with relief at the confirmation that the baby was safe. The doctors had set Mandy's shattered arm under light sedation, but Mandy had refused to take any pain medication. Having already put JT's baby in danger once, she hadn't been prepared to take any more chances.

Thirsty, Mandy tried to lift the water cup from the side table, the movement causing a sharp stab of pain to race up her arm. Black dots formed before her eyes. She cried out, and in a flash her future father-in-law was standing beside her, holding the straw up to her mouth. He looked so pale and tired, Mandy thought as she took a small sip of the refreshing fluid.

"Have you been here all night?" she asked, her voice croaky.

"Of course, sweetheart," Jon Senior answered. "There was no one game enough to ask me to leave you. You, my dear girl, are a very important person in my life, my son's life. Speaking of JT, he should be here in a few minutes. He caught the first plane he could. Caitlin has gone to pick him up from the airport. He's been frantic, angry that he couldn't get here sooner."

Mandy began to sob. "Of course he's angry. He probably won't ever forgive me for being so stupid. I nearly managed to get our baby killed. JT was so happy about the baby. I could have taken that happiness away from him with my reckless actions. Con was my past...and it nearly destroyed JT's future. I put everyone in danger." She could hear the touch of hysteria in her tone, but couldn't stop. "What if Riley had been hurt? Caitlin and he have suffered so much loss already."

Mandy watched as Jon Senior placed the cup back on the side table. He sat his hulking frame down carefully on the edge of the bed beside her, then gently pulled her head against his chest, holding her as she cried. Mandy knew the moisture from her tears was soaking through his crumpled shirt.

"There, there, darling... It's not like that at all. Stop making yourself sick. JT loves you. He was angry because we failed to protect you. *I* didn't protect you." Jon Senior's voice faltered before he continued, "I've been keeping an eye on you when JT was away. June and I have become quite good friends in the process. I usually stay in her flat to be close to you. I should have heard that mongrel before you did. I can't say enough how sorry I am that you were hurt, Mandy. I should have got to you sooner. If it wasn't for Riley coming and getting me from June's, I hate to think..."

JT had reached the door to Mandy's room as his father was lifting the drink to her lips. With the body of his father blocking Mandy's view of the doorway and his arrival, JT had hesitated, giving himself a moment to gather control of his emotions before entering. When he'd heard Mandy's heartfelt confession, JT had been struck dumb. How could she possibly think he would blame her? JT loved Mandy more than anything, and the thought of losing her was worse than any other loss imaginable.

Stunned, unable to comprehend Mandy's words, JT was further shocked at the response from his father.

JT had never seen his father show emotion before. Even after the death of his mother, JT remembered the man being strong and unemotional. Stoic. Thomson men did not cry or empathise—they used power and strength to solve problems.

But there, in front of JT's eyes, his tearful father was holding a sobbing Mandy, apologising for letting her get injured.

Crying.

God, the man had saved her—what was going on in his mind? If it took JT the rest of his life, it still would not be long enough to thank his father for being there to protect Mandy. He needed to set these two people—his wonderful, loving family—straight.

If anyone was at fault, it was him.

"Hey, Pop! You makin' a move on my woman?" JT said, trying to make his voice sound bright and cheery, but in fact sounding hoarse and choked up as his love for the two people before him totally overwhelmed him.

He watched as his father moved away from Mandy. JT stopped breathing as he looked upon the bruised and battered body of the tiny woman in the bed. Mandy wouldn't look at him, seeming to shrink away from him as he reached for her. JT could not bear her withdrawal from him. His heart stuttered. It felt as if a cold, heavy rock had fallen on his chest.

"*No!* Don't you dare pull away from me," JT almost shouted, his words coming from his mouth harsher than he had wanted.

He tried to catch hold of his emotions, forced himself to calm down and, after making sure he had full control over the tone of his voice, JT continued, "Mandy, I love you more than my own life, more than *any* life. Baby, please, I need you. Don't pull away." Sitting down in the spot his father had vacated, JT pulled Mandy into his arms. The longest ten hours of his life were finally over.

Chapter Twenty-Three

Mandy could not believe how much better she felt now she was safe in JT's arms. The things his father had said were so beautiful. Mandy found it difficult to believe that these men had gone to so much trouble to protect her, only to have her nearly get herself killed. JT was always so forthright and open in his love for her, never holding back. Mandy loved JT more than she could put into words. There were not enough colours in the world to replicate her emotions, even though her mind remained void — her colours seemed to have deserted her.

Brodie, having sweet-talked the nurses into allowing them access to the ward before the usual visiting hours, was now also inside the emotion-packed room. Mandy was overwhelmed that so many people were worried for her. Clearly shaken by the recent events, Brodie kissed her gently on the forehead before explaining that Caitlin would be back after she'd collected Riley.

"The boy's finally fallen asleep. Cait said it took hours for him to settle down. June's been watching over him. It's heartbreaking, knowing how much that kid has lived through. One so young should not have had to deal with so much violence and death."

Mandy agreed wholeheartedly with what Brodie had said, and couldn't help but feel guilty that she was to blame for the most recent incident of Riley's distress.

"Just stop that—I know what you're thinking." Reading the look on her face, Brodie was quick to jump in. "Riley is fine honey. Caitlin reckons he's just a bit hyper—kid's full of himself after all the praise he's been getting from old Jon and the cops for his quick thinking. I just meant that Riley has already seen a lot for his age. But he'll be all right. He's got some good people around him. And Mandy, you are one of them. The kid really thinks the word of you. We all do."

Brodie was also quick to praise Mandy, telling her how proud he had been to learn from one of the nurses, who had been speaking with a paramedic about the incident, that Mandy had given back as much as—if not more than—she had received. He added that the chatty nurse had also told him Con had screamed like a baby all the way to the hospital.

Mandy, the memory of the previous night now returning more clearly, shivered as she thought of what could have been. She was thankful that Riley had not been hurt in any way, and was glad he was being hailed a hero.

"Gotta say, Brodes, I owe the kid big time. Brave and smart little bugger, running for help like he did. I've always had a soft spot for him, but that spot has just turned into a whole lot more. He and I will be having a conversation real soon so I can tell him in person how much he's done for me, how much I owe him."

JT's words still sounded choked and emotional, as if he was straining to keep control. Mandy was close to tears again at feeling so much love surrounding her.

"Talking about debt—hey, Pop, I owe you one too." JT turned to his father and embraced him in a big, slightly awkward-looking, hug. "I'll never be able to repay you for what you did for Mandy—for me and Mandy—for my sanity. I just thank God you were there for her, even when I wasn't. You look beat, Dad. Go home, get some rest. You've been here all night. I've got it from here. And...I love you, Pop."

Mandy watched, struggling to hold back her emotions as JT and his father embraced like two big bears, in what JT told Mandy later was the first real hug he had ever shared with his father.

* * * *

A tired Mandy, her arm still very painful, rested in JT's embrace. Her head was pillowed on the familiar and comforting expanse of his broad chest. He had stretched out next to her on the hospital bed. Brodie had stayed and was asleep in the chair beside the bed—both men looked worn out. Mandy wasn't sure if JT was awake or not. His breathing was steady and, comforted by the rhythm, she finally drifted off to sleep.

* * * *

It seemed only minutes before Mandy was awoken by the gentle touch of a nurse, who then checked her pulse and blood pressure. The smiling woman shook her head at the sight of the two large men sprawled out in the hospital room. The nurse informed Mandy that her name was Sally, and that she was about to perform a foetal heart monitor test on 'the bub'.

Sally reassured Mandy that the test was nothing to worry about—just routine, part of normal hospital procedures.

"My son is going to be green with envy when I tell him about you, Ms Magenta. He's a mad Jets fan, and hearing that some of his heroes were sleeping in one of my wards will make me quite popular, I think!" Sally laughed as she went about setting up the monitor.

"Please, call me Mandy. Yes, those two do seem to make a room seem smaller, don't they?" Mandy chuckled at the nurse's words, her own laugh now sounding quite foreign to her ears. "I'm sure JT will be happy to hear your son is a Jets fan. He enjoys meeting or making time for his young fans."

Before long they could hear the rapid sound of a heartbeat, loud and clear. Mandy was so relieved, reassured to hear the beautiful noise. JT's child had a strong and steady heartbeat. She felt JT's arms squeeze her a little tighter. He was now obviously awake and had heard the quick, strong sounds as well. Mandy noticed Brodie was also awake, still sitting in the chair, but now leaning forwards with his hands on his knees, looking enthralled.

"Wow, that's just amazing! Is that the baby's heartbeat? Mandy, JT—that is the most beautiful thing I've ever heard. But don't tell Caitlin I said that!" Brodie added sheepishly.

"I thought you big, tough football players would be different, but you're really just big softies." Nurse Sally laughed at Brodie.

"James might be soft, but I'm as tough as they come. Just like my kid," JT growled back at the nurse.

Mandy smiled, tears in her eyes but brimming with happiness.

The good-natured banter really lightened the mood. Eventually, they were all laughing aloud. Mandy thought it was a good sound after the night they had all been through. Tensions seemed to have slipped away. So as June, Caitlin and Riley peeked around the door, still full of concern, they were greeted by a roomful of light-hearted laughter.

Mandy's doctor came later that day to check on her, only to find half the Jets team camped in her room. Mandy could tell that it was causing quite a disturbance, since the hallway outside her hospital room was filled with staff, other patients and visitors hovering around, hoping for an autograph or just a glimpse of the local sporting heroes. The doctor himself sheepishly obtained a few autographs for his son.

The doc was even promised tickets to the final in exchange for letting the rabble 'break JT's missus out of hospital', as they put it, much to Mandy's embarrassment. She was so overwhelmed with all the support JT's friends were giving her.

The doctor – in a serious tone, but with a big smile – told the group he could not be influenced in making a decision when the health of such an important patient was at stake. The doctor's statement brought forth cheers of "Hear, hear!" and "Good for you!" from the rowdy group. He did inform Mandy that she would be allowed to go home as soon as she felt up to it – which was now, she had replied quickly.

As the last group of well-wishers left the room, Nurse Sally came in with Mandy's discharge papers.

"Time to go home, dear, but you will need to take it easy for a while. Ring and make a follow-up appointment with Outpatients for your arm early next week, and thank you for organising all the autographs. My Josh will be over the moon."

Sitting in the wheelchair as she was transported to the front door—part of hospital policy—Mandy, for the first time, gave some thought to returning to her flat. The idea was so harrowing that she shivered noticeably. JT, having just pulled his car up to the entrance, looked at her and immediately sensed something was wrong, his face becoming a mask of concern.

"Mags, honey, I was wondering if you wouldn't mind spending a few days at my place? I think Dad needs you around—he's been so upset over all that's happened. I still don't understand why he feels so responsible. I think he wants to pamper you a little. It's been a long time since he opened up and showed anyone his feelings. I still can't believe I saw the old man cry. What do you say, you okay with that?"

Mandy would have kissed him if her broken arm had not been in the way. The last thing she felt like doing was going back to that flat in Ashfield. In fact, Mandy didn't think she ever would, and she told JT how she felt. As he gently lifted her into the car, he assured her that it was fine with him if she never went back, just so long as she was always with him. His comforting touch and understanding of her fears was almost as good as any prescription painkiller.

* * * *

Jon Senior had seemed genuinely delighted at the news that Mandy was moving in, and maybe not just temporarily. He welcomed her warmly with a tentative hug and kiss to the forehead, enthusiastically offering to convert the back sunroom into a studio so she could resume her art whenever she felt up to it. He mentioned that he and the police officers who had been called to the Ashfield flat had been quite impressed by her artwork, especially the nudes of a very familiar-looking body, and that he had been wondering if the one of the somewhat large male appendage had been modelled for.

Mandy was a little embarrassed by his comment about her teenage attempt at painting a penis—which she had done mostly to shock her parents—but she was proud of her sketches of JT, knowing she had captured well the strength and power of not just his body, but the whole man.

Caitlin and Riley arrived not long after Mandy, both keen to check up on her. They appeared saddened by her decision not to return to Ashfield, but both admitted that they understood why.

Mandy had been wondering why JT had not been to training in three days. The Jets had won, which did mean they had a week off, but she was surprised they weren't training at all. She mentioned this to Caitlin as her friend was settling her into bed, and noticed that Caitlin looked uncomfortable.

"Okay, what's going on, Cait? Spill."

Caitlin took a deep breath, as if mulling over whether to answer Mandy, before replying, "When they were in Brisbane—after you got hurt—JT told Brodie he was retiring from playing. He blames the game and himself for being away that night, sweetie. I wasn't supposed to tell you, but I'd want to know if I were you."

Mandy could not believe what she was hearing, and was furious with JT. Why would he give up now, so close to the end of the season and with such a good chance at winning the whole damn competition? Mandy was not going to let that happen, and she shouted very loudly for JT to get into their room, quick smart.

Caitlin, probably deciding that was her cue to leave, kissed JT lightly on the cheek and told him it had been nice knowing him as she hurried from the room, leaving an obviously confused and worried JT in the doorway.

* * * *

JT stood and listened to his little fireball as she told him that he was not giving up the game he loved for her, not now she was safe. Con was probably going away for years because of all the charges against him — including attempted murder, as June and Jon Senior had been witnesses, first-hand, to his threats. Mandy went on to list to him how she was just starting to understand the infernal game, and asked him how he could dare to quit now. She was really giving him what for, and all JT could think of doing was kissing her adorable mouth. He heard the sound of his father chuckling behind him — Jon Senior had also come running, worried at the sound of Mandy's shouts.

JT walked slowly all the way into the room and shut the door behind him. He held up both hands in surrender and laughed. *Probably not the smartest move, really,* he thought, too late to stop the book Mandy had been reading from hitting him in the shoulder.

"Ouch, that hurt!" Mandy cried, as the action of throwing the book jolted her broken arm.

"Okay! I surrender, woman! Don't hurt me or yourself anymore." JT laughed. "I will go back to training tomorrow. But we will discuss our future and what I do next season together. What do you think?"

JT didn't give Mandy the chance to answer him. He took possession of her mouth carefully, kissing her into silence and perhaps submission. It certainly seemed to work in his favour, as Mandy was immediately distracted from the argument.

JT decided that he would remember this form of defence for any future disagreements.

Chapter Twenty-Four

The rest of the week seemed to crawl by for Mandy. She was so frustrated at her own lack of mobility – she even needed help to do the most personal of things, such as wash and dress. It was tough not being able to work, as her art was often the best way for her to dispel any unsettling emotions. She found that if she let her mind wander for too long, the events of her attack would come rushing back, often leaving her shaky and panic-stricken in response.

But trying to keep herself busy was frustratingly impossible. She had decided to take up the advice from JT's dad and seek some victims counselling, to help her not only get past her most recent ordeal, but put the entire disastrous relationship with Con behind her and to get on with the rest of her life.

JT, on the other hand, was taking everything in his stride. He was happy to aid her in any way, and nothing fazed him. Nothing was too much trouble – nothing except what she wanted most of all. Needed.

Mandy was sexually frustrated. Having enjoyed JT's insatiable appetite before the attack, she was worried—actually, 'worried' was too mild a word to describe it. Mandy was terrified. JT was acting as if he was not interested in sex at all. Well, not sex with her, anyway. Yes, he cuddled her possessively every night, pulling her bottom tight against his erection, soothing her if she awoke terrorised by her dreams—but nothing else ever happened.

Mandy had tried taking things into her own hand, so to speak. But with only one good hand and various parts of her anatomy still bruised, she was clumsy and ineffectual in her art of seduction. JT, rather than taking the hint and perhaps helping her out, just seemed unaware of her intentions. Mandy didn't know what to do. She was worried that maybe JT didn't want her anymore. She'd begun to question his motives—what if he was too disgusted by all the drama of the attack, and was only staying with her out of a sense of obligation? But that didn't account for his constant erection.

She was too embarrassed to actually talk to him about their lack of intimacy. He was already doing so much for her—cooking, cleaning, helping her to bathe and dress. She didn't want to seem ungrateful. JT had also resumed his training schedule with the Jets team. *Perhaps he's just worn out*, Mandy tried to convince herself. "Yeah, right—as if that ever stopped him before," she actually answered herself.

She was muttering under her breath as she sat struggling to eat her cereal with her right hand, which was her *wrong* hand. Jon Senior looked up from the paper he was reading and raised his eyebrows in a questioning manner.

"Did you say something, Mandy?"

"Oh, no. Just thinking out loud, Mr Thomson."

"I wish you would call me something else, honey. 'Jon', or maybe even 'Dad', if you like. I'd be honoured to think you might one day see me that way." Jon Senior tenderly placed his big, warm hand over Mandy's smaller one.

Hormones were a terrible thing. Mandy, unable to control hers from one minute to the next, started crying again at the man's heartfelt words. As she wiped her teary eyes on the sleeve of her unbroken arm, Mandy managed to sob in reply, "I'd really love to call you 'Dad', if that's okay. You are that in my heart already."

"Good, it's settled then, daughter," Jon Senior replied, then quickly picked up his newspaper and held it up, as if to block his own emotional face from her view.

The sound of knocking at the door ended their sentimentally charged conversation.

"I'll get it," Mandy said as she stood up, carefully trying not to move her still painful left arm. The plaster cast helped with keeping the arm immobile, but Mandy was still refusing any pain medication. It was a relief, though, that the pain seemed to be receding more each day.

It was a nice surprise to see Caitlin standing at the door, holding two large cups of what appeared to be coffee.

"I thought you could use a cup, and a chat. Decaf for you and the bub, though! How are you doing, Mandy?" Caitlin asked as she moved through the open doorway, handing Mandy one of the cups as she tilted the other in mock salute.

"Well! Getting sick of everyone asking me that question." Mandy laughed ruefully as she took the coffee from Caitlin and touched the cup to Caitlin's as if to say cheers. "Who knew you could miss caffeine so much? But decaf is better than nothing, I guess," she said as she took a hesitant sip. "I'm doing okay, Cait. Sick of myself and the fact I'm so useless at the moment...but getting stronger each day. C'mon in — let's go sit down," Mandy said. She led the way to the family room and took a seat on the sofa, gesturing for Caitlin to join her. "How's Riley?"

"Riley is fine. He is still strutting around like a puffed-out peacock, so full of himself after JT made such a fuss over him. Not to mention the way Brodie has been clucking around him...and of course, June and the police telling him he's a hero. It all adds to his now overinflated ego."

Caitlin's smile let Mandy know that she was as proud of her brother's quick thinking in going for help as all the people she had just mentioned.

"But he is a hero, Caitlin. Riley probably saved my life." Mandy shuddered visibly. "Let's not talk about that just now." She quickly changed the subject so as to not get caught up in any memories that might lead to a panic attack in front of her friend.

"How's your personal *hero*?" Mandy asked, using Caitlin's own nickname for Brodie. "What new and wonderful ways has he shown you his undying love recently?"

"Oh, you know my Brodie, always wanting to buy me some new thing or another, as if I need new stuff to make me love him more — pfft! Now he has upped the pressure to move in with him...using the 'safety card' this time." Caitlin mimicked speech marks with her fingers and rolled her eyes at Mandy.

"I'm sorry, Cait. I didn't mean to cause you any trouble..."

"Mandy, stop the worrying. I love the fact that he wants me to move in with him. Just want to see him all squashed up on my sofa-bed for a bit longer. It's *so* cute." She giggled. "Although I think we'll need some extra privacy soon. Riley got up for a drink of water the other night and all but caught us. My goodness, I was so busy enjoying Brodie...you know...down there," she whispered sheepishly, "I didn't hear him. Brodie covered up by saying he was looking for my bed sock. I've never been so embarrassed."

Mandy was laughing, and it felt good. Just imagining the look on Brodie's face as he and Caitlin were caught during oral sex—what a hoot!

"Gee, Brodes can think fast on his feet...or knees, whatever. Good cover-up. Do you think Riley bought it?"

"Oh, I hope so, Mandy. I really do."

They chatted some more before Caitlin finally got to the real reason for her unexpected visit. She explained to Mandy that JT had been talking to Brodie, and Brodie had asked her advice. Mandy was intrigued and listened to her friend closely as Caitlin repeated word for word—or what Brodie had told her was word for word—his and JT's talk. It was so silly, almost laughable, what had been going on.

JT, while usually very private about intimate issues, had been crying—so to speak—on Brodie's shoulder. JT had told Brodie that he was so hot and horny he was going mad, lying next to Mandy's tempting-as-sin body with her luscious booty pressed against him, and he was finding it impossible to sleep. Instead, he was enduring the torture night after night, breathing in her scent and making do with just embracing her, not willing to cause Mandy even the slightest moment of discomfort, so sure that any attempt at making love would cause her pain.

Mandy was both horrified and pleased. JT loved her and wanted her. The big oaf was actually causing her more distress by not making love to her.

"Getting caught having oral sex is not nearly as embarrassing as Brodie and JT talking about our sex life! Love to have been a fly on the wall for *that* chat. Think it might be a wee bit uncomfortable next time I'm face to face with Brodie though." Mandy grimaced at the thought of it, before continuing on more seriously.

"I'd thought he'd gone off me, Cait. He used to not be able to keep his hands off me...and vice versa. I was so scared that he was just doing the right thing by me, you know, getting me well before kicking me to the kerb. Who could blame him, the amount of grief I've caused him...and you all? You can only take so much drama in your life—I can attest to that. But all this time he was worried about hurting me. I could kill him for worrying me like that! Just wait till I see him. 'Luscious booty'... He really said that?"

Caitlin's advice that maybe Mandy and JT should communicate a bit more was, Mandy believed, right on the money. Hearing Caitlin add that she hadn't minded being in the middle of their love life again was a bit of a shock, until Caitlin explained the whole conversation she and JT had shared before, about Mandy's undiscovered pregnancy.

"I can't wait to tell Brodie your side of the story. I bet when you two get this all sorted, the result will be way better than make-up sex." Caitlin's comment had both women giggling again, just as the two men in question strolled through the door, looking slightly apprehensive at what could have caused such amusement in their respective women.

"Doesn't bode well for us when these two get all giggly together, JT. Do you think we might be the subject of their amusement, or is it some other poor human?" Brodie smiled lovingly down at Caitlin as he spoke, then delivered a tender kiss to her forehead. Mandy reached her good hand out and smacked JT gently on the backside, wanting to touch him so desperately. She loved him so much, the big adorable hunk. She could not believe how lucky she was to have found such a caring man.

Brodie and JT explained—well, Brodie, just like the captain and leader he was, did most of the talking— that they were keen to go and watch the preliminary finals being held on Saturday and Sunday, and had been wondering if Mandy felt up to going. Mandy found it so touching that these men worried so much about her. They could have just gone to the game without her, and she would have understood. Watching their competitors play was comparable to research for their jobs, and she told JT and Brodie how she felt.

"Rubbish, woman. If you're not up to going, I can just as soon watch the games on TV," JT growled in his usual loving, gruff tone.

"Yep, and so can I," Brodie added as he winked at Mandy.

Mandy just laughed at the two giant men standing like twin cement pillars, bulky arms crossed over their broad hard chests, with chiselled faces that she could imagine opposition players dreamt of in their worst nightmares.

"You are both so cute, double-teaming me, so I will say yes. It's okay, boys, I should be up to an outing. In fact, Caitlin and I were just talking about going to the game and checking out the Storms' forward pack. We heard that the props in particular are quite a sight—big, tough, macho men."

Mandy heard Caitlin gasp in the background.

"Oh, Mandy, I'm going to pay for that—thanks a bunch," her friend said, giggling nervously.

Amid the grunts, growls and spurts of jealous rhetoric, it was agreed everyone would go to the game together, but the women were to remember JT and Brodie were the toughest, fiercest men in rugby league, and the only men for them.

* * * *

That night, as JT tried to pull Mandy to him in their usual sleeping position, Mandy decided it was time to talk—time for some action.

"He-Man, if you don't give me an orgasm soon I really might look at those other players. Seriously, Jon, I thought you had lost interest in me, but Cait and I had a girly chat today and she thinks I should just tell you how I'm feeling. So I will. I'm totally frustrated and incredibly sad my man is scared to touch me." Mandy outlined JT's face with her good hand, stroking his wide jaw and running her finger over his lip. "You haven't really touched me since we got home from the hospital."

JT stilled Mandy's hand and brought it to his lips, placing a kiss in the centre of her palm, his black eyes so dark Mandy felt she could fall headlong right into them.

"Mandy, how could you possibly, even for a second, doubt my feelings for you? Especially with my hard cock always pressed against that sweet arse of yours?

Honey, you're in pain because you were protecting our child. How could I be so selfish as to cause you any more? Although it certainly would be my pleasure to help you relieve any frustration you may be feeling."

JT's words were instantly arousing. After resting her plastered left arm carefully on a pillow, JT positioned her with her legs spread wide on the bed, ready for him.

"Try not to move, honey," he said as he settled between her legs, grinning up at her. Mandy's mouth went dry, but her body warmed and moistened in readiness, eager for the pleasure she knew was about to follow.

Chapter Twenty-Five

Mandy was spread before him, her pretty pink lips glistening. JT took a moment to enjoy the view before finally lowering his head.

JT loved the sweet taste of Mandy's pussy. Parting her folds with his thumbs, he blew gently on her distended nub. He licked her thoroughly, thrusting his tongue as far into that moist channel as he could, without going near that little bundle of nerves at the apex.

Mandy was begging that she needed more. JT could feel the moisture weeping from her folds as he lapped it all into his hungry mouth. She begged for him to do something, but he kept up with the slow, methodical and exquisite torture. She started moving, thrashing her head from side to side and arching her hips off the bed, trying to get relief.

"JT... Please!"

Watching her buck and squirm was making him wild. JT was so hard it was painful. He ached to feel his cock buried deep into his woman. Deciding it was now time to bring Mandy home, before she hurt her arm, JT grabbed the plump globes of her backside in his hands and anchored her pussy to his face, pressing and swirling his tongue around her nub. It took only seconds before he tasted the sweet cream from her orgasm on his tongue as she writhed, tensed and screamed his name.

JT sucked at her until she begged him to stop.

He needed to be in her. Trying to not to think about his tight balls and throbbing cock, he slid up the bed beside her, unable to resist a taste of her erect nipples on the way past. JT kissed Mandy gently. He loved her mouth—the way it felt, her responsiveness. Mandy never held anything back from him. She always opened herself up fully, never ashamed to show him her passion. He needed to treat her the same way.

"Mandy, I need you, need to bury myself in you. I miss you so much—my cock's throbbing for you. I know it's selfish, but at least you know how I feel."

JT was surprised by Mandy's quick movement, considering she was still hindered by her injury. She grabbed him around the neck with her good arm and pulled him down on her, somehow managing to rub her wet pussy on his shaft at the same time.

"Oh, JT, I need you just as much. Don't ever think I don't. Fill me, make me part of you. Take me, please," she begged.

JT entered her slowly, savouring the moment and the feeling as he pushed through her silken lips. He was unable to stop the moan from escaping his clenched jaw—the pleasure was so great as Mandy's tight, warm channel swallowed his cock whole.

"Oh, baby, you're always so hot and wet for me, makes me feel so fucking good. The way your body responds to me makes me wild. It's taking all my willpower to not slam myself into you again and again. Are you sure you're okay? I really don't want to hurt you, Mags." JT, holding his body still, waited for her answer, unsure how he would survive if she asked him to stop.

"Come for me, He-Man. Make it hot 'n heavy," came her throaty response.

JT began to thrust in and out gently, trying to be careful, leaning his body away to the side so as not to bump Mandy's arm. The slightly sideways angle gave him access to that little bundle of nerves at the apex of her slit. Just before he shot his creamy wad deep into her folds, JT drove Mandy over the abyss to ride the wave of another orgasm. The added feel of her already tight pussy gripping and constricting around his cock in response was all the stimulation he needed to take him to completion.

Chapter Twenty-Six

The days preceding the Grand Final week seemed to roll together in a surge of excitement and expectation. The Jets team, with two resounding victories in the semi-finals, had reached the ultimate game. They were hot favourites to take that final prize. Mandy, Caitlin and Riley all noticed a slight change in the demeanours of the usually calm and collected JT and Brodie. Both men became slightly distant as they were bombarded with media requests while trying to keep the rest of the team grounded.

Mandy knew that JT was hesitant to leave her for even one night. She and his father had repeatedly tried to ease JT's fears, pointing out that Mandy was not alone anymore and that at least, this time, he would actually only be a few minutes away. The hotel the team had booked into was only a few suburbs over. Mandy convinced JT that he had a job to do and that the younger players would need him more, over the next few days, than ever before.

Grand Final day was a fun-filled, festive occasion. Amid plenty of fanfare, noise and colour, the spectator-filled stadium came to life. There were popular bands, sky-divers and cheer-girls, all entertaining the crowds before kick-off.

Mandy sat in amongst a large crowd of the Jets' family and friends, proudly cheering on her man throughout the game. Tears and hugs flowed freely as the final siren sounded, confirming the Jets as winners and season premiers. Mandy and Caitlin were both bursting with pride as they watched Brodie, as captain, lift the shield high and proud. There were excited cheers of approval as Rookie was named man of the match—he had scored all of the sixteen points in the victory over the scoreless Brisbane team.

Mandy found it hard to believe what she was hearing as the exuberant young player at the microphone struggled to be heard over the continuous roar of the crowd.

"I want to thank the Jets fans for giving us so much support this season. You guys are awesome." The crowd's approval of Rookie's words was apparent at the increase in volume of their cheering. "I'd also like to thank the sponsors for this award. I'm truly honoured to be chosen with so many great men playing beside me, but I'd like to dedicate my performance and this award to a very special woman. She's had it tough over the last few weeks and I just want her to know that the whole Jets team is behind her. Mandy—this one's for you."

Rookie's dedication was so unexpected, unbelievably sweet and generous that Mandy was stunned. People around her turned and looked her way as they heard her name, applauding. Mandy felt her cheeks redden at the sudden turn of events had that thrust her into the spotlight.

"Oh, my goodness, he is so sweet. Laura Harris really did a good job raising him. Wonder what JT is thinking. Hope he doesn't go all gung-ho, 'that's my woman you're talking about' on Rookie's behind," Caitlin said, doing a gruff voice to imitate JT before laughing so hard she doubled over in front of Mandy, clutching at her sides.

"Yes, he is sweet, but so is everyone. I love this club, these people. They're just so good." Mandy cried with happiness. Tears leaked from the corners of her eyes, flowed freely down her cheeks as the excitement of the day finally overwhelmed her. "Oh, again with the waterworks... Caitlin, I've got to tell you, pregnancy hormones suck. If I'm not crying I'm peeing. It's a wonder I'm not dehydrated all the time, the amount of fluid I leak..." Mandy hiccupped out the words as she searched her bag for a tissue.

"Here, sweetie — will this help?" Caitlin held out a hanky towards her. "Tell you a secret, Mandy, I can't wait for some of those hormones myself... You look radiant, even with your running mascara."

It was near impossible to get any private time with JT, as the Jets team and hundreds of their supporters partied long into the night in celebration. It was nice to feel so much happiness abound, everyone smiling and having a good time. But in the end, a tired and content Mandy left JT with his boys. She accompanied an incredibly proud Jon Senior as he dropped Caitlin, Riley and June home.

* * * *

It was an unusually inebriated JT who finally stumbled home, noisily, at around sunrise. Mandy had never experienced a drunken JT. The giant of a man looked so cute and cuddly as he flopped happily onto the bed, with a smile that reminded Mandy of the Cheshire Cat—or was that more the big, bad wolf?

The motion of the bed, when JT fell on it, almost flipped Mandy to the floor, she bounced so high. The slurring way he had called her 'woman'—which sounded more like 'shworman'—made her giggle. How could someone so rugged and ferocious on the field be such a loyal, loving teddy bear in reality? Mandy again reminded herself that she was one lucky woman. The fact was proven beyond doubt when, even drunk, JT turned out to be quite the accomplished lover, and spent many hours ravishing Mandy, resulting in multiple earth-shattering orgasms that left her well sated.

* * * *

A sobering JT lay watching Mandy sleep. He loved being able to lie down beside her and just watch her sleeping peacefully, with no frown lines marring her face, no nightmares disturbing her slumber. Gently, so as not to disturb her, he moved a strand of her hair that had fallen over her eyes, tucking the now longer and more feminine, silken, raven-black strand behind her ear. He'd loved Mandy's spiky, short hair, but this new softer, longer style was very sexy. She looked so womanly, feminine. Her curvy, soft body was tucked into his side, the blossoming swell of her belly a promise of a life to come—his child forming within.

He smiled as he reminisced over what had been the most intense few months of his life.

JT had been so happy when his best mate Brodie, after battling some of his own demons, had met and fallen in love with the sweet and caring Caitlin, which in turn had led JT to meet young Riley, and later the love of his life, Mandy.

Dealing with his own emotions over what had happened to Mandy, and his inability to keep her out of harm's way, safe from her abusive ex, had been hard. The frustration of being so far away when she'd needed him most still haunted him. Those feeling of utter helplessness were something JT wished to never experience again. The thought that he might have lost her, or the precious child she was carrying, was just too horrible to contemplate. He had, though, been able to see his father in a different light as the older man had let his own emotions flow freely, openly showing his love and concern for his future daughter-in-law. It had been such a shock for JT to see his usually stoic father so emotional.

JT was also incredibly proud to be a part of the Jets team's success again this season. The young men who were new to the squad had shown such maturity with how they'd conducted themselves on and off the field, and the more senior members had made up a sort of kinship, and had been so supportive of him through thick and thin. Now there was the promise of another season, if he desired, to continue in the game that had given him so much over the years. Whether he played or not, he would always be a Jet.

But as JT watched his sleeping woman, he could not imagine spending another night away from her. He knew that he had, happily, played his last game in the winning Grand Final. It was a fine and fitting way for him to end his career. The future already promised so much—becoming a father and husband, and growing old with the love of his life.

"I am indeed the luckiest man alive," JT whispered to the universe.

Epilogue

In a joint press conference, held shortly after the hoopla of winning the Grand Final had settled down, JT and Brodie had announced that their playing days were over.

Brodie would be taking on the role of assistant coach at the Jets the following season. JT was still considering the offer to become part of the staff at the Jets, but it would maybe be down the track, as he was intending to spend more time with Mandy before making any firm decisions.

Mandy was feeling stronger, mentally as well as physically now, due to some wonderful counselling. JT had accompanied her to some of the more confronting sessions, holding her safely in his arms as she spoke of those terrifying times with her ex, helping her move beyond those memories with his strength and support.

Weeks later, with all the drama behind her, Mandy had stood looking on, teary-eyed once again, as Caitlin had gracefully walked down the rose petal-scattered pathway that indicated the direction of the makeshift altar and her waiting husband-to-be. Mandy had been overjoyed when Caitlin had asked her to be her bridesmaid—albeit a very pregnant one. The warmer November weather had allowed for a late afternoon wedding in the Sydney Botanical Gardens, before an intimate reception had been held—of course—at Mia's Restaurant. Mandy and JT had put on hold any of their own wedding arrangements until after the baby was born.

Caitlin had looked absolutely stunning in her wedding gown. It was a long, silk-embossed satin, cream-coloured gown with a plunging neckline, emphasising Caitlin's full bust before the shimmering material, as if hugging her body, cascaded to the ground, continuing at the back in a short, flowing train. Her beautiful auburn hair had hung loose around her shoulders. Caitlin Walters—soon to become James—had truly looked like a goddess. The three men—Brodie as the groom, and JT and Riley as the groomsmen—had also looked incredibly handsome in their matching suits. Mandy had, of course, silently voted JT the most handsome!

Mandy was now reminded of the adoration and unwavering love that had shone from JT's eyes that day, as he had watched only her during the wedding ceremony. That familiar look was once again apparent in JT's features, but this time the recipient of his gaze was not her, and Mandy could not have been happier. This time, the reason for JT's unabashed emotion was nestled securely in his big hands.

Mandy smiled contentedly, full of love and hope for the future. She enjoyed watching the myriad of emotions that chased across JT's face as he gazed lovingly down at their tiny, dark-haired newborn daughter, Elaina Rose Thomson. The most beautiful and precious design Mandy had ever created.

About the Author

Sydney-born Donna Gallagher decided at an early age that life needed be tackled head on. Leaving home at fifteen, she supported herself through her teen years. In her twenties she married a professional sportsman, her love of sport—especially rugby league—probably overriding her good sense.

The seven—year marriage was an adventure. There were the emotional ups and downs of having a husband with a public profile in a sometimes glamorous but always high—pressure field. There were always interesting characters to meet and observe, and even the opportunity to live for a time in the UK.

Eventually Donna returned home a single woman, but she never lost her passion for watching sport, as well as the people in and around it. Now happily re-married and with three sons, Donna loves coffee mornings with her female friends, sorting through problems from the personal to the international. But she's on even footing with the keenest man when it comes to watching and talking rugby league.

Donna considers herself something of a black sheep in a family of high achievers. Her brother has a doctorate in mathematics and her sister is a well—known Australian sports journalist. An avid reader, especially of romance, Donna finally found she couldn't stop the characters residing in her imagination from spilling onto paper. Naturally, rugby league is the backdrop to her spicy tales of hunky heroes and spunky heroines overcoming adversity to eventually find true love.

Donna Gallagher loves to hear from readers. You can find her contact information, website details and author profile page at http://www.total-e-bound.com.

Total-E-Bound Publishing

www.total-e-bound.com

Take a look at our exciting range of literagasmic™
erotic romance titles and discover pure quality
at Total-E-Bound.